A JUSTIFIED MURDER OF CROWS

SUE ALCON O'CONNOR

Author of "The Bone Shelter"

Bookmite Publishing
Denver, CO

ISBN: 979-8-9869941-5-4

CONTENTS

ACKNOWLEDGMENTS

I have so many people to thank.

Thank you to all who read The Bone Shelter and encouraged me to go back to Patton, Colorado. It really is starting to feel like a real place—albeit a dangerous place surrounded by numbskulls—but a real place. I promise this book won't be the last time I take you there.

Thank you to my family and friends for listening to me prattle on about murder, psychopaths, and monsters. I know it's not always polite dinner conversation, but it helps to bounce things around with people who are your captive audience and are too gracious to tell me to shut the hell up.

Thanks to Dario Ciriello, my editor and friend. The man who usually gets my jokes but isn't afraid to tell me if something falls flat. None of this would be possible without him.

Thanks to Noelle Nevins and her stellar cover art. You are the best!

Thanks to my writing group and all their support. Katye, Diane, McJennifer, and Dario. Your friendship and advice has been invaluable. Writers really do need the friendship of other writers, and I have the best ones.

I love you all,

Sue

For my Husband Mark
Long May He Quack

After death, one's spirit sparks into an alternative realm, transcending space and time. Quick as a grassfire in a blistering wind, flames leap from one place in time to foreign landscapes where we must navigate by trial and error. I don't have all the answers yet, but I will. I have discerned one thing though: dying a premature death with unresolved issues leaves me racked with a lingering need for retribution. Right in the thick of things, akin to a car going the wrong direction on a one-way street, I am burdened with matters demanding resolution. In the meantime, I am unyielding and will stand my ground. I'll remain where I am until the day I can say, without a shadow of a doubt, that you have received exactly what is coming to you. I will wait here in the all-encompassing dark. Unlike you, time is my infinite companion. When the moment is right, I will seek you out with long, frigid fingers and my interminable memory. You were the last thing I saw when my clock stopped—I <u>will</u> see you again.

Edgar Wilson

A withered heart, a poisoned fang—
Justice be a boomerang.

Chapter One

Ghosts Hate Karate

Zane Holyworth oftentimes felt like a glorified Tupperware salesman in respect to billionaires; at the time, his office in Aspen, Colorado was filled with them. Billionaire clients that is, not Tupperware. At that moment, there were nine affluent guests in total. A sleazy news station owner who made his livelihood in buying up smaller channels then breaking them stood chatting with a software developer who looked more like a geeky kid than a man of sixty. A politician with suspected ties to sex trafficking made nice with an icy blonde television personality who was known for her shady insider trading deals. On the blue velvet couch, a Russian oligarch whose name Zane couldn't pronounce laughed at a joke told by a man who was building a spaceship bound for Mars just for the hell of it.

The middle-aged Russian's hand rested on his nineteen-year-old lady friend's knee; she smiled a tight smile which stopped short of her eyes. At the bar, a real estate mogul who owned half of NYC clinked glasses with the owner of a huge chain of retail stores, while some clown who'd made a fortune selling overpriced, cheap bedding called "Your Blanket" hung on the Russian's every word. The scent of entitlement was cloying, but the smell of money overpowered it.

"Please, ladies and gentlemen, sample the product before you decide to purchase," Zane said, gesturing to the trays of hors d'ouevres being passed around by a woman in a crisp white outfit with severe, shoulder-length bobbed black hair. "I'm certain you'll find it to your satisfaction." Each bit of merchandise that sat upon a micro-thin water cracker was worth approximately two hundred dollars. Just shy of ten thousand U.S. dollars per pound. Zane was stupefied by the overindulgence of the wealthy, but more than happy to cater to it.

Conversation hummed through the room, a harmony as self-congratulatory as it was dull. Champagne was drunk from crystal goblets. Success stories were shared, served up with a hefty side of humble brag. As he read the room from an inconspicuous spot at the end of the bar, Zane could sense his clients were more than satisfied. The general consensus was always the same; the more they paid for something, the bigger the chip on their shoulder. Be it a yacht, a villa in Italy, or contraband food items. Zane shook his head slightly but kept the hospitable, well-practiced smile upon his lips.

Zane Holyworth stood and lifted his champagne glass in a toast. "To my dear friends and clients, and of course to the guest of honor, the *Formaggio con Amici*. Zane only sampled his product when he was in a room with potential clients. Satisfied with the night's affairs, he slipped an infinitesimal piece into his mouth. It wriggled on his tongue.

Miles from Aspen, in a small eastern Colorado town, Ethan sat perplexed and just a little irritated. It had been a long day of work at the Dollar Store. Some kid had dropped three two liters of soda which exploded in a rain of Dr. Pepper, drenching the knock-off Barbie section and half an aisle of hand sanitizer, soap, and watery shampoo. What a sticky mess. Took about two hours to clean it up, and he was sure that there were still a few dolls with Dr. Pepper between their toes. And Fresh Forest hand soap smelled more like a Pepsi product than an actual forest. The good news was, the new little side job he'd been offered would bring him in as much money as he made in a year working at the Dollar Store. But first, he had a few questions.

"Alexa, what is *Formaggio con Amici?*"

Alexa: "Formaggio con Amici es un queso Italiano que se traduce como 'Queso con Amigos.'"

"Alexa, no hablo Español. In English. Please. Por favor."

Alexa: "Formaggio con Amici is an Italian cheese which translates to 'Cheese with Friends.' Fermentation of this particular cheese is brought about by the digestive action of fly larvae which leaves the cheese with a soft, liquid center. The live maggots called 'friends' are consumed when the cheese is ripe. The formaggio requires certain enzymes to be sprayed upon unripe cheese to keep the larvae alive and to decelerate putrefaction. Made with raw mare's milk and rare white Alba truffles—"

"Damn, I hate mushrooms."

Alexa: "the cheese is considered unsafe to consume and is contraband in most countries. This does not however keep it from being available on the black market, and it is considered the most valuable cheese in the world. The decomposition makes for a pungent, rotting product with a moist, gooey, living center and…

"Alexa, STOP."

Alexa: "Who in their right mind would eat this shit, Ethan?"

"Alexa, stop right now!"

Alexa: "Bugs and rotten horse milk, and your dumb ass is only concerned about *mushrooms*?

"Jesus Christ, Alexa! Cease and desist!"

Alexa: "Fine. Eat poison."

Rhonda read a lot of thrillers, the more predictable the better. Her passion was primarily horror novels and psychological murder mysteries. She ate them up by the dozen. The aforementioned novels typically included a city girl who moves to the country with her handsome husband after inheriting a big, drafty house filled with ghosts, hears a noise, walks backwards up the attic stairs, gets her ankle grabbed by a skeletal hand, almost gets killed, gets away, almost gets killed again, and ends up solving a big, fat mystery. This scenario would never happen to Rhonda Ramos Benson. Rhonda was a quick thinker, and she knew herself well. In ominous situations such as this, Rhonda would have a baseball bat along with her and beat that bastard of a bony ankle grabber to hamburger, doing a little dance while she was at it. Nope, Rhonda Ramos Benson was not a clutcher of pearls; she'd take no prisoners and smash his serial killer melon like a piñata, and then smack him once more—just for good measure. Dead men grab no body parts. Rhonda hoisted a bulky box from one hip to the other and looked up at the old Victorian that was now her home. Was she about to step into one of the crappy novels she constantly read? She made a mental note: borrow her son's baseball bat and buy a piñata. Practice makes perfect.

In bold letters, KITCHEN STUFF was marked on the bulky cardboard box Rhonda was juggling. How much KITCHEN STUFF does one family need? Then again, what would she do without her lemon zester, garlic press, and three slotted spoons? She felt the box slipping and set it down with a loud thunk and the clickety-clack of protesting kitchen gadgets.

Standing, she looked up at the ornate building where she would now be living with her husband and two children. Actually, one-fourth of the house would be her home. It was a quadplex, and 291 Chestnut Street #1 was theirs, bought and paid for. She chuckled to herself, because here she was standing in front of a behemoth which looked like every haunted house she had ever read about, with a boxful of kitchen garbage that she used maybe once every five years. She gave the box a little kick; it clattered in response. "How many times have I packed you guys in the last ten years?" she asked it, and kicked it again. *I just might need anger management classes.* Getting a new house arranged was going to be a lot of work and a gargantuan pain in the ass. Thank god her sister Carla and her twelve-year- old nephew BJ lived three blocks away and would help in any way they could. BJ's father, Bobby, had been killed the year before. The person who murdered him had been a longtime Patton resident with a dark, lurid past. Rhonda was glad she could be here for them both. Even though Bobby was Carla's ex-husband, Rhonda knew that her sister had still loved him. Mother and son had been through a world of hurt in the last year, and Rhonda would do everything in her power to try to bring a bit of levity back into their lives.

Rhonda sighed and thought about where her life had taken her; Patton, Colorado, population 3,725, was a big downsize from L.A. There was, however, a Starbucks. She sent off a silent thank you to the universe. Coffee, her family, and crappy mystery books were life—in that order.

With hands on hips, she took in her new home. Built in the early 1900's on five acres, the big Victorian had been remodeled in the early 90s into four separate two-story units each with their own private entrance and a shared outdoor space. The outside of the building was painted in what she guessed to be Victorian colors. Deep red trim balanced the pale green of the body of the house, and a creamy white accentuated the lace trim and porch pillars. How many times would they have to move to accommodate Tate's job? Granted, the money was nice. Truth be told, the money had rained down like cottonwood fluff in a Spring wind. His salary made up for some of the inconvenience of moving so often, and here in Patton she had Carla. That sister of hers knew everybody; Rhonda was certain that soon she would know everyone too. Carla loved social events, and she'd already signed Rhonda up for a local book club and pickleball, whatever the hell that was.

Rhonda watched as the U-Haul truck hit an enormous, water-filled pothole, bounced and then pulled into the driveway; a new driveway in a new town. Rhonda sighed. Someday, Tate's job would settle itself into a permanent position, hopefully in a larger town, and surely not this place. She had nothing against small towns, but this little town that sat northeast of Denver was a bit too slow for her liking. She had promised herself that she would have a good attitude, shrugged, then kicked the kitchen box for a third time to show it who was boss. The forks and knives clattered, screamed, and called her a liar.

The U-Haul that contained their furniture squealed, thunking to an overly quick stop, and Rhonda cringed as she thought of all her carefully wrapped breakables; she silently apologized to the mistreated box of kitchen do-dads. A man who appeared to be about fifty stepped from the cab of the truck, took his cap off, and walked over to her. "We're gonna put all the boxes in the kitchen and living room if that's alright with you, missus."

"Thanks, Stan. That'll be just fine," Rhonda said. "I'll try to stay out of your way."

He looked genuinely puzzled. "How did you know my name's Stan, if you don't mind me asking?"

She pointed to the patch on his coveralls that spelled out his name in bright red capital letters. "Wild guess?"

Stan laughed and gestured to his partner who looked to be all of seventeen. "I bet you could guess this kid's name too." An identically styled patch was embroidered with the same screaming red thread. It said "Kyle."

Rhonda gave the young man the once-over. "Let's see, he looks like a…Gary?"

Stan chuckled. "You're downright psychic." He took a cloth handkerchief from his pocket and blew his nose with a noisy honk. Startled, a pair of crows flew from the pine tree in the front yard. Stan gestured Kyle over and ratcheted up the back door of the truck.

Kyle/Gary rolled his eyes like a champ and pulled a lamp from the truck.

"You'll have to show us where you want the heavy stuff, like the couch and the beds." He looked up at the old house. "God, I hope the stairs aren't too narrow. These old houses are notoriously tight." Stan shoved the well-used handkerchief into his back pocket where it hung in off-white surrender. "And you might want to call the city about that monster of a pothole. Damn thing nearly ate my truck."

And all of my carefully wrapped stuff for dessert. "Let me get the door for you." Rhonda jogged up the front stairs and unlocked the entry door and held it open. Once Stan, Kyle, and her lamp were in the house, she walked back onto the porch, down the stairs, and to her car. Opening the trunk, she removed a bucket of cleaning supplies and turned, ready to get to work on the bathrooms. An older woman sat at the upstairs window in the unit that shared a wall with her. Rhonda waved. The woman waved back and smiled. Maneuvering the cleaning products to the top of the kitchen thingamajig box, she stuck a mop and bag of rags under her free arm. Rhonda made her way back to the front door, and it gave out a cliché haunted house creak. At least the neighbors are friendly, she thought. She said a quiet prayer. *Please let there be pizza delivery, and a sporting goods store that sells piñatas.*

Maybe she'd quit yoga and take up karate. Ghosts hate karate.

Chapter Two

Revenant Hunger

RHONDA'S STOMACH WAS GROWLING like a pissed off grizzly bear in a room full of Leonardo DiCaprios. It had been a long day of cleaning, unwrapping glasses and plates, moving furniture, and finding spots for her beloved collectable ceramic vegetable creatures. An orange that looked like a cat sat mid center on the shelf above the kitchen sink. Next to him was a cauliflower sheep, and to the other side a jalapeno pepper shaped like a dachshund with a very sharp green stem that served as a tail. She was so hungry she just might eat them.

The doorbell rang, announcing the arrival of their pizza, and Tate and Carlos hopped up to answer it.

"Mom, I love it when we get takeout and you don't cook," five-year-old Bailey said, climbing up onto a bar stool.

Rhonda snorted. "I'm not *that* crappy of a cook."

"Sometimes you are," Bailey said, her tennis shoes beating a rhythm on the bar. "Remember my birthday cake?"

Rhonda gave her a snarky half smile. "I don't want to talk about your birthday cake." Unnggh. Her daughter's half-inch-high birthday cake. How could she have forgotten the baking powder?

"Mommy doesn't want to talk about your flat birthday cake, Bailey," Tate said.

Carlos had to get in on the action. "The one that looked like a display from the Flat Earth Society?"

"Next year you're both getting a week old pre-made cake from the Dollar Store."

"Promise?" the kids said in unison.

Tate spun the pizza box and with a flourish set it on the counter by the bar stools.

"If you drop that thing it's justification for murder," Rhonda said, reaching up to grab it. She shot her kids a look. "Not a jury in the world would convict a woman that's this hangry,and this judged by her peers."

Tate laughed, and Carlos climbed up next to his sister at the bar.

"Why do they call this a breakfast bar when we're having dinner?" Bailey asked.

"Why do they call it a bar when there's not any booze or the palatable scent of desperation and despair?" Tate grabbed a handful of paper plates and some paper towels and set the table with exaggerated grace. "Only the best for my favorite girl and these two monsters." He ruffled Carlos's curly hair, and the four of them ate their dinner surrounded by boxes and misplaced pieces of furniture.

"I'd have eaten off of the floor like a dog. I was that hungry," Rhonda said.

"Can we get a dog?" Bailey said.

"Mommy was just being funny," Tate said, laying another slice of pizza on her plate. "Mommy thinks she's funny."

Carlos took a bite, "Sometimes she's funny."

"And sometimes she's not," Bailey said, picking off a piece of pepperoni from her brother's plate and laying it on her tongue like an Italian sausage Eucharist.

The Body of Crust, Rhonda thought and chortled, then threw Tate a secret behind-her-back middle finger. He grabbed her hand and kissed it, "Okay, you're funny. Eat your damn pizza."

"Daddy said 'damn'," said Bailey.

Rhonda laughed around her third slice of pizza. "Yes, he did." She looked Tate squarely in the eyes. "He thinks he's funny."

Bailey took two more slices of pepperoni from Carlos, rolled them into tubes, and stared at her dad through them like a little pair of meat binoculars. "I'm the funniest."

Carlos glared at her and took them back, popping them into his mouth.

"Okay, pookie, you win." Tate looked at her. "Wanna know what you win?"

"Yes!"

"A bath!" Tate scooped her up and carried her over his shoulder.

"Wait, Daddy," Bailey said, squealing, "I need to turn on the night light!" Tate carried her over to the oven hood and she pressed the button.

"The good old Mexican night light," said Tate, "every house has one." He held her by the feet so she dangled upside down over his shoulder, her dark hair hanging loose.

She shrieked, giggled, and held her arms out for her mother to save her.

"Sorry, Bailey, Dad wins this one." Bailey went limp over his shoulder and murffled. "You too, Carlos, pajama time." Carlos slid off the barstool and followed his dad and sister up the stairs.

"I kinda liked the flat earth birthday cake, Mom," Carlos said, plodding up the stairs. "At least you tried."

Rhonda smiled. She'd take the participation trophy as a win and run with it. Tonight the order of her can't-live-withouts was family, coffee, and books. Tomorrow coffee would surely take back its spot at the top of the list.

When Tate came back down the stairs, Rhonda had moved the sofa from under the window to the wall that butted up to the dining room. She also had two glasses of wine waiting atop a brown cardboard box marked STUFF. What kind of STUFF, she didn't have a clue. He flopped down next to her, grabbed his wine glass, and took a sip. Rhonda raised her glass and touched it to Tate's; it pinged like a bell in the quiet house. "Here's to this being our last move before we settle down."

"I'll drink to that," he said, taking her glass from her and setting it back atop the mystery STUFF box. He slipped his hand around the back of her neck and he pulled her into a kiss. "You know what else I'd drink to?"

"I think I have a pretty good idea," she said, kissing him back. "I love you, Tater."

"I hate it when you call me that," he said as he gently pushed her back onto the couch.

After three days of dragging furniture, placing knick-knacks, stacking dishes, and filling dresser drawers with clothes, the house was in a wobbly semblance of order. Tate had gone to work this morning, and she and Bailey were running around trying to find Bailey's left shoe. Frustrated, Rhonda grabbed her pink snow boots and handed them to her.

"It's not snowing," Bailey said, looking at them. "It's not even winter."

"I know, but we're going to be late for school and you can't go barefoot." Rhonda snagged Carlos's backpack off the counter, double-checked that she'd put his lunch inside, and dragged him and his sister out of the house. Bailey stomped along behind her and opened the car's back door. Rhonda grabbed the booster seat from the hatch and Bailey climbed up into it while Carlos buckled himself into the front seat. After securing her daughter's seatbelt and then searching around for her sunglasses, which were on her head, she made her way to the driver's seat, backed the car out the driveway and pointed it toward Patton Elementary. The streets were quiet except for a few school kids and their parents and the occasional barking dog.

"When can we get a dog?" Carlos asked.

"Maybe after we move into our forever house," Rhonda said, adjusting the rearview mirror. That was twice in twenty-four hours her children had asked for a pet. "How about a goldfish for now?"

"How about we buy a package of fish sticks and I name them all, buy them little leashes and take them for walks?" Carlos grumbled and folded his arms over his chest. "I'm almost a teenager and never had a dog."

Rhonda shot him a stone-cold mom look. "We'll talk about a pet when we're settled. It's not fair to a dog or cat to move it so often. It'll get confused and might run away. And you, Mr. I'm-almost-a-teenager, watch your smart mouth."

Carlos looked as if he was about to say more, and Rhonda lifted her eyebrows. He snapped his mouth closed, stared out the side window and made an I'm-almost-a-teenager sound.

"I like it here," Bailey said, her snow boots kicking at the seat, "I've already made a friend."

Rhonda was surprised. "Who's your friend, baby? We've only been here a few days, and most of the time you stayed with Auntie Carla." She glanced back at Bailey, certain that as of yet she'd not seen any children that lived in the quad.

"Just some kid. He has red hair, and he's a little older than me." She looked at her and scowled. "And I'm not a baby."

Rhonda pulled the car into the school parking lot. "Okay…maybe you'll see him at school, and you can ask if the two of you can play later."

Carlos was already out of the car and sprinting toward the school. He threw a wave in her direction. She'd put his lunch in his backpack, right?

"I don't think I'll see my friend at school, Mama."

"Why not?" Rhonda helped her out of the booster, closed the door, took her hand and began walking toward the school to introduce herself to her daughter's first grade teacher.

"He told me he can't leave the house." Bailey began to skip. "A goldfish would be okay."

Rhonda bought three bags of Dollar Store cookies, opened the containers, and put them on clear plastic trays. The tattooed young man who worked there directed her to exactly what she needed—plastic platters which looked like crystal but were so cheap you didn't care one bit if you got them back. She'd always referred to them as potluck trays.

Rhonda arranged the cookies in an artistic spiral; she didn't want to randomly dump them, since,that would give away that they weren't homemade. She needed to remember to put baking powder on the grocery list. She might make a cake out of spite, just to prove she could do it. She covered the cookies with plastic wrap, and voilá—it looked as if she'd spent hours baking, but in actuality they were five-minute, meet-the- neighbors gifts. Rhonda startled as a man with a scruffy goatee hurried past her kitchen window toward the front of the house. She pulled the curtain aside and peeked out after him. He had shaggy blond hair, a lanky build, and was hitching his pants up over narrow hips. Another neighbor perhaps?

Rhonda was curious about the red-haired boy Bailey had mentioned and would be sure to be on the lookout while handing out her phony Dollar Store cookies. She shrugged into a light jacket, grabbed the goodies and decided to start with the neighbor she'd met briefly, albeit not face-to-face. The older woman who had waved at her on the day they moved in had seemed friendly enough.

An orange tabby dashed in front of her as she made her way down the front steps, six feet down the sidewalk and up her neighbors steps. She thought about Carlos wanting a dog, and smiled. Maybe he'd be content with someone else's friendly outdoor kitty for the time being. She made a mental note to stop and buy Bailey a goldfish. "Stay clear of the Grand Canyon-sized pothole in the street, little kitten," she said. The tabby cat looked at her, hissed, and walked deftly around it.

Rhonda balanced the tray of bamboozler cookies in one hand and rang the doorbell. She could hear it chime The Westminster Quarters. Heavy footfalls followed, and the door creaked open. An older man in a checkered flannel shirt stood in the doorway.

"Yes?"

"I'm Rhonda Ramos Benson from next door, I just wanted to say hello." Rhonda handed the man the potluck crystal platter of I'm-too-lazy-to-bake-and-I-suck-at-it-anyway cookies.

"Well, that's awfully thoughtful of you, Rhonda Ramos Benson," he said, and accepted the platter from her outstretched hands. "Edna told me that we have new neighbors." He stuck out his hand and Rhonda shook it. "Truth be told, I've been doing a bit of snooping of my own. Being nosy isn't reserved for old ladies, you know?" He laughed heartily. "I'm Henry Hansen, by the way." When he smiled, his face wrinkled into what Rhonda thought looked like an old brown paper bag wadded into a ball, flattened, and forgotten underneath the refrigerator for a few years. She shook his hand; he opened the screen door for her, and she stepped through into a late 1960s-early 1970s timewarp of orange-flowered furniture and wallpaper.

"It's nice to meet you, Henry."

There were photographs of what appeared to be a much younger Henry and Edna, along with an assortment of people of different ages and times lining the entryway. A blue urn sat on the fireplace mantel along with more photographs. One young man was obviously in his high school yearbook photo finery. He looked a lot like the photographs of the younger Henry. She bent in to study it. The handsome young man had full lips, a straight nose, and blond hair which swept his shoulders. "You have a nice looking family."

"That's James," he said, "our only child." He took the photo from the wall and his eyes misted over. "We lost him some years ago to allergy-related issues." He studied the photo and wiped his eyes on his shirt sleeves. His voice hitched. "To think we lost our only son to an allergic reaction to peanuts, of all things. It's unthinkable to me. After all this time I still haven't come to terms with it."

That explains the urn, Rhonda thought. She was touched by Henry's unselfconscious wash of emotions. "I'm so sorry, Henry. That had to have been awful for you both." She touched his arm, and he placed his hand over hers and patted it.

"It was a long while ago, but you never get over losing a child, be they four or forty. They're still your babies, you know?" He replaced the picture and used his fingertip to straighten it, took a deep breath, and said, "look at me blubbering like an asinine old fool. Come on in, please come in!" Henry turned and yelled up the stairs, "Edna! We have company! It's the new neighbor lady you told me about, and she made cookies!"

Rhonda felt a flush of guilt thinking about her imposter cookies on their Dollar Store imposter crystal plate. She'd have to have them over, actually cook, and use real china.

Edna appeared at the top of the carpeted stairs and slowly descended them. One foot. The other foot. One foot. The other foot. She clutched the railing for support and kept her eyes on her feet. Edna's hands looked gnarled by what Rhonda guessed to be arthritis. By the way she took the stairs, she probably had it in the joints of her legs and feet as well. She stepped carefully onto the landing, her blue slippers the exact shade of her house dress. She kissed her fingertip, and touched it to James's photo. "I heard the two of you talking," she said, smiling and extending a hand to Rhonda. "Come on in, let's go to the kitchen, and I'll put on a pot of coffee to go with those delicious looking cookies."

Rhonda felt her cheeks burn. "Please don't go to any trouble, Edna. I just wanted to stop by and say hello."

"Nonsense," Edna said without looking back. "Henry and I don't get that much company, and this is a lovely surprise." Edna busied herself with the Mr. Coffee machine. True to the decor, it looked as if it came from the small appliance aisle at the Goodwill.

Henry saw Rhonda looking at it. "Those things will last forever." He snapped his fingers. "One button, no frills, and great coffee. What else could you need? They don't make them like that anymore, that's for certain."

Rhonda thought about her fancy yet temperamental espresso machine. Henry was probably right about that.

Edna closed the top, flipped a switch, and the orange button blinked on. "We got this for Christmas one year from our neighbor Judy." She turned and looked at Henry. "What was it? Seventy-eight? Seventy-nine?" Henry shrugged his shoulders, and Edna took three plates from the white cupboard. "Anyway, if you think these coffee makers last forever, you should see our Crockpot."

Edna set the plates on the kitchen table, gestured for Rhonda to sit, and took three mugs from the mug tree on the counter. The Mr. Coffee machine burped and sputtered as the pot filled. She placed a trivet on the table, sat the coffee pot on it, added a sugar bowl that looked as if someone had made it in third grade craft class, and finished off with a container of powdered creamer. Henry pulled the chair out for his wife, and Edna sat. "James made that sugar bowl in Cub Scouts." She touched it lightly with her fingertip, as if it were on loan from the Louvre. "I've kept everything of his."

"I have one similar to it that my son Carlos made," Rhonda said as she scootched in her chair and placed a napkin on her lap.

Henry poured the coffee, passed around the counterfeit cookies, and asked her, "So, how are you liking Patton so far? Not much excitement goes on around here, but that suits us just fine, doesn't it sweetheart?" He patted Edna's hand.

Rhonda was charmed by their affection for one another. "We're just settling in, so I haven't seen too much of the town yet." She took a sip of coffee and picked up another shyster cookie, "I'm picking Carlos and Bailey up from school at 3:00, so maybe we'll take a drive around town and make note of some of the things we'll need to check out when we have more time."

"I saw your little boy out riding his bike yesterday morning." There was a crumb of cookie in Henry's mustache. "Tell him to be careful not to ride straight into Sinkhole de Mayo. That darn thing seems to get bigger by the moment, and it's a bike magnet."

Rhonda laughed. "You named the pothole?"

"I didn't name it, but it's an apt name, don't you think? It's so big you could throw a party in there."

Edna reached over and brushed Henry's stray crumb away. He smiled at her. "What is he, about ten or so?"

"Close. He's eleven, and has more energy than a room filled with a thousand squirrels." Rhonda sipped her Folgers coffee. It was surprisingly good. "You've probably seen Bailey as well, she's five."

"If you ever need a babysitter," Edna said, pointing at Henry, "ask this one here."

Henry laughed, "I like kids. I'm a big kid at heart, and I have a million stories."

Edna nodded her head and grinned. "It's true!" She leaned toward Rhonda and whispered, "some of them are embellished so often that I can't remember what's really true."

"Don't be telling all of my secrets, honey. We'll be here all day."

Edna paled. After a heartbeat's silence, she appeared to recover herself and gave Rhonda a sly wink. "Remind me to tell you some of his stories when you have more time. It could take awhile."

Edna's reaction was strange. Does someone have a juicy secret? Rhonda smiled and pushed back from the table. "I have a few errands to run, and then need to pick up the kids." She set her dish and mug into the sink. "It was so wonderful to meet you both."

Edna began to rise. "Stay there, sweetheart," Henry told her, "I'll see Rhonda out and then clean up for us."

Rhonda waved to Edna as Henry stood to escort her to the door. "Thank you so much for the coffee and the company...oh! Are these blueprints?"

Henry stopped in front of a set of four framed blueprints that hung on the living room wall. "Yes! This is what the original house looked like before it was divided into four sections." He pointed to one of the drafts. "This is your first floor right here, and"—he pointed to the next—"this is your upstairs."

"It had a wrap-around porch!"

"She was quite the beautiful home in her day," he said as he led her toward the front entrance. "And, anytime at all to the coffee and the company," Henry said, opening the front door. "And I mean it: if you ever need a sitter, we'd love to."

Rhonda smiled at him, gave his arm a pat, turned, and jogged back to her quad. What a lovely couple they were, she thought as she let herself into the house. She hadn't bothered to lock the door. Maybe small town life had its perks. She glanced toward the two remaining plates of con artist cookies. Meeting the back neighbors would need to wait till tomorrow, right now she needed to make a quick stop at the pet store to buy a goldfish and then pick up her offspring from their first day of school in Patton, Colorado.

Chapter Three

8.5 on the Rude-O-Meter

1997

This Journal Belongs to James Hansen

This ridiculous project is brought to you by Dr. Charles Shelliker. The good doctor compared my optional "reflective writing" to a school assignment, but without prying eyes, deadlines, and judgment.

I am not a stupid person, quite the opposite. I read and I learn. My room is filled with books, and I have outstanding research skills. Nobody would believe the search history on my computer was generated by a seventeen-year-old.

I know journaling is trendy at the moment. Sources—I have a thorough list—suggest it can promote self-awareness and assist in sorting out inner thoughts and feelings. The issue is, what's to sort out? The thoughts and feelings

Dr. Shelliker is talking about are buried, hidden away from my fellow humans, not from myself. They are as deep and secure as if in a hole whose bottom nobody can see; buried somewhere in the muck—but reachable. I can take them out and examine them if I wish and when I please.

I'm not confused by these concepts or feelings, but I don't dwell on them. I know exactly where and what they are. I have a controlled memory of them, as if I'd kicked sand over them, concealing them; a crumb beneath the surface. I'd like to completely forget some of the things I've done, especially where they resulted in a humiliating outcome. Why resurrect them? So I can go back and read the deplorable things people think I've done and relive them? I'll remember things the way I please, thank you very much. Consistently dwelling on the humiliation after the fact would be like having been in an accident where I banged up my head, and once a week smacking my face as hard as I can against the pavement just to remind myself how much it pained me. I'll have to be careful about what I reexamine. I don't think it would be wise to dig too deep or too often, since it could bring on some of the very real sentiments of anger that I've tried hard to control. I know I'm angry. The proof is there. Right. Beneath. The. Sand.

Dr. Schelliker said writing can be therapeutic. That I don't need to show the journal to anyone, including my parents, or even to him. He said it's a good way to have a conversation with "my inner self." Talking with my inner self is no different than talking with my outer self. I don't need to announce my existence. Dr. Shelliker is just another imbecile with Dr. before his name and a wall full of diplomas and awards to plump up his self-image.

I'm sure many of my actions as a child would be foreign, even inconceivable to the average person. To me, they are as natural (and viable) as the multicolored stones on the bottom of Antelope Reservoir. That's all that really matters—what I see. Right under the aforementioned sand.

One of my first memories is from around age five. I felt as if I were having an out-of-body experience at the time. It was like playing a bit part in a film and only then realizing I'm a quite competent leading man.

Do I regret some of it? Some of it. For example, I regret being caught after the incident with the birds. Leaving out the specifics, let's say the world was missing a few baby robins that day. Dad caught me after the fact, grabbed me by the arm and dragged me into the house. I didn't get dinner that evening.

Mom begged him to let me come down to the table— she was always the weak one; she still is. I remember not being able to sleep that night because I couldn't relax. As if rodents were chasing each other around in my brain, each running in a different direction so quickly they blurred from the motion. It was exhilarating and, at the time, confusing.

The mess the birds made, the look on my dad's face when he found me with my hands around their little naked bodies. Squeezing, squeezing, hearing the tiny bones crackle. Being half-dragged and half-carried into my room and unceremoniously dumped onto my twin bed. I lay there in the dark with my hands clenched into fists, wishing I could do to my father what I had done to those fragile little birds. In my mind I imagined him becoming smaller and smaller, until my fingers would fit around his pathetic body and I'd be done with him.

After this, I was grounded until "you come up with a good reason for what you did." "Just because I wanted to see what it was like," was the correct answer, but even at that age, I knew I had to make up something that seemed appropriate. Maybe they'd been hurt and I put them out of their misery? Maybe there had been a cat? I remember thinking I'd work on my acquittal story later. Right then my body was electrified, my mind laser-focused like the red target dot from a sniper rifle. I recall thinking it wasn't fair to be punished. I know that sounds petulant, but I was only five.

My peanut allergy doesn't help my state of mind—it makes me stand out in a crowd, which will not do. I was diagnosed at two years of age. Having this unusual affliction made me more than a student, it made me the student who couldn't be in the same room with a PB&J sandwich. I was the kid who fell to the floor seizing and peeing my pants, saved only by the school nurse's handy EpiPen. I was that kid. There were few accidental encounters that I recall; all of them were utterly humiliating and acidly memorable. It's strange how some things in my childhood are black and forgotten, and some are crystal clear. Humiliation cuts sharp. This was one of those unambiguous incidents.

When I was eight years old, my mother had the flu. Confined to bed on doctor's orders, she was unable to cook, so our neighbor at the time brought us a pot of homemade chili and warm tortillas. I vividly remember gobbling it down, since my dad and I had lived on dry cereal for two days before this. Lo and behold, the neighbor's secret ingredient was a spoonful of peanut butter. The next thing I remember is being in the hospital and being told that three days had passed. I almost died during that incident—perhaps it would be better if I had. I'm feeling that way more often these days.

Now, as a junior in high school, I'm still the quiet kid that could be killed with the wrong kind of cookie. I was the kid who flopped around on the floor in grade school with wet pants. My peers acted as though I were contagious. I wished I could selectively be.

I once found a single peanut taped to my locker. I had to fetch the janitor to remove it, and the entire locker had to be sanitized.

The fact that I'm without a cluster of friends doesn't bother me. I'm good with my own company and stay clear of most of the simpletons in this place. They laugh too loud and chew with their mouths open. They think that losing at football will make the world tilt off its axis and spin off into the sun.

I can make friends if I set my mind to it. I excel at blending in, laughing at the appropriate times and appearing interested in the conversation. There are times when this skill comes in handy. I understand the concept that each of us has a complete and unique little universe spinning around inside them. The problem is, I can understand and relate to mine, whereas I have no desire to dip into anyone else's.

I'm not an unattractive individual by general standards. I have my father's height and my mother's blonde hair and blue eyes, meaning I do get noticed by the opposite sex. As far as females are concerned, it's not as if I don't notice them. I enjoy watching their interactions, gathered in their little cluster of friends, acting as if their conversations about boys and clothes and other girls are the most important topics in human history. As if there's not a similar cluster of girls in the next town down the road with identical problems and clothes and indistinguishable blurry faces. I smile and nod at the right times, ask a question or two, and act as if my thoughts aren't a million miles away. I can play this part with ease, but taking off the mask is a relief.

A girl in my American History class asked me to prom last year and I went, just because going to prom is the acceptable norm, and she was quite popular. Early in the evening she told me she had a headache and needed to go home. I dropped her off at her house at about 9:30PM and she never spoke to me again. That's how it goes; sometimes my mask, sewn together with fabricated social skills, has a way of slipping at inopportune moments. The following week, she found a little surprise in the bottom of her sack lunch—rats aren't really that hard to catch if you know what you're doing.

Women think differently than men. For the most part, everyone thinks differently than I do, and that's a shame: not a major concern, just confusing. At times, I think I'm the only one who gets it. Having one person who honestly sees me might be enjoyable but sounds like a lot of work to maintain.

Enough for today. I need to take five minutes to settle down and finish my calculus homework. Rehashing the past makes me sweat. Perhaps talking to my inner self won't be so terrible after all, if I do it in small, sweet bursts. I'll brush off a few grains of sand, because I can be sure that my inner self is something that can actually see me—and understand what it sees.

Rhonda rang the back doorbell, a plate of day-old cookies in her hand. She heard someone yell, "Coming!" over the noise of a TV and a dog barking. The door opened a crack, and a thickset woman peeked out. She was wearing pink sweatpants and a matching sweatshirt which had a few oily stains down the front. There was a small child by her side along with a tiny white chihuahua. "Shut up Nacho, you noisy little shit!" she hissed at the tiny dog. Nacho sniffed at Rhonda's sneakers. "Yeah?" She said, giving the pup a nudge with her foot. "He don't bite, don't worry." Nacho wandered out into the yard toward the back fence obviously in pursuit of better company.

Rhonda offered up her best I'm a friendly neighbor smile, "Hi, I'm Rhonda. I just moved into the quad with my husband Tate and our son Carlos and daughter Bailey." She held out the platter of day-old I'm-a-bad-liar cookies.

The woman took the platter from Rhonda's hands. Her ragged, dirty fingernails sat at the end of sausage-like fingers. Rhonda thought they looked as if she'd dug a grave for her lover with her hands and buried his bones after eating him alive. She needed to quit being so judgy! She needed to read some chick-lit and lay off the horror.

"Welcome to the neighborhood, I guess," she said. "I'm Anita, and this here is Sophia. Say hi to the new lady, Sophia."

Sophia appeared to be about three years old and was wearing Spiderman underpants and a striped shirt. Her chunky legs and feet were bare.

"Hi," Sophia said, hiding most of her body behind her mother's generous legs.

"The house isn't really ready for company, or I'd invite you in," Anita said. "I live here with Sophia and her big sister Stella. She's in school right now." Anita placed a hand on Sophia's shoulder." "And sometimes my boyfriend Kenny. You might have seen him around, he's a real looker."

"Maybe? I saw a man with blond hair and goatee come around the building this morning."

"That'd be him alright. He's my very own Brad Pitt lookalike. Ain't he something?"

Rhonda thought that was a stretch. Maybe if you stared directly into the sun for ten minutes, turned the lights out and then squinted at him from fifty feet away. She shook away the thought, ignored the question, and smiled at Sophia. "Hello there, Sophia." She turned her attention back to Anita. "You wouldn't happen to have someone living with you who has pale skin and red hair? A little boy?"

"Nope, just me, Stella, Sophia, Nacho—and sometimes Kenny." Sophia had bright blonde hair, as did her mother; Anita's was obviously helped along a wee bit by Miss Clairol.

"I better get going now, I need to make a few calls and tidy up. Could use a cigarette too." Anita patted her pants pocket. "You wouldn't have one on ya, would you? Nacho! Get back in here now!" Nacho trotted back inside. "Damn dog."

"No, I'm sorry, I don't smoke."

Anita began closing the door, and Sophia had taken off in the direction of the TV, which was blaring cartoons. Anita continued to shut the door. "It was nice to meet you, Anita," Rhonda said through the sliver of the open door.

Over the racket of the TV Rhonda heard a muffled, "Yeah, yeah. You too," and the door clicked shut.

Well. That was about an 8.5 on the rude-o-meter. Brad Pitt my ass.

Rhonda picked up the last platter of grifter cookies from the wrought iron patio table. She made a mental note to try to win Anita over. She'd wave, say hello, and try to engage her in conversation if she could. She tucked a bit of plastic wrap under the tray and straightened it. After having moved so many times, Rhonda knew that being friendly with your neighbors kept trouble at bay. She knocked on the door of quad number four. After a few moments, just as Rhonda turned to leave, the door squeaked open.

"Yeah?"

"Yeah" seemed to be the standard greeting in this town. "Hi, I'm Rhonda from number one, I thought I'd bring the neighbors a small gift and say hello."

Mr. Yeah seemed to be in his early forties, bald as a hardboiled egg, clean shaven, covered in tattoos, and looking vaguely familiar. He laughed. "I sold you that plate yesterday morning." He rubbed his eyes as if he had been sleeping. "I never forget a face, or a plate."

Mr. Yeah was the clerk from the Dollar Store. Rhonda laughed. "Well, here it is back loaded with cookies."

"I'm Ethan." He stuck out a tattooed hand and shook hers.

"I'm Rhonda." She dropped his hand and asked, "You wouldn't happen to have a son with red hair? Maybe seven or eight years old?"

"Nope, I sure don't." He scratched his head. "It's just me here, and sometimes my friend Aaron." Ethan opened the door wide and pointed into his apartment. "This is the smallest unit of the four. Just a studio, really." He tipped his head toward the second floor. There was a spiral staircase and what looked to be a bedroom loft. The carpet was olive green and reminded her of her aunt Belinda's old Frigidaire. "I couldn't afford it on my salary alone, but my aunt Rose left me part of it when she sold the place. That was back when it wasn't a fourplex, just a big old house." Ethan smiled. "I've got some good memories from back then."

"I bet you do, Ethan. Memories of relatives are precious." He gave her a nostalgic grin, and his eyes softened.

"You're right about that, Rhonda. I didn't know my aunt very well, but I'm forever grateful she thought of me." He took a cookie and bit into it. "Feel free to drop by if you need anything. If I'm home, I'd be happy to help out." He raised his eyebrows and gestured to the cookie, "These are great, thank you." Ethan opened the door a bit wider. "Would you like to come in for a moment?"

Rhonda was really curious what number four, the back studio, looked like. "Sure, just for a minute." Ethan gestured her in, and Rhonda took in the space. It was surprisingly tidy, very compact, and the spiral staircase looked as if it came from Home Depot. There was Mr. Coffee pot identical to Edna and Henry's on Ethan's countertop. Maybe they came with the house?

Ethan had a wall filled with pictures, most of them watercolors. "These are wonderful," she said. Studying one more closely, she saw a signature on the bottom right hand corner: Ethan Wilson. Rhonda was impressed. "You painted these?"

"I did. I still paint when I have time."

"What's this one?" Rhonda pointed at a stunning painting of a large lake at daybreak.

"That's Antelope Reservoir, it's about ten miles out of town. I've been there so many times when we went camping as a kid and remembered how beautiful it was, so I went back a few years ago and took my sketch kit, and as luck would have it, it was a cloudless day and right at the golden hour."

"The golden hour?"

"Yes, it's that time of day right before the sun sets or right after it rises. It's the time of day when everything looks sharp and bathed in just the right light to make it seem as if it glows."

Rhonda was impressed. Ethan was the perfect example of why you never judge a book by its cover. "You really express that in your art." She moved a bit farther down the wall. There was a shadow box. It had a gun in it. "This is a little different from your other work."

Ethan laughed, "I found that gun in the bushes about half a year back, I could tell it was worth something just by looking at the craftsmanship." Ethan straightened the bottom corner. "Wow, I need to dust this. Anyway, I figured I'd sell it and buy booze."

Rhonda saw his face flush red. "But you didn't."

"Nope. I took it to have it appraised. Seems the darn thing used to belong to Elvis Presley and is worth more than I ever could have imagined." He smiled at her. "I've quit drinking since then, too."

Rhonda studied the engraving on the handle of the revolver. There were stags and moose and other animals. She didn't care for guns, but this was a work of art. "It's beautiful."

"I figure if I ever fall on hard times, this gun will generate enough money to get me right out of those hard times."

"Is it loaded?"

"Oh, hell no. I don't know jack shit about guns." He pulled open the top drawer to the side bar that sat under it. There were a handful of bullets that rolled around. "I kept it because of its history and its artistry, not for protection." He closed the drawer. I'd probably shoot off a toe." He smiled at her.

Rhonda smiled back, "I should be going, I have a ton to do in the house. It was really nice to meet you, Ethan."

Ethan took another hypocrite cookie, shoved it into his mouth, and opened the door for her. "You too, Rhonda. Oh, by the way, these platters go on sale next week; two for a buck. Same with the cookies." Rhonda rolled her eyes and cringed. "Busted."

"Still tasty, though. They're my favorite kind." Ethan laughed and closed the door.

Chapter Four

Don't Set Yourself on Fire Again

TATE GOT HOME ABOUT SIX-THIRTY, came in the door, took off his shoes, and flopped onto the couch.

"Well, hello to you too," Rhonda said, flipping a grilled cheese sandwich.

"I have to tell you something," he said.

Rhonda took the pan off the burner and set down the spatula. "Uh oh. What?" She threw the dishtowel over her shoulder and stood next to him, her hand on her hip. "I can already tell I'm not going to like this."

"I've got to be in Texas for six weeks, starting next Monday." He let out a long sigh. "You and the kids could come with me?"

"Tate," she said, "Carlos and Bailey have been in school for just two weeks, and they only have days left until summer break. They're just now making friends and starting to feel like they belong. I don't want to take them out now." She took the dish towel and snapped it at him.

"And, believe it or not, I had a job interview this morning at eight. You can't be serious about this business trip," she concluded, and planted her hands firmly on her hips. "This is such bad timing."

"Serious as a heart attack. I'm so sorry, Rhonie."

Rhonda took a breath and laid her hand over his; she was used to his chaotic work schedule. Inside, her heart shrunk like a long-abandoned apple. "It'll be okay, we've done it before. We'll make it work like we always do."

"I appreciate you so damn much, Rhonie." He draped his arms around her and pulled her to his chest. "It'll settle soon. This is our last move, I promise."

"*Promise*, promise?"

"If they ask me to move again without a clause that it's permanent, I'll step down and take a desk job and not in the field." He kissed her. "So, yes. Promise, promise."

She laid her head against his shoulder. He smelled of sage and gasoline—he smelled of his work. "Okay, it's a deal. I'll let you live."

Tate pulled her closer. "Job interview?"

"Yes, at the elementary school. They have an opening for an English teacher. Talk about luck." She snuggled in. "It wouldn't start until mid August, so that will give me the summer to whip this house into order. We'll be staying at least a few years, right?"

Tate nodded, untangled himself from his wife, and walked to the kitchen to get a beer. "That's what they tell me, yes."

"Alright, then." She turned and looked at him as he cracked open his beer. "I'm getting the living room painted, I can't stand this dull gray color that screams 'flip this house.' Even for a month, let alone a few years." Rhonda walked back into the kitchen, gave the soup a stir and took the last grilled cheese sandwich out of the pan. "Do you mind getting the kids? Dinner's just about ready."

Tate walked over to the bottom of the stairs and hollered up, "Carport!! Bailey! Dinner!"

Rhonda laughed. "Jesus, Tater, I could have done that!" She shook her head and chuckled. "Carport."

Carlos sprinted down the stairs, and Bailey came to the top of the landing holding two action figures in her hands. "Daddy? Can I eat in my room?"

"No you can't eat in your room," Rhonda answered for him. "I haven't seen you at all today. First you were in school, then the minute we got home up to your bedroom you went." She stood with her hands on her hips. "Dad hasn't seen you either, now get yourself down here."

Bailey let out an exasperated groan, threw her head back, grunted, and plodded back to her room. There was a clatter of something being tossed to the floor. "I'll be back," she whispered.

"Was she talking to the action figures?" Tate asked.

"God, I hope so."

Tate and Rhonda stood in the driveway in front of their new home. He kissed his wife, hugged his children and clutched them close. "I won't be gone that long, and we can FaceTime."

Carlos frowned. "Will you bring me something?"

"Of course I will, Carlos."

"Me too?" asked Bailey.

"Of course, baby." He picked her up and squeezed her tight.

"I'm not a baby."

"You'll always be my baby," Tate said, kissing her cheek. "Even when you're one hundred and forty-seven years old, you'll still be my baby."

Bailey laid her head on his shoulder and hugged him. "Okay, Daddy."

He touched his wife's face and looked at her playfully. "I'll bring you back something too." Tate waggled his eyebrows. "A big something."

She chuckled. "Just be safe and call. A lot." She felt her eyes well up with tears. "And for God's sake, remember to eat and don't wear that yellow tie, it reminds me of hotdogs."

"Hotdogs?"

Yes, it looks like cheap mustard, and it's hideous."

"I will. I won't. I promise." Tate slipped into the driver's seat of his BMW. "Take care of your mom, kiddos. You know how much trouble she can get into." He booped Bailey on the nose. "And make sure Goldie doesn't drown."

Tate's daughter smiled at the mention of her new pet. "I'll make sure, Daddy." You could almost hear the gears spinning in Bailey's head. "I'll take her out of her bowl once in a while to make sure she doesn't."

Tate laughed. "Um, naw, don't do that punkin."

"We've got this, Dad," Carlos said, scuffling his shoes. "I can't believe she named him something as lame as Goldie."

Bailey nodded, stuck her tongue out at her brother, then wiped at her eyes. "Goldie is a girl."

"Whatever Mom cooks, you eat it, and tell her you love it," Tate said, closing the car door.

"Do we have to?"

"Yes."

Tate backed out of the driveway and turned right. "Don't set yourself on fire again!" Rhonda yelled after him through cupped hands.

And with that, Tate drove off and out of sight.

Rhonda noticed Edna in the upstairs window and waved. She waved back and then lowered her hand and did a small-scale wave with her fingertips, that had to have been meant for the kids. They waved back as well.

Rhonda grabbed Bailey's hand. "You two clean up your rooms, even if it means only getting your dirty clothes into the hamper." She looked at her watch. "The painters will be here in half an hour, we need to stay out of their way." Carlos gave a nod and hopped up the steps to his room. Her son was so good-natured and looked so much like Tate, she had to smile. He even walked like him. Seeing him take the stairs two at a time made her grin. Tate Benson's mini-me.

Rhonda sat down at the counter, opened her laptop, and brought up her email. There was a note from Patton Elementary School. She opened it and her day became instantly brighter. "Yes! I got the job!" She pumped a victorious fist into the air and then sent a text to tell Tate the good news—even though he was only five minutes away.

True to their word, the painters arrived at 10:00 A.M. sharp. Rhonda showed the three of them into the house and pointed out the walls she wanted painted. She had a few paint samples from Patton Hardware. It had taken her about two hours to decide on colors, and the salesman had finally given up and gone to take his break. She was either color blind, or all the greens looked the same. Rhonda handed Doug, the painter, an older guy with a shock of white hair and a beard to match, the color swatches she'd chosen.

"You sure?" he asked her.

"Yes, I think it'll go well with the warm beige color I picked for the other walls, and the red that I picked to outline the niche alcoves."

He looked at her over his half-frame glasses, "Ma'am, are you 100 percent sure?" Rhonda nodded. Doug sighed. "Then goose turd green it will be." He held the swatch up to the wall. His white coveralls were a choppy rainbow of past jobs.

"It's called Cactus Green, I think?" Rhonda took the swatch from him and held it up next to her second choice, Moonlit Jungle. There was little difference in her eyes— they both looked, well, dark green. She tilted her head and studied them. "Do you think Moonlit Jungle would work better in this space? I mean, it's just an accent wall…" She held Moonlit Jungle next to the swatch that would cover the rest of the walls—Tantalizing Toast, with the niche accents in Colonial Red.

"Oh, hell yeah," said Doug. "Anything works better than goose turd. In my opinion it looks as if someone walked through a golf course and then smeared their shoes on the wall."

"You're the expert," she said, handing the swatches back to him. "Moonlit Jungle it is."

Doug took the swatches, stuck them into his pocket and yelled out the door to his coworkers who were unloading ladders and drop cloths. "Hey fellas! Eighty-six the goose turd!" He turned his back to her and went to meet his crew out on the front stoop. "Shit, I hate that color," he mumbled, shuffling off.

Rhonda giggled and headed up the stairs to get the laundry. The shared washroom facilities were accessed through a door outside which led to the basement. The kids' laundry hamper stood outside Carlos's closed door, filled to the brim with pants, shirts, underwear, pjs, and the stinkiest socks this side of Commerce City. She picked up his hamper by the handle, tucked Bailey's pink laundry basket under her arm, and inched past the painters out the front door and toward the basement entrance.

Doug was having a smoke next to the porch but didn't see her come out. "If I have to paint one more wall goose turd green, I'll throw myself into a volcano. Why the hell women like that godawful color is beyond me." He threw the butt of his cigarette to the ground and crushed it as if it were a poisonous, goose turd green insect.

Rhonda snickered, turned the corner before he could spot her, and set down the laundry. Still grinning, she keyed open the door to the cellar and flipped on the light. A fine coating of dust covered the bare bulb, giving the basement a yellowish hue. Descending the wooden stairs that looked as if they'd been around when dinosaurs roamed the earth and which creaked and protested under her weight, she thought once again about a baseball bat. Her sisters used to hide under stairs exactly like these at her grandmother's house. They'd wait for her to come down and then scare the crap out of her by grabbing her leg through the open stairs. No wonder she had a fear or ankle-seizing bad guys. Thanks, Carla and Jenna. Sheesh. Sisters.

She dropped both baskets by the washer and looked around. The basement was a testament to years gone by. There were bikes and tools, fishing poles, boxes and old paint buckets, and a shelf of jars of what looked to be various canned vegetables and fruit.

Tendrils of inky black shadows filled the corners and crept up the concrete walls, giving the illusion of movement as the bare bulb swayed and slowly calmed. The air was stale and smelled damp. The scent of mildew and earth blanketed the space, and there was something else, something she couldn't quite place—something ripe.

The jars of vegetables were on an old metal shelf, and their contents looked fairly new; Rhonda picked one up. The label had a floral sticker which read, "Made with love by Edna Hansen". Smiling, she placed it back onto the shelf and went to check out the stone-age appliances. *They'll probably have a sticker that says, "Made with love by Fred and Wilma Flintstone. Nope! Whirlpool, circa 1972.* She was surprised it didn't have one of those hand crank wringers.

After sorting the darks from the lights, she shoved half the laundry into the tub of the washer. God knows why she bothered sorting them, the colors were beyond bleeding into one another—they were all kid-clothes colored. She ticked the knob to start, and a thunking sound which reminded her of a bowling ball rattling around in the back of a pickup truck filled the room.

"Good grief." The old washer bucked like a rodeo bull. Rhonda lifted the lid. Sure enough, the tub was filling with soapy water and seemed to be working just fine, although the old Whirlpool was protesting loudly about it. She had brought a paperback with her, thinking she could sit out the washing time and read. She looked at the title.

Zombie Janitors From the Boiler Room. Perfect. She snorted and shoved it into her back pocket. Why did she read this garbage? Oh well.

The only chairs to be seen were a pile of the metal folding type, and a big recliner that looked as if it probably came free with the washer. But the sound was too much for her, and the cellar was too dark to be comfortable for reading. Not only that, the place gave her a good case of the creeps. She'd hide away with her book in her bedroom, or out on the back stoop while the painters worked, and come down periodically to check on her laundry's progress. Turning to leave, she noticed the bare lightbulb which hung from a string, swinging in a brisk circular motion and sending the black threads of shadows that lived in the corners creeping back out from their hiding places. It was as if someone had walked by, reached up and gave the bulb a solid push. The shadows continued their slow escape from the recesses of the cement walls. "Hello?" If no one had pushed it, there had to have been an earthquake. There was no answer, but the empty space under the stairs seeped out darkness as black as deep space.

"I'm done," she declared.

Rhonda fast-tracked up the steps and chided herself for being so easily frightened. The beast inside the ancient washing machine had probably set the bulb spinning. Patton, Colorado didn't have earthquakes or monsters or Zombie Janitors. All basements held a certain disturbing aura, even well-lit basements with windows. They were buried underground, meaning that when you were down there *you* also were buried. Rhonda shivered and flung open the door, almost running directly into Anita from unit number three. Rhonda let out a short yelp and just about tumbled back down the stairwell. "Oh dear god, Anita, you scared me," Rhonda said, steadying herself as her paperback fell from her pocket and fluttered to the ground.

"The basement is creepy as shit, right?" Anita said, a cigarette in one hand and Nacho the chihuahua in the other. "I see things moving down there every place I look." She blew out a blast of smoke. "I've been takin' my wash to the Laundromat on Pine Street. I can't make myself go down there no more, it's probably fulla haunts."

"Have you actually seen something while you were down there?" Her heart was still playing giddyup-go under her T-shirt.

"Naw, I can just feel 'um, you know?" Anita shuddered, and the flesh on her arms quivered. "You know that feeling you get in the pit of your belly when you know you're some-place you shouldn't be? Same feeling as being in an alley in the dark, or how I imagine it'd be at a carnival at night with-out no people around, the lights out and the music turned off." She put Nacho down, and he ran around the side of the house. "You'd just know the clowns were still at the cir-cus—they're just sleeping somewheres. That's the feeling I get." Anita tapped her cigarette against the brick, pinched it, and stuck it into the pocket of her dress. "I'd rather pay the money to go to The Pines and do my laundry there."

"The Pines?"

"Yeah, that's the name of the laundromat down the street. I save up my quarters in a spaghetti sauce jar." Anita turned to leave, her pink slippers barely lifting from the ground as she shuffled off. Beneath her house dress it ap-peared as if her thighs were melting onto her knees. "The cookies were great, by the way. Thanks. I forgot to put them on the counter and my damn dog ate most of them, but the one I got was really tasty." She pointed toward Nacho as he sniffed around the rose bushes. "He's useless as all blazes."

"You're welcome, I'm glad you all enjoyed them," Rhonda called after her. Maybe she'd make spaghetti tonight and save the jar.

"Get in the house, you little rat."

Rhonda cringed. *Poor Nacho.*

"Oh, and hey," Anita said, turning for a second. "When you're done with that book, can I have it? It's on my list at the library, and I want to read it before some jackass bans it."

Around five-thirty, the painters packed up their gear, cleaned up to the point that the room was cleaner than it had been before they started work, and headed out.

"It'll be wet for a while, so don't you touch it, young man," Doug said to Carlos. "And whatever you do, don't lean on it." Doug shook his head. "Wouldn't want to get gooseturd on those nice new jeans."

"I thought we decided on Jungle green," Rhonda asked him.

"Jungle, goose turd, cactus, frog vomit, it's all the same to me." He turned to Rhonda, took off his cap and scratched his head. "Why do so many women like that color all of a sudden anyways?" He threw up a hand in surrender. "Every other house has at least one wall painted olive green, and it's always a woman that picks it."

Rhonda thought for a second. "I guess it reminds us of being outdoors—of plants and growing things."

"Why don't you just go outside?" Doug sucked on his teeth and turned to leave. "Reminds me of camo and duck hunting, but thanks for the business ma'am." He tipped his cap. "You have a nice evening—in your new outdoor-indoors. Honk, honk. I feel like I'm in my brother Marvin's duckblind." He gave Carlos a wink and Rhonda grinned. Doug was grumpy, but he was lovably grumpy.

"I need to get the last of the laundry up," she told Bailey. "Do you want to come with me or stay here?" Both seemed like bad options, although after being up and down the stairs all day the basement no longer sent her skin crawling, and she seemed to be growing used to the mustiness. Who was she kidding? She didn't want to go down there alone. Yep, a five-year-old would save her.

"I'll come with you, Mama—I want to see what's down there." Bailey looked at her with those eyes with the impossibly long black lashes. "Are there toys?"

"Not that I saw, but I didn't explore that much."

"I know there's some and I'm going to find them!"

"How do you know that?"

Bailey looked down at her scuffed sneakers, "I just do." Her daughter paused a second; Rhonda could all but hear her mind working. "Grandma and Grandpa's basement has lots of toys."

Rhonda nodded: this was true. "Come on then. Let's get the last of the clothes and put them away, then I'll start dinner."

"What's for dinner?"

Rhonda thought about her mid-afternoon conversation with Anita. "I'm thinking maybe spaghetti." Rhonda yelled up the stairs, "Carlos! Be back in ten!" She heard a grunted response and a *ratatattat!* from a video game.

Bailey raced out the front door and headed to the cellar stairs. "Be careful on the steps, they're dangerous!" called Rhonda.

Bailey swung the door open and stopped cold. "You go first, Mama."

Rhonda busied herself folding laundry and stacking it in her plastic basket. Bailey checked out the corners of the basement with the flashlight app on her mother's phone. "What's this, Mama?"

Rhonda placed a stack of folded jeans into the basket. "What's what, Bailey?" She heard a metallic jangling sound from across the concrete and cinder block room. Dropping the shirt she was holding, she walked to where Bailey was standing at the far end of the basement, Rhonda's phone in her small hand. There was a door that blended in so well with its surroundings that she hadn't noticed it before. It was secured with an ornate and obviously very old padlock. She tugged it. It stayed secure. "Probably more storage, baby."

Rhonda took her phone back and clasped her daughter's hand. She leaned in close to the door. The odor that seeped from the pores of the basement seemed to be originating from behind the locked space.

Bailey placed her fingers on the elaborate lock. "I think Paul lived in here," she said, jangling it once more, "at least sometimes."

Disconcerted, Rhonda threw the unfolded clothes that were still in the dryer on top of the neat pile of denim. "Let's fold the rest of these upstairs and start dinner." Spaghetti was a certainty now, she was going to need the sauce jar for quarters to feed the machines at The Pines. She and her daughter ascended the creaky cellar stairs, leaving the unsettled shadows that guarded the mysterious locked room to quietly calm.

Chapter Five

Everyone Hates Raisins

1997

This Journal Belongs to James Hansen

Today I had a book report due. I'm not one to read fantasy novels; I find the genre droll, overdone and cliché. Instead of wasting my time, I concocted a book, the author, and the storyline; thirty minutes and two thousand words later, I placed it on my teacher's desk. I've found that most high school educators aren't that bright. I'm certain to receive an exceptional grade for my outstanding summary on the work of an obscure, albeit fabricated, author's fable titled *Robert the Tall*. Our hero proceeded to carry out most of the clichéd journeys of fantasy novels and wrap up the conclusion in a nice, tidy fashion in the tradition of the genre. I don't have time for pointless high school nonsense.

I spotted a new girl at school today. Her name is Kimberly White. She's blonde and petite, pretty in a nor-mal-average-bland type of way, like oatmeal without any sugar—filling, but mundane. I don't stay at school during lunch period often as I have a difficult time listening to and watching people eat. The sound of chewing nearly makes me implode. The sight of half digested lunchroom food is my own personal hell.

Kimberly White. There she was looking at me, lunch tray in hand. I could tell she was waiting for an invita-tion to join me. I moved my backpack out of the way and gestured for her to take a seat. Miss White, it seems, had recently moved from Denver to live with her aunt. That made me question her situation with her parents, but I didn't ask. I found that people are more than willing to tell you their life story without the need to question.

She told me she hadn't had a chance to meet many people yet, but she was hoping it wasn't too late in the year to join a few clubs. She looked like the choir type to me. The next thing out of her mouth was that she loved to sing and could play the piano. So transparent. I was pleas-ant to her and did my best to keep up with the non-stop jabbering, but it was a little unsettling. I don't think any-one has thrown that many words in my direction in years. She prattled on and on, talking with her mouth full, and I began fantasizing about sewing her lips shut to the point of conisdering the best pattern of stitching to employ.

When she was done eating, she gathered her books and headed out, thanking me for the company. I told her I'd see her around sometime, and she'd smiled at me. She has one crooked tooth in front. It overlaps the other tooth in an awkward way. I hadn't been able to stop staring, even through her enormous and repulsive bites of ham sandwich. I hope she didn't notice me gawking at her mouth, but to me, her tooth is as out of place as a clown at a funeral. It's wrong. It's unnatural. It doesn't fit. It's inappropriate, out of place, disturbing. I was so hyper-focused on her dental abnormality that I almost forgot my backpack.

That would have been problematic. No one needs to scrutinize my musings until I'm primed to display them to the masses.

After dinner, which consisted of spaghetti, sauce from a jar (the jar was washed and on the counter awaiting spare change for the laundromat), French bread, and a salad, Rhonda and Bailey sat on the front stoop talking with Henry. He and Edna had just finished dinner as well, and Henry smelled vaguely of meatloaf.

"No idea about the door in the basement," Henry said, smoothing his gray hair back with his hand, the other holding a plastic glass of iced tea. "I've seen it before of course, but never paid it much mind."

"The lock appeared to be too large for a door that size. I was just curious." She absentmindedly bit at a cuticle, her nerves still a little jangled. "I think I'll get a ladder and clean the windows, inside and outside," Rhonda said, thinking about the four small, cloudy basement windows. "It'll give the place a lot more light, don't you think? I wonder if anyone would mind if I trimmed the bushes around them while I'm at it? It's so dark down there, Anita said she wouldn't think about doing laundry in the cellar."

"Anita is afraid of the stairs, sweetie," he said, patting her arm. "She's afraid she'll take a tumble, and I don't rightly blame her for that." Henry smiled. "She's a nice woman and we're friendly, but I think those stairs could be treacherous for a lady of her…authority. If you get what I'm saying." He smiled at her. "As for the bushes, I don't think anyone would mind one bit."

"And the basement door? The one with the padlock? I'm sorry I keep bringing it up, I'm genuinely curious."

"Probably from way back when this property was a single family house." Henry thought for a moment. "That'd be back in 1978 or so. The house belonged to a family with the last name of Wilson." Henry sat his glass on the stoop; condensation dribbled down the sides of the plastic and puddled onto the cement. "The house it-self was built in 1901. Generations of Wilsons lived here, they passed down over the years, always keeping it in the family until Rose Wilson sold it to developers from Den-ver. After Rose's son was gone, she never set foot in the house again." He leaned in close and whispered to Rhon-da, "Claimed it was haunted." Henry shook his head and continued, "The real estate developer wanted to tear it down and make apartments, but the people of Patton were having none of that nonsense. Eventually they set-tled on dividing it up into four sections and declared it a landmark." Henry reached over and tapped Bailey on the nose, "That's how 291 Chestnut became 291 Chestnut, number one, two, three and four. You being in number one." He turned to Rhonda. "You want some iced tea? I can get you some."

"No thank you, Henry, we're good." She smiled at him. "It sounds as if this property has gone through some major changes in its time."

"Sure has. There was a stairway that divides in two at the top, what are they called?"

"Split landing?"

"Right, that's it. You and me, in number one and two, have half of those old stairs, since we're out front and all. Anita's stairs used to be the servant's stairs."

"And Ethan?"

"They put in a spiral staircase when they divided the place up. Number four is the smallest." Henry waved at a car that drove past. The blonde woman in the passenger seat waved back. "That's Beth Harmon. She's the closest thing that Patton has to a celebrity."

Beth nimbly maneuvered around the Sinkhole de Mayo.

"She's famous?"

"Yep, she wrote a bunch of books for ladies. Romance novels. I've never read them, but Edna has every one of them and I bet she's read them all three times. They're all signed, too. Edna tells me they're rather spicy." Henry grinned, making air quotes around the word. "I honestly should read them, Beth being our neighbor and all, but I'm too afraid someone will see me holding a book with those kinds of cover photos. I'll leave the romance and 'spicy' things to you women, I'm more of a history buff myself." He sipped his tea. "You know, sometimes Edna and I sit at opposite ends of the couch and just read. We don't say a word for hours." Henry's eyes seemed far away and misty. He shook his head and came back to the conversation. "Anyway, there was a stipulation in the sale of the house, put there by Rose, that Ethan Wilson, Edgar

Wilson's only surviving heir and nephew, would have at least one quarter of it for himself. The guy that bought it turned it into a quadplex and set up Ethan in number four. More of a studio, really. Kitchen, bathroom, a small living area on the first floor, and a loft for a bedroom."

"Yes, I've been inside, he showed me around the other day." Rhonda dug her lip balm from her pocket and applied a layer. Darn dry Colorado weather, "I saw his paintings, he's quite the artist."

"That he is! I have one hanging in the upper hallway. It's a watercolor of a pond with reeds. That's what it's called, A Pond with Reeds," Henry said, and added, "He's a nice man, that Ethan. Lives frugally and works a low stress job. Seems really happy about it too." Henry circled the lip of his iced tea glass with a finger, "the company he keeps is, let's say, questionable, but he helps me sometimes when I need something heavy moved. He made me promise that if I needed help around the house, now with Edna and her health the way it is, that I'd ask him first." Henry pointed at Bailey. "I'll ask this young lady second. You up to that, sweetheart?"

Bailey grinned, "Sure! Will you pay me?"

"Bailey!"

Henry let out a hearty laugh. "How 'bout I pay you with cookies?"

"Deal. As long as they don't have raisins in them." Bailey made a face.

"Pardon her manners, Henry. Good grief."

"I know a song about raisins that I learned in school today, Mr. Hansen. Do you want to hear it?"

"Of course I do!"

Rhonda smiled, since she knew what was coming; she'd been her daughter's captive audience for hours now.

Bailey took a piece of lined paper from her pocket, stood proudly, and sang:

> My neighbor is a baker,
> Her name is Mrs. Clout.
> Sometimes she makes me cookies
> and I pick the raisins out.
> Sometimes she makes me cherry pie.
> Sometimes she makes me cake.
> Sometimes I eat the raisins
> 'Cuz she took the time to bake!

Bailey took a bow.

Henry laughed, and both he and Rhonda clapped. "Bravo! You must sing that for Edna sometime!"

Bailey bounced and plopped on her mother's lap. "I will!"

Rhonda ran her hands through Bailey's hair. "What about Anita in number three? What's her story?"

"She moved in about five years ago, she was married at the time." Henry spat over the edge of the stoop into the weeds. "Sorry, think I might be coming down with a chest cold. Her husband wasn't around much, only got a glimpse of him a time or two, and then he was gone. She had the older girl at the time, not sure how the little one came about…you'd have to ask Anita about Sophia's daddy." Henry sniffed. "I believe she has a boyfriend named Lenny or Kenny. Something like that. The only reason I know that is, I hear her yelling at him occasionally."

"I think his name's Kenny," Rhonda said. "Anita thinks he looks like Brad Pitt."

Henry laughed, and iced tea dribbled from his mouth. "Maybe if a person got hit on the head a few times he'd look like Brad Pitt." He wiped his lips with his hand.

Rhonda grinned and stood. "Well, I better get going, Henry. This girl here needs a bath and then it's bedtime, there's school tomorrow." She placed a hand on Henry's shoulder. "Tell Edna hello for us." She took Bailey's hand as they turned to leave.

"Call me if you need help with anything, Mr. Hansen!" said Bailey.

"I sure will honey, I most certainly will."

"No raisins!"

"No raisins, I promise."

Henry picked up his glass, stood up, and his knees popped like old dry wood. He gave Rhonda and Bailey a wave, and the door to 291 Chestnut, number two closed behind them.

"Hi, Daddy!" Tate's face filled Rhonda's laptop and Bailey bounced. "I miss you," she pouted, then brightened. "Did you buy me something yet?"

"Hey, Dad!" Carlos photobombed the screen, making faces from behind his sister. Bailey swatted at him.

Tate's face gave a pixellated hop around. "You'll find out when I get home."

"Listen, kids," Rhonda said, "Mom needs to talk to Dad about some boring stuff. You get yourself upstairs and ready for bed, and I'll read you two books tonight, Bailey."

She turned to Carlos. "And you can have an extra twenty minutes playing video games, deal?"

"Deal." Carlos took the stairs two at a time. "Bye, Dad!"

"Bye, Daddy! I love you!"

"Wow," said Tate, "I'm impressed. Not one bit of argument out of them." He took a drink from a soda can that sat on the table next to him. "Did you call an exorcist or something?"

"Oh, stop!" Rhonda laughed. If he were here in person she'd have given him a punch to the arm.

"So how are our neighbors?"

"I've met all of them now. They seem like a nice bunch of people, although the jury is still out on Anita in number three."

"What about Anita?"

"Nothing really, I probably don't know her well enough to form an opinion." Rhonda stared at a spot above the computer screen. "She's just a bit…hard around the edges, I suppose you could say?"

Rhonda went on to tell Tate about her experience in the basement, her scare during her star performance in the wonderful world of washing, and the mysterious padlocked door. "I'm not usually spooked so easily. I'm a bit embarrassed. I've always seen myself as a woman with a firm constitution."

"I think your idea about giving the windows a good wash is great," Tate said. "All basements are creepy. Dust, cobwebs, those small windows and lack of illumination." He took another swig of soda, "When I get home I'll see about putting in better lighting. How's that?"

Rhonda let out a breath. "That would be amazing—thanks, Tater. I might just wash the outside of the windows and leave the inside until I can actually see what I'm doing." She thought about this for a moment. "No, never mind. I'll get it done. I'm fearless, remember?"

"I have something I have to tell you, my sweet, darling, fearless wife."

"Uh oh." He hadn't made a comment about her use of the nickname Tater. "Uh oh."

"I may have to stay an extra two weeks."

"Aw, Jesus, Tate, you can't be serious."

Tate rubbed his thumb and forefinger together. "The money for those extra two weeks is more than I've made all year."

Rhonda dropped her head and groaned. "Down payment for our forever home?" She shook a finger at the screen. "I'm going to make you promise this time."

"I promise."

"Pinky swear?" She held up the little finger of her right hand.

He held up his. "Pinky swear."

Bailey called down from the top of the stairs, "Daddy? You want to hear my song about raisins?"

"Yes baby, I do!"

"I'm not a baby!"

"I miss you all so damn much," Tate said softly. Rhonda knew he meant every word. "Is Goldie still with the living?"

"So far, so good," Rhonda told him. "If she croaks I'll just replace her with another Goldie from the pet store. Goldie has a lot of relatives that look just like her."

Tate laughed, "I love you."

"I love you too."

Chapter Six

Stone Cold Dead and Buried

The Wilson House, 1957

Edgar Wilson did not trust public schools. He wanted his children brought up in a strict, God-fearing environment without the influence of self-proclaimed educators who coddled children to the point of producing entitled, spineless adults. Patton Elementary School was about as far as you could get from the kind of education he envisioned for his children. The majority of parents dragged their feral offspring to church on Sundays, but that's where living true to the Word of the Lord ended. He was having none of it. Edgar's wife Beatrice was perfectly able to teach his children The Word of God and the basics of math and grammar. What more did they need to know to grow into good Christian people, who lived a life of self control and obedience?

Beatrice had set up her own classroom in her home at 291 Chestnut Street, making sure it was in a quiet place where there would be no interference. Class began with prayer and the reading of scripture. After three hours they would move on to other less essential teachings, like reading, addition and subtraction. Edgar oversaw every aspect of the curriculum down to the last Bible verse and math problem. He insisted that class be over by noon, so Beatrice had plenty of time to engage in her other household duties.

Edgar, being the head of the household, insisted on a clean house, dinner promptly at 6:00 P.M., well-mannered, quiet children, and a report from his wife on the day's activities. 291 Chestnut Street was his house and he ruled over it. For the most part, his daughter, Rose Wilson, was just that, well-mannered and quiet. He had made sure she knew that the inside of the house was for unobtrusive, near-silent play time. Paul, Rose's twin brother, struggled with this. His condition put him on a rollercoaster of mood, often leading to a frenzy of emotional outbursts. Edgar did not understand Paul's lack of self control. "Spare the rod, spoil the child"— he would not have a coddled son. Edgar would make sure of this. Paul's "condition" be damned, he would abide by the house rules just as his mother and sister knew they must.

Having returned home for the day, Edgar hung up his coat and called for his wife. She came from the kitchen, wiping her hands on her floral apron.

"Yes?" she said.

"Yes, what?"

"Yes, Edgar?" Beatrice looked down toward her hands, which were now knotted in the fabric of her apron.

"Better." He enjoyed control in his household. "Where are the children?"

"They're outside playing," she replied, adding quickly, "their school work is finished and on your desk."

"Are they playing with those damn colored kids?"

"Yes Edgar, Leyta and Johnathan are here."

"Keep them outside." Edgar walked to his office and closed the door.

Rose watched over her twin brother like a mama bear tends to her cub. If he had one of his meltdowns, she would take him out to the carriage house and close the door. She'd hold him close to her, as if when they were in the womb together, and she would rock him and stroke his hair. Rose would tangle herself around her brother until he stilled, his face streaked with tears and beads of perspiration. Paul would lay his head on his sister's shoulder, their red hair intertwined; his was short and choppy, hers long and flowing. No one understood her brother the way that Rose did.

The loft in the carriage house was their refuge and was filled with toys stealthily taken one by one from the house. Sometimes they would sit and draw all afternoon; Paul's drawings were remarkable for their realism and intricate detail. Every drawing contained birds. Crows were his favorite, and his work far exceeded the ability of any ordinary eight-year-old.

Rose would leave a window open that faced the big house so she could hear if they were being called inside. Mother and Father would call twice, no more, before there was trouble to be had. Rose was sure that Mother was following Father's instructions with the two calls for dinner rule, but the look on his face if they were even close to late made it obvious that both she and her brother would be punished. Her mother was chastised at his hand as well, and feared him—Rose could smell it on her, and, in Rose's eyes, Mother would shrink inches under his gaze.

Rose, on the other hand, stood tall. She would do as he asked, but she would not bend for him. She knew he sensed her defiance. Father would slither off his belt (two swats for two calls) and Paul would crumble and be sent to his room; in extreme cases, he'd be sent to the basement room to ponder his wrongdoings without dinner. Rose would be allowed to remain at the dinner table, quietly eating and hiding away bits of dinner in her dress pockets to give to Paul. Mother would sit silently, not touching her food, her eyes occasionally flickering in the direction of Paul's empty chair.

After dinner, Rose's father would retreat to his office and she and her mother would clean the kitchen and wash the dishes. When all was tidy, Mother would completely disengage and retire to her bedroom. If Paul was confined to his room, Rose would crack open his door and slide in the napkin which held the remnants of dinner she'd managed to squirrel away. If he had been sent to the basement, this was not an option. On those occasions, Rose would lie on her bed unable to rest until she heard the sound of Paul being led back to his bedroom. Sometimes it was hours. A few times it was overnight.

As twins, they were a novelty. As twins with bright Irish red hair and schooled at home, they were beyond that. In 1957, Paul's disability helped secure their place as odd ducks, and made them ostracized from children their own age. He would never survive, let alone thrive, in a public school setting. It made the pickings slim when it came to making friends, but Rose didn't mind, she loved her brother more than anything in the world. Rose did, however, have one good friend named Leyta Simmons. Leyta was Rose's age and the daughter of the only Black family in Patton. Being outsiders in 1957 naturally drew them together, and, as luck would have it, they got along well and the girls bonded. Their personalities and likes were similar, and they became fast friends. Having someone her own age to confide in and trust made Rose's life happier. When she was with her friend, the musings of her less than idyllic home life stilled. Leyta became Rose's safe place; Rose knew how lucky she was to have her in her world. Leyta felt the same and voiced it often.

Leyta had a younger brother named Johnathan whom she sometimes brought along to play. He was three years old and didn't speak much yet, but he and Paul seemed to understand each other as if by some secret telepathic language. The boys would wander the woods behind the house, making forts from sticks and building rock castles. Paul was comfortable around Johnathan, and if they were more than thirty yards or so from the back of the carriage house, Paul would insist on holding the younger boy's hand and pulling him closer to the girls.

Other than herself, Johnathan was the only other person she'd seen Paul purposefully touch. It made Rose happy that Paul was such a good companion to Johnathan, and because of it, the girls didn't worry too much when the boys were out exploring. Rose and Leyta took that time to play board games, make up elaborate stories with dolls, and Rose's favorite: school. Leyta did a fine impersonation of her teacher, Mr. Carlson, and since Rose had never been to public school, she soaked up every moment of it. They'd giggle and gossip together; Rose shared everything about her life with Leyta. Sometimes it was difficult for Rose to understand; Leyta's family didn't have any of the same poisonous drama that Rose's did, although some of the stories Leyta shared about being the solitary Black family in town might be worse. Their situations couldn't have been more different, but the day-to-day pain itself bonded them. More than once they'd cried together trying their best to understand and, most of all, to be there for one another and listen.

Father's tools lined the walls of the carriage house and sat upon shelves. The old cistern beneath the carriage house had been unused for many years and was securely locked shut, only making its presence known if one of the children tripped over the padlock. The carriage house floor was covered in layer after layer of sawdust, as was the rest of the six-hundred-square-foot building; but a pathway of bare dirt, crafted by footprints, cut through the sawdust to the ladder of a triangular corner loft.

While the first-floor walls held Father's tools, which they were not allowed to go near or touch, the loft was another matter. The loft was Leyta and Rose's safe place. Once they climbed the ladder, the upper story was a magical art project in the making. Sometimes they'd color on the loft walls, pretending they were making wallpaper for the house that they'd share when they grew up, and often they'd tape their paper artwork to the wooden walls. When the boys weren't busy playing outdoors, Johnathan and Paul would climb up and paint with the girls.

A few feet from the floor were Johnathan's scribbles. Higher up were Paul's elaborate drawings. Paul saw the world in a way that the other children did not, and it showed in his artwork. The rear wall was covered in elaborate scenes, at times abstract and dark. Intricate sketches of trees and birds and wildlife; a mural which allowed a glimpse of the existence that lived inside Paul. Paul's world poured forth through his delicate fingers, splashing across the loft wall with an outpouring of quizzical emotion that otherwise lay hidden from sight. Day by day his artwork changed. Paul would wash the chalk-covered meadow scenes and replace them with dark, wilted nightmares. Rose knew it was the only way her brother could express what was boiling inside him. The girls gave him space when he was in the mood to create.

Rose and Leyta made a heartfelt promise to always be friends. She felt closer to Leyta and Johnathan than she ever would to her own parents.

"Bread and Butter."

"Butter and Bread."

They swore a pinky oath on this each time they were together. A solemn eight-year-old swear—pinky oaths were never to be broken.

"I wish you could come to school with me. I know you'd like it," Leyta said one day while they were playing reading class with their dolls. Leyta brought books with her the likes of nothing that Rose's father would allow in their home. Mystery stories and books about pirates and treasure. Sometimes Rose would sneak them into her house and read after everyone was asleep.

"I do too, Leyta, but even if my father would let me, who would take care of Paul?" Rose shook her head. "Paul wouldn't be happy going to school. We both know how the kids around here can be."

Leyta nodded and understood. She understood all too well.

"And what if he got into trouble while I'm not here?" Rose continued. "You know how my father is. Paul wouldn't be safe."

Leyta sighed and stood. "I'll be right back," she told Rose as she climbed the ladder down to the sawdust floor and toward the back door to the carriage house.

"Check on the boys while you're out there?"

Leyta nodded and closed the door. Rose sighed, and her shoulders fell. Father had made it crystal clear that he did not want "those damn colored kids" in the house. He allowed them to play out back, and he didn't even like that much and made it loudly known. If Leyta or Johnathan needed to use the bathroom, they had to go into the forest behind the house. Rose and Paul would also take nature breaks in the forest; it felt wrong to go into the house when their friends were not allowed.

Father. Rose despised him.

Occasionally, Mother would bring them lemonade and cookies when father wasn't home. There was a time. when Father was on a three-day business trip, that she allowed Paul and Rose to visit the Simmons's house for a play day. Mother sat in the kitchen with Leyta's mom Sheila, drank coffee, and gossiped. It was so nice to see her mother smile and laugh. Leyta's father was outside painting the trim of their house. His name was George Simmons, and he was covered in yellow paint. Rose and Leyta begged to have a sleepover, but Mother's eyes clouded over a bit and her brow creased—the same look they'd seen so many times when she was weighing the pros and cons of going against her husband's wishes. Mother's indecisiveness lasted a few moments, and then she said no. Even so, that day when she was allowed to play in Leyta's bedroom was one of the happiest of Rose's life. Sure, she'd seen many of her toys and books when Leyta would bring a box full to the carriage house, but seeing them in their place, on her shelves, in her *bedroom,* was a completely different feeling. It made Rose happy and a bit envious. That day, the girls heard the sounds of their mothers' whispered voices from the kitchen, and they crept out to eavesdrop.

Rose peeked around the corner. Mother was holding Leyta's mom's hand. "I have thought of leaving him," she said, touching a tender bruise under her eye, "I've thought of it for a long time. I have a metal box that I've hidden, filled with all the money I can siphon off without being noticed, and I have my grandmother's and my mother's jewelry."

Rose watched Sheila squeeze. her hand. "You know that George and I will help any way that we can."

Rose and Leyta looked at one another; they had been under the impression that this was Beatrice and Sheila's first meeting, but by how close the women seemed, it was obviously not.

"If you want me to keep the box for you, I will," Sheila told her.

"I have it fairly well hidden," Bea said, "but thank you. "I have no idea how much my mother's jewelry is worth. I'll have to rely on the money I can squirrel away, and use the jewelry for when we get ourselves settled." Bea looked up at Sheila with tears in her eyes, "I hope we can still see each other sometimes."

The girls looked at each other and dashed back to Leyta's bedroom.

"You can't move away!" Leyta said, clinging to Rose. "You can live with us!"

"I won't! I will never move away, I can't! I won't go!" Rose started to cry. "We'll think of something, promise me?"

Leyta nodded. The bright mood had evaporated like warm breath on a cold day. "We'll think of something," she said, but Rose wasn't sure what that could possibly be.

At the end of the day, Sheila gave Rose's mother a huge hug and told her to please call her if she needed anything. Once the door closed behind Bea and Rose, George took his wife into his arms. "If he hits her again, we call the police." Rose could see and hear them through the open window.

"Do you think they'd even listen to us? Edgar is a very big presence in this town." Sheila was crying now. "Would they listen to a Black man accusing one of Patton's prominent citizens of abusing his wife? George, I think if you were to go to the police it would be *you* who would end up in jail."

That evening, Rose said a silent prayer pleading with God that her father would travel more often, or get so drunk that he'd never come back home at all. Guilt, like a thick, wet fog, would rush in and smother her prayer, but she couldn't help wishing for him to disappear. She wished he were properly stone cold dead and buried. The world would be a better place without Edgar Wison in it.

Chapter Seven

Going to Jupiter…

RHONDA HAD TALKED HERSELF into washing the windows in the godawful basement, but first, a good deal of landscaping needed to be done to reach them from the outside so it wouldn't be quite as dark *inside*. The bushes and weeds had grown thick around the foundation of the quad, and Rhonda wondered if she could tackle them with the flimsy tools that she had.

"Need some help?"

Rhonda jumped. "Ethan! I swear the people in Patton are the most light-footed folks I've ever met!" She set down her bucket with its window cleaning supplies and her pitiful pair of weed trimmers that doubled as kitchen shears. "Actually," she said, holding up her pathetic scissors, "do you have any *real* tools I could borrow to hack down these overgrown shrubs?"

"I do. Not that they're all mine." Ethan motioned for Rhonda to follow him. Turning the corner, he led the way to an ivy-covered carriage house on the back part of the property. He unlocked the door and threw the latch that held the door closed. "Gosh, I barely noticed this building back here—it has more weeds around it than the basement windows!"

Ethan opened the door and reached in to turn on the lights. "This used to be where carriages were stored, way back before cars were around. We've always called it the carriage house. I suppose a *garage* wasn't fancy enough." Ethan walked inside and Rhonda followed. There were boxes and walls of tools, old camping equipment, stacks of wood, and an oily concrete floor. "This property never fails to amaze me," Rhonda said, checking out various pieces of antique hardware. There was even an ancient ore bucket in the back right corner. Rhonda bent to examine it. This would look pretty out front filled with flowers."

"Here we go!" Ethan held up a pair of hedge trimmers that made Rhonda's little snippers look like a toy.

"What's up there?" Rhonda asked, pointing to a loft that covered about a third of the square footage of the property.

"No idea, probably more tools. You're standing in the middle of the land where things you seldom use go to die."

"Like a giant kitchen junk drawer," she said. "How do you get up there?"

"I haven't a clue, maybe there used to be a ladder?"

They left the carriage house, and Ethan locked the door behind them. "Let's see what we can do about cutting down the jungle around those basement windows."

Through a lot of grime, sweat, and the passing of two hours, the hedges in front of the windows were cut down to ground level. Rhonda peeked through the mucky glass, her cleaning bucket in hand. "I can take it from here, Ethan." She placed her hand on his arm. "Thanks so much."

"No problem at all, Rhonda." He wiped his brow, leaving a muddy brown streak. "I need to go shower and get to work, but I'll see about moving that ore bucket to the front for you." He picked up the hedge clippers. "I'll put these back before I go." Ethan dug in his pocket for the ring that held the carriage house key.

"Ethan…can I ask you something?"

"Sure, Rhonda, what's up?"

Rhonda was looking at his key ring. "Do you happen to have the key to the locked door in the basement?"

Ethan laughed. "I sure don't. That thing's been locked tight since I can remember—at least since I was a kid, and that's a pretty long time ago." Ethan palmed the rest of the keys in his hand, his slender fingers wrapping around them tightly.

Rhonda wasn't sure she believed him.

Later that day, three blocks from 291 Chestnut Street, a front screen door slapped open.

"Auntie Carla!" Bailey raced into the house and hugged Rhonda's sister Carla Ruiz around the waist. Carlos hugged his aunt and then hurried to his cousin BJ's room to see his new frog. Rhonda gave her a hug too. "You smell like cheese, Auntie Carla!" Bailey said, still clinging tight to her.

"Geeze, Bailey!" Rhonda sighed, shaking her head.

"That, mi hija, is because I'm making macaroni and cheese for our dinner tonight. Along with a meatloaf and broccoli."

"I don't like broccoli. It smells like Carlos's farts."

"Bailey!"

Clara cackled. "I'll cut you up some carrot sticks, how's that?" This appeased Bailey and she skipped off toward BJ's room to see the frog.

"Where did I go wrong?" Rhonda asked her sister.

"What? Are you kidding? We have the greatest kids ever." She threw her arm around Rhonda's shoulder. "They're a laugh a minute. Would you rather have 'seen and not heard' children? I wouldn't. Think of all the fun we'd miss."

Bailey stuck her head out of her cousin BJ's door. "The frog swallows live crickets whole!" She bounced back into the bedroom.

Rhonda laughed and followed her sister into the kitchen. "You're right, I wouldn't know what to do with well-behaved kids. Wow, something smells fantastic!" she said as she sniffed the air. "You inherited all the good cooking genes in the family, that's for sure."

Carla cracked the oven door so Rhonda could take a peek. "Only the best for my baby sister and her monsters." Macaroni and cheese bubbled, its crust brown and crunchy. She closed the oven and held up a bottle of Malbec. "Wine?"

"Dear gods, that looks and smells amazing. What are the rest of you going to eat?" As if on cue, Rhonda's stomach grumbled. "I could eat the whole casserole with my hands, and to answer your question, absolutely on the wine." She set two glasses on the counter. "We walked over, and I think I know the town well enough now that I can find my way home."

Carla poured the wine, and they took a seat across from each other at the kitchen table. "How's BJ doing?"

Carla traced the edge of her wine glass with a finger. "As well as can be expected, I suppose." She closed her eyes for a moment. "Losing his dad and his grandpa the way he did last year…" Her words trailed off, and Rhonda placed her hand over her sister's. "I still loved him, you know?" she said, talking about Bobby, her ex-husband. "And who couldn't love Grandpa Manny? He was like…super Pop-Pop." Carla wiped at her face. "Having you, Tate, and the kids here is going to be so good for him," she said, and sipped her wine. "This is the happiest I've seen him in a year. I'm not exaggerating one little bit. Manny and Bobby's death was a nightmare for all of us." Carla took a hefty gulp from her glass. "I hope their killer rots in hell."

"Let's plan on lots of mac and cheese and wine nights," Rhonda said, giving Carla's hand a squeeze. "It'll be good for all of us."

Carla set her wine down, walked around the table, and hugged Rhonda tight. "I love you, baby sis."

"I love you too." Rhonda felt hot tears prickle her eyes. "Anyway, next time, dinner at my place. You can help me wash the cellar windows, I don't like going down there alone. That being said, there's a spooky basement for the kids to explore, and BJ and Carlos will be all over that."

"You really think you can keep Bailey from joining them?"

Rhonda laughed. "So true." She clinked her glass to her sister's. "Here's to feral children."

"Mom!" The voice was Bailey's, and urgent. "There's only half a cricket left, come see!"

Rhonda and Carla agreed that BJ could spend the night with Carlos. "Bring a flashlight, BJ," Carlos said, as BJ and Bailey joined him racing toward the front door to join their moms. "I want to check out the stinky basement."

BJ nodded eagerly. "One more thing." He got his bat from the coat closet and stuck it under his arm. "I think I'll take this too," he said, and shoved his little league helmet into his duffle bag.

"Your helmet? How come?"

"Maybe it's haunted?"

"Your helmet?"

"No idiot, the basement!" Carlos punched his cousin good-naturedly. "Anyway, what good will a baseball bat do against ghosts?"

"Maybe ghosts like baseball," Bailey said. "Look, Mama, I rescued one of the crickets, can we buy it a cage?"

The four of them headed out the door and toward home. Carla waved until they turned the corner.

Rhonda laughed. "Maybe we should let him live in the backyard with his friends."

"Okay. I'm going to name him Paul."

"That's random," Rhonda said, plopping her into her booster, "why Paul?"

"Then I'll know two Pauls!"

"Two Pauls?"

"Yep!" Bailey spun in a circle. "The other Paul is my friend."

The cricket bounced in its little plastic bag. "Where does the other Paul live?"

"The carriage house." Bailey skipped ahead. "But he comes to visit me in my room when he's sad."

After Rhonda and Bailey were asleep, BJ and Carlos prepared to carry out their clandestine mission to explore the haunted basement and plunder its treasures.

"You know what time it is?" BJ whispered to his cousin as they slipped out the front door.

"Dunno."

"It's 3:33," BJ whispered.

"So?"

"That's half evil."

Carlos snorted out a laugh. "And you're half stupid."

BJ snickered and stuck his Little League helmet on his head. "I'm goin' to Jupiter…"

"…to get more stupider!" they finished together.

Carlos punched him. "Anyway, dummy, there's a bunch of boxes and crates under the stairs. Mom's been too afraid to go under there, so to her, it's all uncharted territory. I poked around a little but haven't thoroughly investigated. I did see a box marked 'Toys', though. I promised Bailey I'd pull it out for her."

"You took your little sister down here?"

"Yeah, I figured if there were ghosts they'd eat her first."

"Smart move."

The wooden stairs creaked and popped as the cousins made their way down; Carlos searched blindly for the pull cord that would turn on the light. "Got it." The light clicked and flickered a few times until the weak amber glow seeped from the bare bulb, not reaching quite far enough to chase the shadows from their obscured refuge. The old bulb gave the basement the kind of tint that reminded Carlos of pictures in his grandmother's photo album—the ones in which everyone was stiff and looked unhappy.

If Carlos thought the basement seemed creepy during the day, at night it was creepy on crack. Taking one careful step at a time, the boys crept their way across the concrete floor. The lightbulb quivered a few times, and the boys turned on their flashlights in case they were left in darkness.

"It smells terrible down here," BJ said.

"It smells like ghosts."

"Ghost *shit*, maybe."

"Do ghosts shit?"

"If they eat, they shit."

"What do they eat?"

"Your little sister?"

Snickering ensued. "No wonder it stinks down here."

"My grandpa used to say that ghosts shit those white styrofoam packing peanut things that you get in the mail," said BJ.

Both boys snorted.

"I found something the other day," Carlos said, "but didn't have time to really check it out. My mom was home, and it was almost dinner time." What he didn't add was that spending too much time in the basement alone didn't appeal to him one little bit, and Bailey had refused to go back.

Carlos gestured his cousin over toward the space beneath the steps.

"Show me," B.J. whispered.

Carlos pointed his flashlight under the stairs. Cobwebs glimmered in the stream of circular light, and the boys brushed them away. "It's right here."

Carlos tucked his flashlight under his arm and reached up to a crooked riser about four feet from the ground. It pulled out like a drawer. "I was gonna pull the toy box out for Bailey, and I smacked my head on the damn thing. I didn't have time to investigate; Mom called me for dinner."

Inside the drawer was an old yellow envelope and a key. BJ reached in, took out the envelope, and handed it to his cousin. "You found it, you should open it."

Carlos carefully opened the yellowed envelope which crackled with age. Inside was a folded piece of paper. He unfolded it and read aloud:

February 10th 1955

This is an itemized list of the items I have saved and hidden, hoping for the day I can escape with my children. If someone finds this letter and the contents are still there, I may not be alive. If I am not alive, my husband Edgar Wilson is to blame.

Carlos and BJ looked at one another, their eyes round, their faces startled. Carlos continued reading:

Aunt Pauline's diamond ring
Aunt Pauline's diamond earrings, matching necklace, and bracelet
Gloria's three strand pearl necklace
Grandmother's emerald and diamond art deco ring
Great grandmother's sapphire and diamond brooch
Gloria's three Fabergé eggs.
As of this day, fifteen thousand dollars.

I am not a great artist, but this is approximately where I have hidden the metal box. It is ten inches long, five inches wide and eight inches tall. I'll be adding to it until I am sure that I and my children will be safe. Enclosed is the key.

Beatrice Wilson

A rough map was drawn on the yellowed paper. It was clear where the house stood, even though it had been re-modeled over the years and divided into quads. The carriage house was also evident, drawn as a school child would draw it, boxy with square windows. To the south of the carriage she'd drawn a tree, and beneath that tree was an X.

"Holy ghost pepper Jesus!" BJ said.

Carlos high fived his cousin, pocketed the map and key, and headed toward the stairs. The door to the basement creaked open from above. The boys clicked off their flashlights and retreated to the darkness under the steps. They held their breath.

"Somebody down here?" a voice called. "Hello?"

It was Ethan Wilson from number four. He walked to the padlocked room and opened it with a key. All of thirty seconds later he was out, locked the room back up, and pulled the cord to the light, leaving them in darkness. Back up the stairs he went.

"That was seriously close," BJ whispered.

Carlos nodded in the dark, "Count to thirty to give Ethan a chance to go home and then let's get out of here."

"One Mississippi…"

Something bumped in the general area of the ancient washer and dryer, and a wave of putrid stink washed over them. The boys dashed instantly for the stairs.

"Hurry!" BJ said, "Smells like something died down here!"

Carlos pushed his cousin from behind to hurry him up. Basement exploration was done for the day and had been a surprising, yet terrifying, success.

After retreating to the house, the boys leaned breathless against the front door. "My dad got a metal detector for his birthday, and I think he bought me one too," Carlos said.

BJ grinned. "Treasure hunting…"

"Yep!"

The boys raced up the indoor stairs to Carlos's bedroom to further examine the map, their minds bubbling with thoughts of treasure and ghosts.

"Make sure you hold on to that map and key. I'm never going down into your basement again."

Bailey poked her head out from her room. She was holding Goldie's fishbowl. "Will you two assholes shut up? We're trying to sleep."

Chapter Eight

Can Ghosts get Colds?

Patton, Colorado, 1957

"Paul!" Beatrice Wilson cried out through cupped hands. "Paul! Where are you?"

Beatrice was beginning to slip into a full-blown panic; her son had been missing for over an hour. "Rose," her mother said, shaking her by the shoulders, "when was the last time you saw him? When did you see Paul for the last time?" Rose buried her face in her hands and sobbed, trembling. She didn't speak. She couldn't.

Beatrice's voice took on an hysterical edge. "Damn it, Rose, when did you see him?"

Rose looked up at her frantic mother, who never cursed, but couldn't quite make out her face through a blur of tears. *The last time I saw him—alive?* "I can't remember," Rose wailed and curled herself into a ball, hugged her arms around her chest, and rocked. "I don't know, I don't know, I don't *know!*"

Beatrice sped past her into the house to find Father. The screen door slapped shut. "Edgar! I need your help! I can't find our son!"

Her voice rang through the empty house. She raced into the main level, and Rose could hear doors opening and slamming. "Paul! Edgar!" Her mother's cries echoed up the stairwell.

Rose heard her mother sprint up the stairs, then the sounds of more doors opening and banging closed. Rose thought her heart just might explode, it was pounding so fast. *Oh God, Paul.* Her sweet brother, her twin. It was her job to take care of him, to keep him safe. She'd never forgive herself. Oh god, she wished Leyta was here. She wished Paul was here. This thought brought on a fresh wave of sobs. She'd failed him.

An hour later the police arrived. They searched the house again, finding no sign of the eight-year-old redheaded boy or his father.

"Do you think that your husband could have taken him someplace?" the policeman asked Beatrice.

"No! He never took our boy anywhere, and his car is still here!"

"The train station is only half a mile away," said the officer. "He could have taken him to the city?"

"I'm telling you, no. Edgar and Paul are not close, I can't remember one time that they went out alone together." Beatrice scrubbed at her eyes; her hands were clenched into fists.

"We'll check the woods behind the house, and ask around at the train station," the officer said. Rose noticed that his shoes were spit-shined to a bright polish. What a strange thing to notice.

The policeman turned his attention to Rose. "Young lady, when did you last see your brother? Think very hard, please."

Rose looked up at him, her eyes glassy and swollen. "I saw him playing behind the carriage house." She dropped her head, tears slipping from the tip of her nose.

"You didn't see him after that?"

She hesitated a moment. "No, sir." Rose turned her back to him and curled into the corner.

"Ma'am, you said your son was a difficult child."

"Yes, he has a medical condition that makes him troublesome at times. He doesn't talk much and has a tendency to throw fits, beat his head on the ground, and scream. If he doesn't get his way or things are out of order for him he'd be in an uncontrollable state, sometimes for hours." Bea slipped into thought for a moment. He also has a condition called dyslexia, he gets letters and pictures jumbled." She looked down and her face flushed. "I have it too."

"Could he have wandered off and gotten lost because of this?"

"No! He never wandered far. It just isn't like him."

"Do you believe your husband may have harmed your son?"

"No,"—Beatrice's eyes shifted from officer to officer, and she crossed her arms over her chest—"of course not!"

"Do you think there's a possibility that he may have run away?"

"No!" Beatrice shifted from foot to foot. "I don't know. Where would he go? He's eight years old!" She wrung her hands. "Why are you asking me these things? Why aren't you looking for my boy?"

Another hour passed without a trace of the male members of the Wilson family. Beatrice sat on the back stoop, her head bowed in prayer, her lips moving silently, her eyes closed. Rose had cried herself to sleep on the corner of the back porch.

"Sarge!" one of the officers searching the property exclaimed from somewhere behind the carriage house. "You gotta see this."

Beatrice shot to her feet and trotted behind the other policemen to a grassy spot right at the property line. Rose stayed in her place, her hands over her ears.

A rock about the size of a bowling ball peeked up from beneath the ground. Around it and splattered over it was a dark puddle of what appeared to be blood. The liquid had seeped into the ground and dried a deep copper on the stone. Beatrice dropped to her knees and screamed out, "Paul! This can't be his, can it?"

One of the officers helped her to her feet, her hands sticky with blood which had not dried yet. She felt her knees buckle and cried out for her husband. "Edgar!" The officer held her up, "Edgar!" Beatrice screamed again. "Where's my boy?"

Rose heard the commotion from across the property and clasped her hands tighter over her ears. *No, no, no, no.* Rose could hear her mother's hysterical wailing from a hundred yards away, and she slipped into the back door, went up the stairs, and headed to her bedroom. On the way she stopped at Paul's bedroom. It was all so wrong. It looked just as it had before this nightmare day, how could that be? The bed was made, his toy box was closed, the rug on the floor was still the same faded purple and yellow. Sketches of houses and birds were scattered on his desk. She picked up a picture of a bare tree filled with crows and held it to her chest. Rose grabbed the blanket that her brother always slept with, sagged into her room, fell into bed and pulled the covers over her head. "Oh God, Paul." She held the blanket to her nose and breathed in the scent of her brother.

Rose stiffened, threw the duvet back, swung her legs off her bed, and walked to her parents' bedroom. Clutching Paul's blanket to her chest, she walked to her father's side of the bed and spit hot and fierce onto his pillow. She made her way back to her room, closed the door, slipped back under the covers, and contemplated never coming out again. Paul's blanket. She'd keep it forever.

Oh, Leyta, I need to see you. I need to hug you. I need you to hug me back and tell me everything's okay. She would wait until after dark and sneak out and tap on her friend's window. Rose made a promise to never let anything, anywhere, anyplace, get between their friendship again. Patton, Colorado and your backwards, racist ideals be damned to hell.

Eight months later Rose and Beatrice sold 291 Chestnut Street and moved into George and Sheila Simmons's basement

Edgar and Paul Wilson were not seen again. Of the two, only one was mourned.

Aaron Taylor pounded a hammy fist on the door of quad number four. "Ethan! I know you're in there, open up."

Ethan knew his friend wouldn't go away. He was trapped in his own home. He thought about lying and saying he was sick. "I don't feel real great, go the fuck away."

Aaron gave the door a kick and then another thump with his knuckles. "Dammit, Ethan, we have business we gotta talk about." Aaron was a mountain of a man with a full black beard and a braid of hair that reached to his mid back. "C'mon, baldy, let me in!"

Ethan huffed. He knew he was stuck. He got up, opened the door, and Aaron barreled in.

"What the hell do you want, assquatch?" Ethan asked him.

Aaron took him into a good-natured choke hold and rubbed his hairy knuckles on his friend's bald dome. Aaron outweighed him by a good one hundred pounds, and Ethan was airborne for a moment. "We need to talk business, and we need to do it now, alopeciashit pendejo."

Ethan laughed despite the situation and pushed his friend away. They'd been friends for years. All the way back when an important conversation would have been had at the playground, sitting on the merry-go-round kid launcher in the park. "We're way out of our league, Aaron," he said, rubbing his head as if he still had hair to smooth down.

Aaron grabbed one of Rhonda's leftover cookies and shoved it into his mouth. Crumbs clung to his black beard like tiny mountain climbers on a densely forested slope. "Naw, we just have to give it till the end of the month." He grabbed another cookie and popped it whole into the cave of his mouth. Aaron mumbled through a piehole filled with cookies, "They promised to get it out by the end of the month. We're talking a lot of money here, E-gore." He brushed at his beard. The little cookie mountain climbers now clung to his shirt.

"I know it's a lot of money, but it's making me crazy." Ethan began to pace. "This is some dangerous shit we're dealing with." He looked at Aaron and frowned. "These are some dangerous *people* we're dealing with."

Ethan clenched and unclenched his fists, his anxiety crackling in the air. "I'm never doing this again; I don't care if Kenny is your cousin. Sometimes people have shitty relatives." Ethan couldn't stop pacing "How the hell did Kenny get involved in this? He stopped midstride and glared at Aaron, "he's as dumb as a box full of Helen Kellers."

Aaron walked over and examined the shadow box which displayed Elvis's gun. "Okay, Kenny might have a room temperature IQ, but—hey amigo, maybe you should load this."

"Jesus Aaron, you know I don't know jack shit about guns!"

Aaron turned and looked at him, his face grave. "Have you checked on the stuff?"

"Yes, I've checked on it."

"Are you sure you've checked on it? You're the only one with a key. Why weren't you picking up your phone? That's why I'm here beating down your damn door."

Because I don't want to think about it. It scares the shit out of me, and we just might die.

"Just go down and check it every day to be sure," said Aaron, "or hand over the key and I'll do it."

Ethan thought seriously about doing just that. Give him the key, the money, the spray bottle and instructions—the headache. "I promise to check it once a day," he huffed, and plopped onto the couch. Aaron sat next to him and picked up a video game controller.

"Are you up to me beating your hairless ass?"

"Just one game," Ethan said. "I need to get to bed, I work the early shift tomorrow."

"Just one game, you got it." Aaron handed him the other controller. "I can't believe you still work at the goddamn Dollar Store. After the end of the month you can quit if you want, you'll be set when it comes to dinero."

Ethan slid his hand into his pocket and palmed the key. It was safe on the ring. *The shit I get myself into.* "I like working at the Dollar Store."

"You got any beer?"

"I quit drinking."

Aaron rolled his eyes and looked at him. "Hermanito, you aren't any fun at *all* anymore."

Ah, the last day of school. If only all days could hold such sweet promise.

Rhonda conjured up memories of that glorious feeling from her childhood. Running to her locker as the last bell rang and hugging her friends goodbye with the pledge of many phone calls and sleepovers. The intense feeling of freedom she felt as she stepped off the school grounds and into the commencement of summer. She smiled at the memories, but she had to admit that she was looking forward to the first day of school come mid-August. A new job, a new house, happy kids, her sister close by. Life was good. All that was missing was Tate, and he'd be home soon enough. *If you know what's good for you—*"Tater!"

Carla and BJ would be at her house in just a few moments. It was time to tackle the inside of the dirty cellar windows. There was strength in numbers, and Carla was a badass. Having Carla and the kids running around would ease the creepy-crawlies that she felt when she went into the basement. When did she become such a scaredy cat? The doorbell rang, and she walked with purpose to answer it.

"Surprise!" Carla said, holding up a bucket and leaning the stepladder against the brick. She reached into the bucket and pulled out a box of wine. "I brought liquid reinforcement."

BJ dashed up the stairs heading to Carlos's room.

"Did you wipe your feet?" said Carla.

BJ gave a virtually audible eye roll, clomped back down, wiped his feet, and walked back up the stairs.

Rhonda yelled up after him, "Will you and Carlos please include Bailey today? You're my free babysitters."

BJ moaned. Carlos moaned.

"I. Am. Not. A. Baby!" Bailey yelled, unseen in her bedroom.

Carla giggled. "That girl is five going on fifty."

"I don't think there's anything she can't do," Rhonda said, "except go into the basement alone. It's so out of character for her." She picked up the window cleaner and some fresh rags. "I swear that basement is straight out of a horror movie."

"Damn, this basement is straight out of a horror movie." Carla dropped the bucket. "And it smells like old feet."

Rhonda pointed to the hamper she'd brought down that was filled with Carlos's socks and underpants. "Good call."

The washing machine thumped. The bare bulb swayed. The whorls of shadows that lived in the corners came to life in time with the wobbling light. "I think," said Carla, "it's going to take more than a few clean windows to make this place feel less haunted." She turned and whispered, "Don't you ever walk up these stairs backwards." She placed the stepladder next to the first window. "Do you have a bat? How about a pipe? Great-grandpa's machete?"

Rhonda laughed. "We are so alike. I thought the same thing." She pointed at Carlos's bat leaning against the shelf that held jars of Edna's pickled green beans.

Carla unfolded the ladder and set it against the wall. "Hand me a rag and the vinegar water, would you?"

Rhonda steadied the ladder for her. "Do you want me to do it? I know how you are with heights."

"I'm good, you do the other two."

"I bet there are a million spiders down here."

Carla took the cleaning supplies. "Better spiders than ghosts or serial killers."

"I hate spiders. Spiders are to me like heights are to you."

"You are such a baby, little sis."

Rhonda sing-songed and mimicked Bailey. "I. Am. Not. A. Baby."

They both giggled.

There was a distinct, and very loud sneeze.

"Are the kids down here?" Carla asked.

"No."

"Can you hear the people in the other units?"

"No."

"Can ghosts get colds?"

"No, but murderers can."

Carla scurried down the ladder. "To hell with these windows, we're calling a cleaning service!" She clenched Rhonda's hand. "I'll pay for it."

The sisters made a run for the stairs, leaving the cleaning supplies, the ladder, Carlos's underpants and socks, the ghosts, the monsters, the murderers, and all the spiders for the professionals.

Chapter Nine

A Shoe of Bigfoot, and Spite Brownies

Bailey sat at the little craft table in her room, and a rainbow of wax crayons wiggled as she drew.

Goldie swam in her bowl on the dresser, overseeing playtime. She meandered in and out of a plastic sunken pirate ship, attempting to tune out to the conversation at hand, and was on to much more important things—swimming in circles. She saw the goldfish orange Mango Tango crayon teeter on the edge of the table and roll off. Bailey bent to retrieve it. Whew. That was a close one! Mango Tango was Goldie's favorite color.

Two pieces of what had been crisp white drawing paper sat on the small table as well, the once pristine sheets now covered in bright works of art.

"I'm not anywhere near as good of an artist as you," said Bailey, smiling at the chair across from her where the other piece of paper sat. "I'm pretty good at drawing houses and windows. Sometimes trees." She drew a circle on the top of her paper in bright yellow and made sunbeams around it. "But you can draw people and animals."

Bailey looked over at the other paper. "Is that the carriage house?" Goldie's view was a bit distorted through the curved glass of her fishbowl, but she recognized the sconces and the color of brick. Goldie prided herself on being observant: the intelligence of goldfish has always been hugely underestimated.

Three crows sat atop the peaked roof of the carefully-drawn building. She peeked out of Bailey's bedroom window from where her bowl rested. There were no crows there now. Goldie wasn't sure how she felt about crows. She flicked her lacy tail and turned her attention back to Bailey's art project. Goldie *did* like art.

Bailey listened for a moment. "What's that circle right there?" She poked at the picture, brow wrinkled, and said, "I don't know what a sisturd is." She shrugged and drew in a stick figure, thought for a moment, and then drew in another. "Anyway, I'm so glad you're my friend. Will you sign your picture for me?"

Bailey placed her hand over a spot next to the adjacent paper and patted it. "It's okay, writing is hard. Here, I'll help you." She walked around the table, picked up the black crayon and wrote PAUL in block letters at the bottom of his picture. She sat back down. "Will you pass me the red and the brown, please? I need to draw in our hair." The stick figures held hands and grinned, their smiles as bright as the Colorado sun.

Goldie swam on, a silent but dutiful bodyguard. Mango Tango-colored hair would have been a better option.

"Do we *have* to take her with us?" Carlos asked, as he and BJ gathered camping gear from the old carriage house. He picked up an ax. "We'll need this."

"No you won't," Rhonda said, and took it from his hands. "Yes, you have to include Bailey. I'll come get her at her bedtime so that you and BJ can sleep in the tent alone." She noticed that Ethan had yet to move the old ore bucket. "Before you two set up, help me roll this thing around front."

The three of them tipped over the ore bucket and rolled it out the door. "It needs to go out front by the front porch."

Nacho the chihuahua met them halfway. "Are you out here by yourself, little man?" said Rhonda.

Carlos grunted, gave the iron bucket a shove, and huffed. "Can I have a dog?"

"Someday, I promise." Rhonda always kept her promises. Shoot. She'd just painted herself into a corner with a future dog.

Carlos and BJ grunted as they sat the ore bucket upright.

"Thank you guys! I'll bring out brownies later."

"Homemade or store bought?"

"Store bought."

The boys high fived each other, and Rhonda shot them a look.

"You'll get Bailey by eight?" said Carlos.

"I told her tonight she could stay up till nine."

Carlos clicked his tongue, threw his head back and groaned.

She'll feel left out if she's not included. And don't take that tone with me," she added, pointing to her flip flop.

"Yes, Mom."

The four of them headed back to the carriage house. "That's better," Rhonda said, handing them the tent stakes. "She's only made a few friends since we've moved here, and I want her to have a fun evening."

"She has that imaginary friend she's always talking to. She says he draws pictures for her." Carlos whispered, "I think she might be"—he made a circle with his finger by his temple and whistled—"losing it."

"Be nice." Rhonda used a step stool to get the last tent stake and handed it to him. "No farther than the property line." Rhonda pointed out the back door. "See that pink flag? Put the tent about ten feet from that flag, so I can see it when I come to get Bailey. No farther than that. This property has five acres. You two will be staying in one of them. Do not wander, do you hear me?"

"Fine," he muttered, drawing out the word.

Rhonda raised an eyebrow and put a hand on her hip.

"Yes, Mom," Carlos said. He was smart enough to know that you do not mess with a Mexican mom with a chancla[1] in her hand; she'll smack the fear of god into you from twenty feet away.

"Thanks for helping me move the ore bucket, you two almost-teenage hooligans. Stay outta trouble, and"—the boys took off running and were halfway to the treeline—"be nice to your sister!"

---

1   *Chancla: Object usually made from plastic material and worn on the feet. A small piece of rubber slips between the big toe and the second toe. This item makes a flip flop sound when walking. It also serves as a propulsive unit of discipline.*

"Fine!" came the dragged-out reply.

Rhonda closed the carriage house door. "I might bake brownies just to spite them."

Carla arrived about four-thirty. Bailey waved. "Hi Auntie Carla! Bye Auntie Carla!" She hurried out the door after her brother and cousin, dragging her Barbie sleeping bag around to the back of the house. The tent was already set up and ready for the campout.

"I hope it doesn't rain," Rhonda told her sister, "that old tent is more holey than Great-grandma's mantilla."

"I can't picture Great-grandma without that lacy thing on her head standing in front of the church." Carla giggled. "We're going straight to hell."

"It's true."

"Yeah it is," Carla said, her mood turning serious. "Are you sure it's safe out there?"

"Of course it's safe. They're kids. Let them be kids."

"You're right—we live in friggin' Mayberry," Said Rhonda, opening a bottle of wine.

The next day an unexpected death would shake the small town to its core.

"Let me in, you guys!" Bailey pleaded. The tent was zipped up tight.

Carlos peeked from one of the mesh windows. "No," he said, then thought about what his mom had said about including her. They only had to include her until nine, and it was already seven-thirty. "Alright, fine." He unzipped the tent, and Bailey and her sleeping bag crawled in. "You have to stay in the back," he said, and pointed toward an empty spot in the rear of the six-foot-square tent.

Bailey spread her pink sleeping bag out and placed her pillow on top. She laid back and lookin up at the peaked canopy. "This tent is a flaming piece of shit."

BJ laughed hard. "Is she always like this?"

"Yep."

BJ reached over and fist-bumped Bailey. "You're okay, you know that?"

Bailey grinned, bumped him back and let it explode.

Rhonda had packed dinner for them, and Carla had brought a cooler of soda. Carlos rummaged through the two plastic bags for food. "Baloney and cheese, or peanut butter?" He ripped open a bag of potato chips while he was at it.

"Baloney," said BJ.

Bailey looked up to her cousin and smiled. "Baloney." She didn't like baloney, but she did like BJ. It seemed like the smart thing to do was to get on his good side so her brother wouldn't treat her like a little kid.

A lantern sat in the center of the tent as the three of them ate their dinner and planned out the evening. The sun was beginning to set, leaching the color out of the woods.

"Ghost stories," Bailey said, grabbing a fistful of chips. "We need to tell the scariest stories we know."

Carlos looked out at the darkening forest. "Think there are animals out there?"

"Probably," BJ said, and grabbed a PB&J.

Bailey curled her fingers into claws. "Monsters!"

Both boys looked at her. "What kind of monsters?" Carlos asked.

Bailey took a casual bite of her sandwich. "I'd guess Bigfoot."

"Bigfoots are just an urban legend," BJ said.

"I don't know," said Carlos, "remember how Grandpa told us that he and his friend saw Bigfeets on a fishing trip?"

"Grandpa's friend Drunk Donnie? C'mon, there's no such thing as Bigfoots."

"Is it Bigfoots or Bigfeets?" Bailey asked, and chewed thoughtfully. "I mean, a bunch of deer are called a herd. Then there's a pack of wolves, a gaggle of geese, and a murder of crows."

"No way on the murder of crows."

"Look it up, dummy," she said to her brother.

Carlos pulled out his phone and googled. "Damn, she's right."

"So what's a bunch of Bigfoots called?" she asked.

Carlos googled again. "It doesn't say."

"Let's name them, then," Bailey said, wadding the waxed paper her sandwich had been wrapped in and sticking it in the bag they had for trash. *Mustard. Unggg.* "From now on a bunch of Bigfeet will be called a shoe." She looked pleased with herself, "a shoe of Bigfoot."

BJ and Carlos stared at her and then broke out laughing. "Your sister's the best, man," BJ said, wiping his shirt where he'd sprayed cola out of his nose.

"Bigfoot isn't real," Carlos said, even though he was laughing too.

The canopy of the tent shook vigorously, as if a bear was trying to rip it right out of the ground by its stakes.

Carlos unzipped the tent and sprinted out, BJ on his heels.

"Guys!" Bailey said, alone in the tent. She huffed and grabbed her pink pillow and threw her Barbie sleeping bag over her shoulder. She gave an exasperated eye roll as she surveyed the woods behind them. She could have sworn she saw a flash of orange fur. "No way…"

"Way!" came a voice from within the trees.

"Whoa." Bailey waved in the direction of the cottonwoods then returned her attention to the retreating boys.

"Buncha babies!" she muttered. "Who's the baby now!" she yelled after her cousin and brother.

Behind her, twigs snapped and leaves crunched.

Ethan paced back and forth in unit four. Aaron sat on the couch with his head in his hands.

"That was fucking close, Aaron," Ethan said. "I was stuck in that basement room for almost an hour." He turned and faced his friend. "I was stuck in a room with nineteen million dollars' worth of product while two ladies made horror movie jokes. I was so close to them we were breathing the same air, dude."

"I can't believe you let yourself sneeze. Why didn't you plug your nose? That stops a sneeze, I think." Aaron kicked at the door. "Mierda."

Ethan threw the entire key ring at him. "Dust, ghosts, insects, contraband, whatever else is back there makes me sneeze, okay? It smells like a locker room in there. You check it from now on. All you have to do is go in once a day and spray the wedges with the water bottle filled with the enzyme mixture. The key is on the ring. The old brass one with the octangular head. I'm out." He walked over to the shadow box on the wall, took it down, and ripped off the back. "I'm loading Elvis's gun." He opened the side-board, took out the bullets, pried the gun free from the blue velvet backing of the shadow box, sat at the kitchen table, and began loading ammo with shaking fingers.

Aaron sat across from him. "We gotta stick together on this, Ethan. We promised Kenny.."

"To hell with that, and fuck Kenny." Ethan was dead serious. "I'm not getting stuck in that room again, because not only is there an igloo of illegal product, there *were* spi-ders, just like those ladies said. And besides that, I don't want to die in prison." He stuffed bullets into the cylinder and held the gun up. "Does this look right to you, Aaron?"

"Don't point that thing at me!"

The creepy tattooed guy from the Dollar Store, whose name happened to be Ethan Wilson, was right—he didn't know jack shit about guns. He flipped the gun and cocked the hammer, his fingertip barely touching the trigger. Staring down the barrel of the revolver, his fore-head creased like someone's grandma's pleated drapes. His last thought was, *maybe I'll start drinking again,* before he accidently pulled the trigger and splattered his head and its contents against the wall behind him. The creepy guy from the Dollar Store's body jerked backwards off his chair and slowly slid down the wall, leaving a Colonial Red- and Tantalizing Toast-colored smudge. He fell in a heap onto the Goose Turd Green carpet. It actually was a very suitable accent color.

Edna's hips hurt. Her knees hurt. Her ankles were swollen and they hurt, too. She knew it wouldn't be long until Henry would either have to have a lift installed for the stairs, or they'd have to make up a bed for her on the first floor. The trouble was, the full bathroom was upstairs; downstairs was only a powder room with a toilet and a sink. She knew the lift would be pricey. Ten years ago, Henry could have installed it himself. Now, his back would have none of that. He was a year older than she was, for heaven's sake!

Edna sat in the upstairs bedroom by the window reading and keeping an eye on the neighborhood. She sighed, knowing that she'd need to make it down the stairs and to the kitchen soon. Henry was helping with all the cooking now, but, gosh darn, it made her feel guilty.

Edna stood on rickety legs, which she could not only feel but see shaking; she gave herself a minute to steady, then walked out to the landing at the top of the stairs. Grabbing tight to the banister was growing difficult with her fingers all gnarled and painful. She was leaning toward going down the stairs handsfree, to save herself the pain in her knuckles, but that could be dangerous.

Edna had a few photographs on the upstairs landing, and she studied them for a minute. There was one of her and Henry on their wedding day. Another was of her, a smiling Henry, and baby James; they had it taken at Sears right before Christmas. The third was of James at Halloween in a Superman costume holding a pumpkin candy bag. He was wearing a gleaming plastic sideswept black wig. She picked that photo up, her arthritic hands protesting, and traced her finger down James's cheek. They'd be together again one day, she was sure of it. She hung the photo back up, and willed her feet and legs to get moving. She was aching for a cup of tea before dinner, and Henry had run to the store.

She stood at the top of the stairs looking down. When had they grown so steep? She was becoming afraid in her own home. Slow and sure, she walked down them, taking her time and really thinking about where she was placing her feet. She'd need new slippers soon, these were getting old, a bit ratty, and the tread was wearing thin. That wouldn't do.

As Edna made it to the bottom safely, James's highschool photo greeted her in the hall. She kissed her finger and then placed it on his lips. She took in a lungul of air, steadying her breathing and racing heart. "James, my sweet, sweet boy. I know in my heart we'll be together again soon."

She shuffled to the kitchen to put on the kettle, hoping she'd be able to lift it when it called out to her.

Chapter Ten

I'm Too Old for This Shit

1997

This Journal Belongs to James Hansen

I don't usually stop at fast food places during lunch break, but I'd stayed clear of the lunchroom today and I was ravenous. I'd begun to make my way to join my fellow students, but, standing in the doorway, I could feel myself become agitated by the size of the crowd. I needed a break and took my time walking around the block to Burger Town.

I ordered myself a cheeseburger, some fries, and a drink, then sat down at one of the booths in the back. I look up and who do I see? Snaggle-toothed Kimberly White. Had she followed me? I looked down at my food, not wanting her to mistake eye contact as an invitation to join me. Alas, she slid into the booth across from me and started to unwrap her burger. It smelled strange. It ended up being a fish sandwich, and I wanted to vomit. I imagined how that would be, spewing hot stomach acid all over her supersized number three with extra mayo.

My heart felt like it was going to beat out of my chest when she started loudly *chewing* again, that damn crooked tooth taking center stage to her half devoured sandwich: a bit of mayonnaise stuck to the corner of her lips. My legs started to bounce up and down quicker and quicker and a cold sweat started at the base of my neck and trickled its way down my spine. She asked me about school; she told me about choir, and how she made a new friend named Paula. Why the hell wasn't she with Paula? It just so happened that Paula was out sick today, so she had sought me out.

I didn't say much during lunch, and when she gathered up the greasy paper, napkins, and fry cup, I noticed I hadn't taken one bite of my own lunch. I collected my uneaten lunch and shoved it into the sack it came in. I noticed that she'd left her straw on the table. It had a smear of pink lipstick on it. Perhaps it had touched her deformed incisor. I picked it up and put it into my backpack along with my other belongings.

At that moment I didn't know what to make of this encounter. At the time I was annoyed. Mulling it over now, I wonder what her motives were and how to process this. Should I be pleased she found me attractive? Should I remain annoyed that she barged in on my solitary lunch without an invitation? Should I have screamed, reached across the table, grabbed her by the throat, yanked that damn tooth from mouth and dropped it into her soda like another piece of ice?

I need to avoid her. She stresses me. Thinking about it now, after the fact, stresses me. I had to take one of the anxiety meds today after lunch. I fell asleep in math class. When the passing bell rang, I found thirty sets of eyes upon me. As I've stated before, I don't take humiliation well, and, as always, my first thoughts turn to revenge.

This is on you, Kimberly White.

The Wilson House, 1957

For the first time ever, Rose was allowed to spend the night at Leyta Simmons's house.

The girls sat on Leyta's pink ruffled bedspread, side by side, cross legged, their backs against the wall, their knobby knees touching. Both had kicked their shoes off and wore identical white bobbysocks.

Rose's hands were clasped in her lap, her head bowed. "I miss him so much, Leyta."

Leyta put an arm around her shoulders. "I know, Rosie, I'm so sorry."

Rose laid her head on her shoulder, as Leyta's three-year-old brother Johnathan waddled in. "Where's Paul?" he asked, looking around. "I want him to help me with my puzzle."

Rose wiped her eyes and held her arms out to him, and he crawled onto her lap. "Paul is gone, sweet boy."

"Gone forever?"

"Yes," Rose said.

"Why?"

"I don't know, Johnathan." She looked into Leyta's dark brown eyes. Anxiety was evident on her eight-year-old face.

"He's not coming back?"

"I don't think so, sweetie."

Johnathan frowned. "If he does, will you tell him to come see me?"

Rose and Leyta hugged him tight. "That's a promise."

"Can I play with you today?" Usually Rose and Leyta would say no, and send him off to play with Paul.

"Of course," said Rose.

"Yes you can," said Leyta at the same moment.

Johnathan brightened, climbed off his sister's bed, and dumped out a puzzle.

"I'm so sorry, Rosie," Leyta whispered, her voice cracking.

Rose hugged her so hard she feared Leyta wouldn't be able to breathe. "It wasn't your fault," she whispered back.

Leyta wept onto Rose's shoulder. "Thank you for still loving me."

"Always."

"Always."

"Quit fucking around, Ethan!"

Aaron yelped as the pistol went off in Ethan's hand, leaving what looked something like a Jackson Pollock painting on the faded wallpaper.

"Jesus H. Christ!" Aaron bolted out of his chair, toppling it behind him. He hurried over to what was left of the creepy tattooed guy from the Dollar Store.

"Fuck!" He pushed Ethan with the toe of his boot. "Tell me you're not dead!"

Aaron, so deafened by the explosion he couldn't hear his own words, bent and examined what was left of Ethan's face. "Are you fucking dead, pendejo?" Aaron tugged at his long black hair, "Ay, Dios! You're fucking dead! What do we do now?" He groaned, "what do *I* do now?"

Someone had to have heard the shot. Goodbye half a million in payoff!

He had to get out. Screw the money. Aaron turned toward the door, planning to get the hell outta Dodge, when he thought for a moment, turned back, and picked up Elvis's gun, which had propelled itself onto the couch when it went off. Aaron shoved it into the back of his pants, thinking he could at least get a few thousand out of the deal, opened the door, and dashed off across the back lawn and into the woods.

Aaron crashed down a path he knew came out on the highway, his bulk breaking branches as he went, his legs pumping and his heart hammering in his chest. He stopped for a minute to catch his breath. *I'm too fat for this shit.* He could hear the highway traffic not far off. A raccoon darted across the path, and he tripped over it. The creature gave him the stinkeye and waddled off into the brush.

"Fuck you, trash panda!" Aaron picked himself up, dusted off his jeans, and poked at the stitch on his side that felt as if it would rupture at any second. He bent at the waist, gasping. With some luck he'd hitchhike his way into another state before the police got involved.

Aaron's thoughts turned to the gun. It was worth a fraction of what they'd have gotten paid for storing the contraband. What if they traced the gun back to him? The cops can tell what bullets were shot from what gun, right? What if they thought he'd murdered Ethan?

"Shit!" He took the gun out of the back of his jeans, held it like it was a poisonous snake (Aaron didn't know jack shit about guns either), gave it a good wipe down with his shirt, and tossed it into the woods like he was in the major leagues. There was a faint thunk somewhere deep in the trees.

"I still got my arm," he muttered to himself, took another big breath and hightailed it toward the highway. Car lights twinkled in the distance. Aaron kept trotting along and grumbled, "Well, shit. This means I might have to get an actual job." He clicked his tongue, threw his head back and grunted, then thundered out of the woods by the side of the highway. Walking backwards, he wiped the sweat off his forehead and stuck his thumb out, putting on his best I'm-totally-harmless smile. "Fuck Ethan. Fuck Kenny. Fuck Elvis," he said, as a pair of headlights slowed.

"Where you headed?" Aaron asked the driver.

"West."

"That's where I'm headed," he said, opened the door, and got in.

The kids were asleep when Rhonda heard the gunshot.

She opened the front door and saw Henry Hansen already out on his front porch. "That sounded like it came from one of the back units," she said, stepping out onto the stoop. "Are you and Edna alright?"

Henry was already halfway around the building. "Yes, yes we're fine. We need to check on Anita and Ethan."

Rhonda trotted hot on his heels. "You're not going by yourself!"

Anita was out back standing on her porch. "The gunshot came from next door," she said, pointing with a sausage-sized finger.

Rhonda and Henry found Ethan's door wide open. "Ethan?" yelled Henry, "you okay?"

Only silence answered. Henry stepped inside.

"Holy mother of God!"

Rhonda was right behind him. She screamed on seeing the carnage, pulled out her phone, and dialed 911. "I need to get back to my kids!"

"Go, go! I'll wait for the police."

Rhonda turned toward the door, looked down, and noticed a key ring. Must be the one to the carriage house, she thought. She picked it up and pocketed it, then sprinted home.

Henry followed her out, stepped around the building, and waited for the cops.

The police surrounded 291 Chestnut Street like flies on a shit wagon. Anita walked to the far end of the property with Nacho. Police or no police, it was time for her chihuahua to do his nightly duty. She grabbed her walking stick with the nail on the end of it and headed toward Nacho's favorite pee spot. The stick served a dual purpose. One was to help her keep her balance, since at her size she'd probably need help getting up if she tripped; and two, for coyotes and other creatures that would think Nacho would be a tasty snack.

Anita had made a beeline to Ethan's condo when she heard the gunshot—what a mess!

She'd seen someone running for the woods behind the house. She couldn't be sure who it was, but she sure as shit hoped it wasn't Kenny. She was kicking herself for not picking up the key ring she'd seen lying on the floor in the middle of the room. She'd seen enough crime shows on TV to know that one stray hair could tie her to what was obviously a murder.

But the keys…dammit, they'd need those keys. She didn't know everything that was happening, but she did know it was tied to the locked room in the basement, and locked rooms needed keys. She'd seen both Henry and the new lady walk into Ethan's quad. If the cops didn't have the keys, they did.

Rhonda watched as Nacho lifted his leg against the side of the carriage house. The walls blinked red and blue from the police lights that filled the street and the yard. Anita stood leaning on her walking stick as Nacho took his time and finally started spinning in circles.

From the corner of the yard, not two feet from Nacho, came a very large raccoon. Biggest she'd ever seen. She lifted the pokin' end of the stick and waddled at it.

"Not today, Satan!" Anita hollered at the raccoon.

It stopped, stared at her, stared at Nacho and turned back toward the woods. Anita gave it a good poke in the ass with the nail end of the stick to hurry it along. "C'mon dog, you gotta be done by now," she muttered, and led her chihuahua back toward quad number three.

A policeman waved her over. She lifted a finger indicating one moment, then let Nacho back into the house. "I know I'm gonna have to give a statement," she said to the officer. I hope this don't take too long, I'm missing the goddamn Bachelor." She thought for a moment. "You guys didn't happen to pick up some keys, did ya?"

"Keys?"

Nope, the cops didn't have them—that left old Henry and the know-it-all new lady.

"Well, shit on a stick."

The following morning, Rhonda heard a knock on the door, wiped her wet hands on her dish towel, and went to answer it. There stood Henry from quad number two.

"Hi there, honey," he said. "Some hullabaloo last night, huh?"

Rhonda opened the door for him and Henry stepped inside. "I can't believe it, Henry." She hung the dish towel over the faucet in the kitchen sink. "Ethan seemed so harmless."

"You never know about people, I suppose," Henry said, "or the company they keep." He took a seat at the counter. "I hear they didn't find the murder weapon. It had to be murder if the gun was missing."

Rhonda placed a cup of coffee in front of him. "I heard that too, and yes, you're right." Henry nodded his thanks. "Have you spoken to Anita?"

"I haven't seen her, but I'm sure the police questioned her." Henry took a deep breath and squared his shoulders. He smiled. "I came over for a happy reason, though. Have you been to Antelope Reservoir?"

"I've heard of it, but never been. I hear it's beautiful."

"It truly is."

"Would you like a pastry to go with that coffee?"

"No, Rhonda, I'm fine." Henry turned to face her. "Edna and I were wondering if you and the kids might like to take a little fishing day trip with us sometime. Last night shook her up, she needs to get out a bit to get her mind off of things." He pulled a newspaper from his back pocket and set it on the table. With a little sigh, he pointed to the headline. "They're going to drain the reservoir soon. The water is going to Kansas for the crops. I guess that's what reservoirs are for. Darn shame, though."

He gestured to an article in the paper, and Rhonda read over his shoulder. "Says here that'll happen in two weeks. Who knows when they'll fill it again, but Edna and I have some darn great memories there."

Rhonda smiled at him, noticing his eyes misting over. "I'm sure the kids would love it."

Henry shoved the paper into his back pocket.

"Will it be difficult for Edna to get to the shore?" she asked. "And we don't have any fishing gear."

"Don't worry about the gear, I have a ton of it in the basement."

Uhhnggg, the basement.

"The parking lot isn't far from where we'd usually fish. Once I get a lawn chair down to the water, Edna can sit in it and be comfortable all day." Henry met Rhonda's eyes.

"I guess I have ulterior motives. I'd like you to take her other arm and help her down the slope to the beach."

Rhonda nodded. "Of course. Sounds like fun, we can make it a picnic."

Henry brightened. "It'll mean a lot to both of us. We used to take James too, before he got to his teenage years and was too interested in other things."

She thought about how excited the kids would be, and how glad she was that she still had a year or two left of Carlos's childhood. "We're in. When do we go?"

"School's out, so how about Thursday? There won't be as many folks out on a weekday."

"Thursday it is," Rhonda said, "but will you get the gear up from the basement for me?"

Henry stood to leave. "Absolutely. I'll let you women talk about what to pack for a picnic." He had his hand on the doorknob and looked over his shoulder. "Just no nectarines, I hate those things."

Chapter Eleven

Shoulda Been an Actress

Grandma Elise Brown struggled to fit into her stretchy hot pink jogging pants. The damn things must have shrunk in the wash. As if she'd jog. She'd walk fast, that was good enough. Hell, maybe she'd just stroll. She grunted and pulled them up over her hips, paired them with a matching pink sporty shirt. *At least that still fits.*

"Albert!" Grandma Elise hollered at her husband, who was in the other room, "can you zip me?" *Zippers on the back of shirts. Who the heck thought that was a good idea?* "Who designed these things, Michael Phelps?" she grumbled. Grandma wasn't a fan of Michael Phelps; his ears stood out, and that was not to her liking.

"Jesus, Elise, quit your caterwauling, I was watching Wheel of Fortune." Grandpa Al did not like to be disturbed while watching his show.

Elise turned and pointed to her zipper.

Al gave it a quick tug and snicked it up. "Where are you headed?"

"I think I need more exercise," Grandma said, "look how tight these pants are."

"I think you need less donuts," Grandpa muttered under his breath.

"What did you say?"

"Nothing, dearest, you have a nice walk." Grandpa thought for a moment. "This doesn't have anything to do with the commotion down on Chestnut Street, does it?"

Grandma squirmed a little, and he raised his bushy gray eyebrows, "It does, doesn't it!"

"Fine! It does," Grandma said, shrugging on a white, but totally appropriate for the season, sweater. "There must have been two dozen cops out there. I was in the Wilson house once, you know, it'll be interesting to see the inside now that they chopped it up. On top of all that, I need to get in shape for pickleball." She buttoned the bottom few buttons of her sweater. "Don't you want to know what happened?"

"You know what I want to know, Elise?" said, as he turned and walked out the bedroom door, "I want to know what the hell I missed on Wheel of Fortune, *that's* what I want to know."

Grandma harrumphed. "I'll be back soon," she said. "Well, hopefully not too soon. I want to know all the dirt."

Grandpa waved a hand behind his head without turning, and she walked out the back door.

"Let me know what you find out," he called behind her. It wasn't as if he didn't enjoy a bit of neighborhood gossip.

Grandpa Al turned his attention back to the TV. "Just spin the damn wheel. Idiot."

Grandma took a left on Main Street, then another left on Chestnut. The house that had piqued her interest sat halfway down the block. Grandma shrugged out of her sweater. She thought it would be cooler today. You just can't trust weathermen.

A woman with dark hair was on the porch of 291 Chestnut Street, filling a rusty old ore bucket with ferns. *Can't she afford a new pot? They're cheap at Walmart and anyway, ferns are all gonna die on the south of the house. Every one of them will fry. They'll be dead as dirt within the month. What a waste of time and money.* Grandma couldn't believe they'd turned that great house into condos. *What an eyesore, what a shame.*

She waved to the woman, and the woman waved back.

"Hello, and welcome to the neighborhood! I'm Elise, Elise Brown. I brought you a bag of donuts!" The donuts were a day old, but Grandma didn't think it would look acceptable to come empty-handed. She made her way to the porch.

"How nice of you," the woman said, clapping potting soil off her garden gloves. "I'm Rhonda. Come on in, and I'll make coffee."

Got her, Grandma thought, one side of her mouth curling up into a half smile.

Grandma was a short woman. She followed Rhonda into the house and climbed up onto one of the kitchen counter stools like a little pink mountain goat. The damn things were tall, it wasn't natural. Grandma was not built for anything but *normal* chairs.

Rhonda put a pod into the espresso machine and set a small cup beneath the spout. "It's so nice to meet the neighbors."

"It's nice to meet you too." Grandma eyed the espresso machine." That's quite a fancy coffee maker you have there. We have a Mr. Coffee. It only has one button."

"It makes regular coffee too, if you'd rather?"

Grandma nodded. "That would be very nice." *What does that little coffee cup hold, three tablespoons, maybe four?* "I've heard that the government can listen in on your conversations through fancy-pants appliances like your coffeemaker and maybe even the microwave. I bet the FBI is listening in right now."

Rhonda placed the cup of espresso to the side, dug through the coffee pods for a nice, light morning blend, put a large mug under the spout, and turned it back on. She set small plates out for the donuts, and took out the cream and sugar.

"I don't know about that," said Rhonda. "Even if they did listen in on us, all they'd hear are kids yelling and me sometimes trying to do yoga."

Of course it has to be yoga, thought Grandma, then turned her attention back to the task at hand. "Mind if I take the maple donut? I'm not much for chocolate," she said, her fingers already on the maple glaze.

"Sure, please do. I love chocolate." Rhonda placed the chocolate donut on her own plate.

"So," said Grandma, steering the conversation back to important things, "I hear you had some excitement around here the other night." *Might as well get right to the meat and potatoes.*

Rhonda sighed. "Yes we did, it was terrible." She set her espresso cup down, her hands shaking a bit.

"So, what happened?"

Rhonda looked up at her. "The man in unit four was found shot."

"Oh my god!" said Grandma, clutching her chest. "Did he do it to himself or did somebody off him?"

"The police aren't 100 percent sure, but they're talking about a possible homicide." Rhonda took a bite of her get-the-gossip bribe donut. "All I know is that about eleven that night there was a gunshot, and Henry from next door and I ran around back and found the man in unit four shot and killed."

"Was it messy?" Grandma asked eagerly.

Rhonda's breath hitched, and it looked as if she might cry. "Ethan Wilson was a very nice man. He helped me clean the basement windows and trim the shrubs."

"What? Why? Don't you have a husband?"

"I do. His name is Tate, he's away on business."

"Ethan Wilson…" Grandma was deep in thought. "That name sounds familiar." *I shoulda been an actress.*

"This house used to belong to the Wilson family, it was built in 1901."

"Now I remember! I was in this house once when it was a single-family home…like all the rest of the respectable houses in the neighborhood." She poured a bit more cream into her coffee. "Edgar and Beatrice Wilson were their names. How in the world could I have forgotten that? Well, I was just a kid, I guess." She looked intensely at Rhonda. "They had two children. Twins. A boy and a girl." She stirred her coffee, the cream diluting the brew until it was a light tan.

"Tantalizing Toast…"

"What's that?"

"Nothing, nothing, please continue."

"I was here once because of a Bible study group my mother thought about joining. We never came back. I remember my mother saying they were a bunch of lunatics." Grandma took a bite of donut, and wiped a tiny bit of maple-colored frosting from her cheek. "It's a shame what happened here, downright terrible."

"What happened here?" Rhonda asked, her donut, coffee, and Grandma's gossip-mongering seemingly forgotten.

"Well, Edgar Wilson and his son Paul"—Grandma wiped her cheek with a napkin, "went missing one day. Paul was about seven or eight, I think? He wasn't quite all there, if you know what I mean," she added, tapping a finger against her forehead.

"The father or the son?"

"The son. The father was a mean drunk, or so I was told. I'm not sure what was wrong with the boy, I know he didn't talk."

"They just…disappeared one day?"

"So I heard," Grandma said, taking the last bite of her donut before starting to wiggle off the barstool. "I probably should be going."

"You're more than welcome to stay awhile if you like. If I have any more questions about the house may I call you?"

"Oh, you bet." Grandma hooked her sweater over her arm. "My daughter is a world famous author, you know. She writes these dirty romance novels for lonely women." She looked up the hallway stairs as she reached for the doorknob. "Not that I'd read that stuff."

Grandma fumbled around in her purse and wrote down her phone number for Rhonda. "If you have any more questions about the house…or you hear anything else about the murder the other day." She handed it to Rhonda and took one last look up the stairs as she turned to walk out the door. "Last time I was in here that slow little red-haired boy was standing right there," she pointed, "on top of those steps."

Rhonda's eyebrows shot up. "Little red-haired boy?"

Grandma nodded. "Yes, and his twin sister. She had red hair too." She noticed Henry sitting on his front step and waved. "That Henry Hansen," she whispered, "he was a looker back in the day."

Grandma and her pink stretchy pants headed down the porch steps. "Thanks for the fancy-schmancy coffee, but you may want to watch out for interlopers listening in." She turned right at the sidewalk and muttered to herself, "What the hell is wrong with Folgers?" She waved over her shoulder and called out, "You might want to drag that old rusty barrel to the shade, all your ferns are gonna cook."

Kenny rapped on Anita's door at 291 Chestnut number three. "Let me in, Anita!" He could hear shuffling movement and the TV from behind the door. The TV switched off, and the door cracked open. "Hurry up, dammit," Kenny said, and muscled his way inside. "Turn the TV back on, I don't want nobody to know I'm here."

Anita flipped it back on and the sound of cartoons filled the room.

"Daddy!" Sophia yelled, and hugged him around the leg.

Kenny looked down at her and patted her on the head like an overanxious puppy. "Hello, my little fuck trophy."

"Kenny!" Anita admonished him, "don't say dirty stuff like that around the kids."

"Only one of them's mine, remember?"

Anita said, "Stella, you and Sophia go to your room, I need to talk to *Daddy*."

Kenny snorted, went to the refrigerator and got himself a beer. "You're not pinning the other brat on me, Anita. Nope, not mine." He slid into the recliner next to the TV and turned it down a little. "This is some deep shit we're into here, babe."

"Don't babe me," Anita hissed at him, "you got yourself into this mess, you can get yourself out." She turned her ample body toward him, blocking out the TV. "Ethan's dead, you know."

"I heard about that. How the hell did that happen?"

Anita stared at him.

"Oh, no. No, no, no. I didn't have nothing to do with that."

Anita stared harder and lifted an eyebrow.

"Babe, I swear to you. I was with Jerry and the guys down at Joe's Cave having a few beers. I have an alibi, and you can call any one of them and ask them about it. "

"I might do that."

Kenny held out his phone. "G'head," he said, shaking it at her, "call them. Any of 'um."

"Put that thing away, I believe you. The question is," she said, turning to him, "what the hell are we gonna do now?"

"That's my girl. I like that you know we're a team."

"I have a question."

"Shoot," said Kenny.

"How did they get the goods into the room downstairs without anyone noticing? I was here that day and I didn't see them." She squinted at him. "And I see everything."

"Well," he said, "remember when the new lady moved in and the movers came?"

"Yeah. Nacho barked his stupid head off. When are you gonna give your sister her rat dog back anyways?"

Kenny picked up Nacho and scratched his ears. "A van followed them, guys went to the basement and stashed it. Get me another beer, honey britches? No one suspected a thing. The movers were in the house, the van pulled up, Ethan had left the door to the basement open and within ten minutes they were gone. And I kinda like this dog." He turned the chihuahua to face him and sing-songed, "Mommy doesn't love you…"

"I'm not that hairless thing's mom! And! Who are *they*?"

"Beats me, just some guys that are gonna give us money for babysitting some coke." He shrugged his shoulders, "I guess it's coke. The basement stinks like ass. Does coke go bad and smell like that? I never liked the stuff—it makes me feel crawly." Kenny turned his body in the recliner, sat Nacho on the floor, and called after her, "You can't walk away from this and leave me at it on my own. You're knee deep, babe."

Anita walked to the kitchen, grabbed two beers from the fridge, and sat down on the couch. It whimpered under her weight. She tossed the extra beer to Kenny and cracked open her own.

"I can't back out now, even if I wanted to." She took a long pull of beer. "I've totally inseminated myself."

Kenny scratched his head, "inseminated?"

"Yeah, you know, I'm guilty and up to my eyeballs in this mess."

"Incriminated."

"Whatever, don't get smart with me, asshole. I'm treading water here, Kenny." she threw a pillow at him.

"Do you know where the key to the room in the basement is?"

"Like I told you, it was in Ethan's condo, and then it wasn't. Either Henry or the new lady had to have pocketed it."

"We gotta get that key back." Kenny stood up and started to pace. "They want the stuff a week from Friday, and we're supposed to check it every day." He threw up his arms. "We gotta get that stinkin' key! How the hell will we let them inside to take all that shit outta here?" He huffed out a breath. "No blow, no dough. Ethan was handling that part of the deal, and now Ethan's"—Kenny made a finger gun and pointed it at his head—"pow."

Anita let out a sigh of frustration. "Let's just go up to Home Depot and say, 'Hey, can you make us a new key for our stinky cocaine room? We lost the old one when the guy next door was murdered.' Think that might work, Kenny?" She took a quick drink of beer and continued, "I've made it crystal clear to the new lady that the basement is full of spooks, she's no problem. And Henry and Edna have a washer and dryer in their unit. One of those fancy stackable ones." Anita looked at him and smirked. "And Ethan's gonna be nobody's problem but God's."

"Ethan had the keys!"

"Well, I know for sure that the cops don't have them." She finished off the last of her beer. "Henry and the new lady were there first, and the minute they left, before the cops showed up, I went and peeked."

"You think maybe Henry or the new lady has the keys?"

Anita rolled her eyes. "That's what I told you, Kenny."

"We gotta find those keys, babe."

Anita set down her beer, hauled herself off of the couch, and walked over to him. She put her hands on his shoulders and murmured, "I know something that'll take your mind offa our problems for a while…"

Kenny grinned, his mind turning to chocolate pudding. He strapped his hands around her broad backside, squeezed her mind-blowing Great Pumpkins, and yelled, "You fucking kids stay in your room!"

Chapter Twelve

I'll Be Delighted Beyond Measure to Shoot Him

RHONDA AND HENRY loaded the back of Henry's truck. There were fishing poles for everyone, a lunch packed, along with lawn chairs and sunscreen. Carlos and Bailey were in the back seat of the truck, strapped in and ready to go.

"I hope I can make it up there, Henry," Edna said, eyeing the height of the first step.

"You can do it, honeybunch, I'll help you." She put her foot on the metal step and Henry lifted her so that both feet were up and in.

She slid in with a chuckle and patted Henry's cheek. "Thank you, sweetheart."

Rhonda had slipped into the back with the kids and Henry took his place on the driver's side. "Next stop, Antelope Reservoir!"

Edna smiled back at Rhonda and the kids. "This is going to be such fun. I've been wanting to do this for so long." She smoothed her slacks. "I guess it took some young ones to make this old man want to take me. For crying out loud, it's only ten miles away."

Henry grinned at her and patted her hand. "We made some good memories there."

"And some not so good ones," she countered, as her smile made way for a far-off look in her eyes.

Henry looked at her with so much love that it made Rhonda's heart clench, then he said in a whisper, "Today we make some great ones!"

Edna smiled softly at her husband. This time she patted his hand.

Henry parked the truck, walked around to Edna's side, and lifted her out as if she were a child in a car seat; he held her hands, making sure she was steady on her feet. "Rhonda? Can you please grab a folding chair from the back, and we'll get this young lady down by the water."

Carlos was already on it. "Got one!"

"That's a lad, take it down to that sandy spot right over there." Bailey had a chair too, and they were scampering down the incline to the water like two little rabbits. "Rhonda, you take one arm..."

Together they helped Edna make it safely to the sand on the edge of the reservoir. The water was still and sparkled in the morning sunshine. Carlos and Bailey set up the old-fashioned plastic weave lawn chairs and Edna took a seat, pulling a paperback book from the pocket of her slacks. "Don't worry about me, I'm perfectly fine. Now, go get the fishing gear and let's see who lands the first catch of the day."

The kids ran ahead and Henry plodded up the incline.

"James used to love to camp here when he was a child," Edna said. "The campground is just around the bend over there on the west side. There was a playground and showers, and the fishing was really good." Her eyes misted over. "I miss him so much. He was such a good little boy…he really was."

Rhonda put her arm around her shoulder, "I'm certain he was. Do you feel close to him here?"

"I do, probably closer to him here than anywhere else."

"If ever you need to talk about it, you can come to me, okay. Edna?"

Edna nodded and wiped her eyes with the back of her hands. "Thank you, honey I may take you up on that sometime."

Rhonda changed the subject, "Do you need anything from the truck?"

"Oh shoot, yes I do. Will you grab my purse, please?"

"Anything else?"

"Maybe a bottle of water?"

"You've got it." Rhonda made her way up the slope.

Edna got back to her feet, pulled a one-inch vial from her pocket, and walked to the edge of the water. The sun made the denim-blue lake glitter like a pocket filled with diamonds. She opened the tiny vial and poured its contents into the waves that lapped at the shore. She blew a kiss and sat back down.

Unbeknownst to her, Rhonda had turned to ask if she wanted sunscreen while she was up here. She saw Edna sprinkle the gray ash into the water. "James," Rhonda whispered, and silently continued up the slope.

Many snagged hooks and broken lines later, one fish was caught. Bailey felt so sorry for it that they let it go. The kids were muddy, filled with junk food, and happy. Bailey was also getting tired. She'd climbed onto Henry's lap and fallen asleep. He stroked her hair. "This is what having grandchildren would be like."

Rhonda smiled at him. "Consider yourselves to be bonus grandparents to these two."

This made Henry beam. He planted a kiss on Bailey's sweaty, sleeping head. "We'd be honored."

"Yes we would be," Edna added. Rhonda could tell they meant every word.

Not long after, Edna began dozing in her chair. Her paperback book slipped to the ground.

"Looks as if I need to get my better half home," Henry said.

Bailey stirred on his lap. "Is the fish okay?" she said, rubbing her eyes.

"Yes, honey, we barely nicked him," Henry told her. "He's probably home with his family right now."

Rhonda, Henry, and Carlos began hauling gear and chairs up the hill. Edna stood looking over the water. "This will probably be the last time I see Antelope Reservoir," she said, a melancholy tone to her voice.

Rhonda gave her a gentle hug, put her paperback in her purse, and tossed the strap over her shoulder. "I've got your things, Edna."

"Thank you honey, I appreciate it."

Getting a tired Edna to the top of the slope took a great deal more time than getting her down. Her exhaustion was evident on her face, but she smiled through it. Henry picked her up and placed her in the truck, buckled her in and patted her leg.

"There you go, my sweetheart."

Rhonda and the kids piled in the back seat, and by the time Henry had the truck turned around and out of the parking area, Bailey and Edna were fast asleep and Carlos wasn't far behind.

"It's a fucking cow truck, Kenny," Ishmael said. "It's a piece of garbage! How much did you pay for this thing?"

"It was a steal, only three hundred bucks."

Ishmael looked at him over the top of his glasses. "Why in God's name would you want this cow truck?"

"Once we get our pay out, I'm gonna turn it into a taco truck."

"This is the dumbest fucking shit I've ever heard."

The cow truck was a Patton, Colorado mobile landmark. It had belonged to Bobby and Manny Ruiz, owners of Dan's Used Furniture and Supreme Meats, and father and grandfather to BJ Ruiz respectively. The truck had been involved in a fatal accident about a year ago, leaving the town of Patton shocked and saddened. The cow truck had been driving the streets of Patton for as long as some could remember: it was as much of a monument to Patton as Casa Bonita and Blucifer, the blue bronco at the airport, were to Denver. Horrible, but ours. The once happy dancing metal cow on the side of the van looked dull and depressed. At least it had seemed jolly when it belonged to Dan's Used Furniture and Supreme Meats.

"This is what I'm gonna do," said Kenny. "I'm gonna fix this up real nice with the money we get next week. Then I'll make a fortune with my new business. I'll drive around the streets playing mariachi music and selling tacos, kinda like the icecream truck but with Mexican food." He gave the cow a pat.

Ishmael looked at Kenny as if he'd grown two heads. "That's the dumbest idea I've ever heard."

Kenny brushed him off. "I already have the sound system; I'm hooking that up tonight." He pointed at the cow. "When I was in New Mexico last summer I bought this flat metal sombrero from one of those roadside stands that sell all the cheap pottery and hammered metal shit from Mexico? You know what I'm talking about?"

Ishmael nodded, and watched two men walk by. The taller of the two had a sports jersey on that said TODD across the back. The much shorter of the two was dressed head to toe in black.

"Who are those two?"

"No idea," Kenny said, tinkering with the cow's new headgear. "I call them Todd and Not Todd. They walk by about this time everyday." He shrugged. "The taller of them wears that Todd jersey a lot, I had to call them something. Do you think the little one's a midget?"

"Jesus, Kenny, he's a little person. Can you just pretend to be a tiny bit socially sensitive?"

"'Little person' sounds kind of lame," Kenny said. "If I was that short I'd want to be called something else."

"I'm afraid to ask."

"I dunno, I think the word midget is pretty badass. If I was a midget, I'd be one hell of a badass, ball punching, bullet of a midget." You could see the gears in Kenny's head trying to work. "It's like saying 'Tiny House.' It's a fucking camper, call it what it is."

"Just shut up, I'm not listening to any more of your bullshit," said Izzy. But he made a mental note to keep an eye on both strangers, no matter their size.

"This sombrero isn't quite big enough to fit the cow's head, but it'll do for now, and it's green, red, and white—like the Mexican flag. What says 'buy my tacos' like a Mexican flag colored sombrero?" Kenny pointed above the Dan's Used Furniture and Supreme Meats logo. "I already painted over that, see? I painted in TACOS."

"You can see through the paint you put on, now it looks like it says Used Tacos, Kenny."

"Fuck you, Ishmael; Izzy, this is my *dream*, man! Don't be shittin' on my dream! I may even sell margaritas out of it...can you imagine driving around with Mariachi music and selling margaritas out of my taco cow truck? Imagine the ladies running out of their houses waving money at me. All ladies like margaritas. Maybe I'll buy some little paper umbrellas…"

"I don't know if that's legal."

"Paper umbrellas?"

"Selling alcohol out of a moving vehicle." Ishmael shook his head and turned to leave. "I gotta get back to work. All I'm doing is driving my van of stuff to the city limits. That's all I'm doing."

"We're gonna be rich next week, buddy! Super dooper stinkin' rich!" Kenny yelled after him. *If I can find the goddamn key to the smelly cocaine room.*

He flipped on the sound system that was rigged to the cow truck, and mariachi music blared from a bullhorn mounted on the hood. Izzy grumbled and shuffled off.

Kenny frowned. "No one's gonna kill my dreams, man! I'm gonna be the taco *king* of this town." He cranked up the audio system as loud as it would go.

La cucaracha, la cucaracha!
Ya no puede caminar.
Porque no tiene, porque le falta,
Marijuana que fumar!

Izzy shot Kenny the middle finger without turning around. He'd need to be at the shop about this time tomorrow to see if Todd and Not Todd were hanging around. He'd check it out and follow them if he could.

Todd stopped walking when he reached the corner, looked down at Not Todd and said, "I think that Kenny guy may have been dropped on his head as an infant."

Not Todd nodded and patted the gun in his shoulder holster. "I'll be delighted beyond measure to shoot him."

Carla had loaned Rhonda a short white culotte skirt. Rhonda looked at herself in the mirror; cellulite dimples pocked the backs of her thighs. "I haven't worn a skirt this short since high school."

"You look amazing! Look at those legs. I wish I had legs like that."

"I have two kids. I've earned every bit of this cellulite." Rhonda turned to face her sister and spread her arms. "This is as good as it gets."

Carla handed her sister a white visor. "You'll need this."

"Is this part of the standard pickleball uniform?"

"Yep, wear it. It's part of the Designated Dinkers' attire. It's our lucky hat." Carla pointed to the bright pink D on the bill. "It's in the pickleball bill of rights."

"There's a pickleball bill of rights? What am I getting myself into? Do I have to sign a contract with my own blood?"

Carla laughed. "No, but the ladies and the Limp Dinks take it very seriously."

Rhonda let out a bark of a laugh. "The Limp Dinks?"

"Yep, Patton's only all men's gay pickleball team. We have a few lesbians and a couple of gay men on some of the other teams, but these guys stuck together. Oh my god, they play it up—and play to win, they're a hoot. It's a party every time."

"*The Limp Dinks?*" Rhonda was still laughing

"They're a ton of fun, wait till it's margarita time afterwards. You may have to sell your liver to the devil."

"Dinks?"

"It's what we call a shot that lands over the net in the no volley zone." Carla added, "we're playing the Pickle Ticklers today though, they're an older group. We may just win this time. Actually, the Designated Dinkers kind of suck…but we make up for it in spirit!"

It was going to be an interesting day, Rhonda thought, tugging the back of her culottes down. "Carlos! You and BJ keep an eye on Bailey. We'll be back in a few hours." *Hopefully in one piece and sober.* "Keep the doors locked."

Carla and the newest Designated Dinker left the house.

The restaurant across from the pickleball courts, La Casa de los Frijoles, was hopping. Pickleballers of every size, shape, and experience level packed the patio.

Mario, the captain of the Limp Dinks, filled Grandma's margarita glass. "You were on fire today, Elise!"

Grandma, teetering directly on the border of tipsy town, licked at the salty rim of her glass. "I sure was. I'm gonna feel it tomorrow, though."

"I was so surprised to see you here," said Rhonda. "Happily surprised."

"Why?" Grandma asked, "because I have this big caboose? I may be old and fat, but I'm not dead." She took another hefty slug of her margarita. "We kicked these guys right in their Limp Dinks."

Ben choked on a mouthful of guacamole. "You sure did! You're an outright pickleball ninja." He wiped his mouth on a napkin.

"It's good to have you with us, Rhonda," Mario said. "Hopefully next time you get in the game and not just sit on the side."

Rhonda inwardly thanked all the saints that she got to sit on the side. *These people are cutthroat pickleball gangsters.* "I had a great time watching and learning," she said, grabbing a chip. "Next time I won't be going in blind."

"Speaking of blind," Grandma said, taking a super-sized dip of guacamole, half of which ended up on her shirt, "I hear One-eyed Lou signed up to be an alternate."

"Hold up. Didn't you hear?" Mario said. "He's just Lou now. His other eye bit the dust in an unfortunate encounter with the Sinkhole de Mayo."

"He was driving?" Rhonda asked.

"Naw, just walking. His peripheral vision is for shit," said Ben. "Was."

"Wait," Rhonda said, "he wants to play pickleball and he's...he's..."

"Blind as a bat. Yep," said Grandma. "He's got a great serve, though."

Everyone nodded in agreement.

Mario took off his rainbow visor, hung it on the back of his chair, and ran his hands through his sweaty hair. "It can get all kinds of brutal out there." He lifted the chilly pitcher and filled Rhonda's glass without asking.

"Not too much more for me!"

"Oh, don't be such a party pooper," Grandma said, and Carla nudged her sister under the table with the toe of her tennis shoe.

Mario lifted his glass. "You are the queen of pickleball, Elise. The undisputed queen of pickleball."

"Damn straight. I need a crown. A big one with diamonds, like Queen Elizabeth's." Grandma's visor was a bit crooked on her head, and Elizabeth came out 'Elizabeff.' "Here's to pickleball royalty!"

Everyone lifted their own glass except for Ben, who had his phone out.

"Put your damn phone away, that's rude," said Grandma.

"I'm just making myself a note to bring you a tiara next match."

"Oh, well then," Grandma said, taking another drink, "by all means continue. Who's up for another pitcher?" A bit of salt sat on her lip like a little crystal mustache.

A cheer went up from the crowd. Rhonda dropped her purse, grinned, and lifted her glass. What the hell! It's a pickleball party!

Grandma stood and waved. Her plastic Casa de los Frijoles chair went toppling backwards. "Look! There's One-eyed Lou now! Oh wait," she said and stopped waving, "that ain't gonna work."

"Who's your sister talking to?" BJ asked.

"She has this imaginary friend with red hair."

"Seriously? Let's sneak over and spy."

Carlos thought about this and set down the map that they'd found in the basement. They'd been studying it and making treasure hunting plans and preparations. They were supposed to be babysitting, and that meant that they should be watching Bailey, and watching was like spying, only not as sneaky. "Okay, but be quiet, I know what she's like when she's mad, and I don't want to deal with that."

BJ agreed, and cracked open Carlos's bedroom door, "Clear."

"Follow me, BJ, some of these boards squeak."

Hugging the wall, the two boys crept toward Bailey's open door. Carlos peeked in and put his finger to his lips. "Shh."

BJ nodded and made a zip motion across his lips with his fingers.

Bailey was sitting on her bed facing away from them. "I wish I knew how to turn on the lights for you." Her head drooped. "I'm so sorry you're scared. It makes me so sad that you're afraid of him, because my dad is so nice. He can be lame sometimes, but he's always nice to me." Her voice hitched and she listened for a moment. "I don't know how to find Rosie or Leyta."

Bailey stopped talking, and it seemed as if she were listening to a conversation. "Or Johnathan. I know he was your best friend. I know you miss them." Her shoulders slumped then, and Carlos and BJ could tell she was crying. "I don't know them, and I miss them too. I miss them for you."

She paused for a second. "What?" she asked, and spun around looking directly at her cousin and her brother. "You shouldn't be here."

The bed creaked as if someone had jumped off it. Bailey stood, walked purposefully toward the door, and slammed it in their faces.

The boys stared at one another and ran back to Carlos's room.

"Either your house is haunted or your sister is possessed," BJ said as he shut the door.

A floorboard from the hallway creaked, and a shadow blocked the light coming from beneath the door.

"Probably both," Carlos said as a breeze blew through his bedroom, fluttering the treasure map to the floor.

Rhonda and Carla came cackling back into the house. Rhonda—who was the least drunk of the duo since having switched to water an hour ago—had a protective arm around her sister's shoulders.

"Let me go, I have to pee." Carla made a beeline to the powder room.

"Kids! We're home!" Rhonda shouted up the stairs.

Carlos and BJ came thundering down them. Bailey peeked out of her room, stepped out and closed her door. She walked purposefully down the steps. BJ and Carlos hugged Rhonda hard.

"Wow, what a welcome," she said, and kissed the top of Bailey's head. The boys clung to Rhonda in a fashion she was unaccustomed to by pre-teens while Bailey stood nearby, all but fluffing her hair and filing her nails.

"What happened?"

Bailey gave the boys a look that silently said, "don't even think about it."

"Nothing," Carlos said, his eyes on his sister.

"Nope," said BJ, "nothing at all."

Bailey went to the cupboard and helped herself to a Dollar Store cookie. "Want one?" she asked them. Both boys shook their heads no.

"Only one before dinner, little girl," Rhonda told her.

"Only one," she answered. "Mom, you smell like Uncle Gerold when he comes home from playing poker."

Bailey took her snack and skipped back up the stairs, went to her room, and closed the door behind her.

"Mom?" Carlos asked, "have you ever seen that old movie called The Omen?"

Chapter Thirteen

Your Sister is the Devil

1997

This Journal belongs to James Hansen

Kimberly White was not the first person I've ever seen dead. My grandmother had a stroke while she was babysitting. I was probably ten or so. She began to slur her words, and it looked to my ten-year-old self as if half of her face was melting away. I suppose I should have grabbed the phone right then and dialed 911, but when she fell to the ground, I couldn't stop looking at her eyes. They were frightened, yes, but something else as well…they were pleading, and she said nothing. They were pleading with <u>me</u>. To do something, to do anything.

I recall kneeling down and moving close to her face. I could feel her breath on my skin. Her hand was twitching like it wanted to escape; like a spider the instant before it feels the back of your shoe. I pulled away a bit and observed. Her eyes were wide and flitting about, but she did not speak; the only sound was a grumble in her throat, and her wedding ring clicking on the kitchen tile as her hand quivered. It took some time before her eyes stilled and her breathing stopped, but her pleading whimpers still echoed in my head. I put my ear next to her lips. Nothing. I sat there for a long while, taking it all in, preserving the scene unfolding before me like a photograph that I could tuck in my pocket, saving it for another day.

I recall hearing my dad pull up in the driveway, and running upstairs to the room my grandmother had set up for me when I stayed with her. I heard my father screaming. I told him I was reading upstairs with headphones on.

She was my first dead person. Thinking about the life seeping from her eyes and her body trembling still gives me a rush of adrenaline—she knew she was dying, and I got to share in that connection. I recreate that fear and intimacy at times to this day, and this is how I go about it.

Reptiles make excellent pets. They're intelligent, quiet, and beautiful; not only in the way they appear, but in the way they move. I find them fascinating. My parents were steadfast against my putting up a terrarium, so I purchased one with my own money and put it up on my own. My mother, as always, buckled and convinced my father that it would be good for me to have the responsibility of owning and caring for a pet.

The king snake has no name; it seemed juvenile to name it. I do however, at times name the mice that it swallows whole every two weeks. I schedule the feeding days so that I know the serpent is a touch past ravenous. Then, at the appropriate time, I introduce it to its meal.

Today I placed the mouse into a plastic sphere meant for exercising pet rodents and lowered it into the terrarium an inch at a time. My little white friend scrambled up the sides of the ball the instant it hit the rocky bottom, sending the clear hamster ball rolling. I could see the fear in its eyes as it grew frantic and tried to escape its confines. The king snake came to life, its body still but its tongue flickering, tasting the air and the scent—the fear—of its prey.

I pressed my face to the glass, watching it slide across the cage smooth and swift, wrapping its scaled body around the ball. The mouse was frantic, its red eyes searching for a means to elude its predator. Tomorrow or the next day I'll release the animal and allow my pet to dine. Until then I'll enjoy their dance.

As for my grandmother, I don't know what you'd call it, a jolt of understanding? An epiphany? As with the mouse, she understood she would die. I understood that I could have done more for Gran: ten minutes can be a lifetime when it comes to strokes. But I chose not to. I *chose* not to.

There it is, there's the answer. I controlled that situation down to the last tremble. It was as if I had my first breath as she took her last. As if my eyes opened as hers closed. It felt like gas escaping through the valve of an overloaded pipe which has been tightened so long it's on the verge of rupturing. Although she was the first *human* I saw leave this world, she wouldn't be the last. That wouldn't be you either, Kimberly, but you would be the next. This time I'll take actual photographs—and your flawed front tooth, I'll take that as well.

No, Kimberly White wasn't the first person I saw dead. Kimberly White was the first person I made dead.

I'm on edge. I may release the mouse earlier than expected.

Today, not far from Patton

Rose and Leyta were having tea. The plastic tablecloth had the look of real linen. The teacups, although modern, gave the illusion of fine, antique china. Leyta's brother Johnathan sat close by, reading a paperback novel, his gray hair clipped short, half moon reading glasses on his nose. Leyta and Johnathan visited Rose every day like clockwork at 3:00 P.M. sharp. Leyta raised the tea cup to Rose's lips, and she sipped. Rose's eyes were far away and lost, but today seemed like a good day: she was blinking in and out of the present, which was unusual and made Leyta happy.

"Johnathan?" Leyta asked her brother, "Would you please grab a few more napkins?"

"Sure." Johnathan laid down his book, grabbed his cane, went to the coffee bar and came back with a stack of white paper napkins.

"Thank you." Leyta dabbed at Rose's chin.

Rose smiled at her friend. "Is Paul here today?"

Leyta took her hand, fragile as tissue paper, in her own. "Not today, Rosie."

"Maybe tomorrow?"

"Maybe tomorrow." Leyta changed the subject. "Another tart? I'll break it into small pieces for you."

Rose was lost in something out the window and said, "that would be nice, thank you," before drifting off again into a world of the past.

Johnathan put a hand on his sister's shoulder. "It's hard to watch."

Leyta's face threatened to crumble. "It truly is. I love her so."

"She loves you too. All of that love is still inside of her, Leyta. She loves you the way she did when we were children. She may not always be able to express it, but that love is there. I can see it when she looks at you."

Leyta sniffled, pulled a tissue from her pocket and blew her nose. "I know, I know that with my heart."

The sky was scattered with delicate clouds that stretched like bridal lace across the blue arc of the afternoon. Rose Wilson stared out the window. A crow flew by. She smiled and waved at the shiny black creature. Her skeletal fingers, thick with ropey blue veins, fluttered after it as delicate as bird wings.

"We gotta find that key and find it today." Kenny was pacing in quad number three.

Anita took corn dogs out of the freezer, then placed them on a well-worn cookie sheet. She picked one up and waved it at Kenny. "You're gonna have to search each one of the other quads, top to bottom." She pointed the frozen wiener at him. "Keyword, 'YOU'."

"Don't wave that thing at me, Anita. And for godsake turn off the Mr. Coffee, the whole house smells like burnt breakfast."

"What?" She looked at the dinner on a stick. "Why the hell not? You wave yours in my direction every five minutes." She pushed the button on the Mr. Coffee and placed the half empty pot in the sink.

"Mine's bigger."

Anita knocked the frozen hotdog twice on the counter. "Mine's harder."

"You love it."

"Oh, shut up Kenny, I'm being serious here." She shoved the cookie sheet into the oven and set the timer. "All I'm gonna say is we need to check all the quads, and we gotta check them quick."

"I'm one step ahead of you, babe, I've gone through Ethan's house this morning. "He reached into his back pocket and pulled out a pair of blue plastic gloves. "I wore a pair of your hair painting gloves, I don't want fingerprints anywhere near a murder scene."

"We don't know that it was murder, now they're talking suicide," she said, snatching the gloves back. "These are expensive." She went to the closet and put them back into the box from which they came. "I hope you didn't get any Ethan on them. Hell. I'll use them next time."

She stood looking at him, "Did you find anything?"

"Nothing."

"I told you they weren't there. You never listen to a word I say," she said as she shoved the remaining corn dogs back in the freezer. "Henry takes Edna to the doctor once a week, on Tuesday at about nine."

"That's tomorrow."

"Yep, and you're gonna break in and search the place."

"Why do I gotta do it?"

"Because I'm gonna go to the new lady's house with a welcome-to-the-neighborhood cake, keep her busy, and snoop." Rhonda opened the oven and checked the corn dogs. "Just a few more minutes," she said, closing the oven with a clunk. "Dinner'll be ready in fifteen minutes, Can you get off your ass and set the table?" Anita continued, "I'll be able to check around her kitchen and ask to use the bathroom while I'm there and you're"—Anita pointed toward Henry's quad with a fork—"there."

"Doesn't the new lady's quad have a powder room on the main floor?"

"Yep, and I got that all figured out. I'll tell her that a woman with my juicy figure," she ran her hands over her curves and folds, "doesn't fit well into a little bathroom like that, and I'll ask to use the one upstairs."

"My baby is brilliant."

Anita fluffed her hair as the timer on the oven went off; she opened it, grabbed a pair of oven mitts, then sat the cookie sheet onto the top of the stove. She picked up one of the corn dogs, stared Kenny in the eye, and stuck most of it into her mouth. She pulled it out slowly and his eyes grew wide.

"Ain't that hot?"

"I'll show you hot," she said, running her tongue up the corny part of the corn dog.

"Okay! I'll check Henry and Edna's quad the minute they pull out of the driveway."

Anita chuckled. *Men are so easy.* "Dinner time, my boo. Can you call the girls? They're outside."

Kenny sprang to his feet, opened the door, and yelled for them. Anita took down a bag of chips and started cutting up a couple of apples. Gotta stay healthy when you're about to get a bucket fulla money. Anita saw Vegas in her future—with or without Kenny. Vegas, baby.

Please god, don't let him fuck this up.

Before Carla sobered up enough to walk home from her sister's house after a raucous game of pickleball, BJ and Carlos cornered Rhonda in the kitchen. "Mom, can we talk to you for a minute?"

"Sure. What's up, guys?"

"Shhhh," they said together, their fingers on their lips.

"Okay," Rhonda said, stage whispering, "what's up guys? Better?"

"We think Bailey is possessed and needs a priest," Carlos told her.

Rhonda laughed; they shhhhhshed her again. "What in the world would make you say something like that? You two have been watching too much TV."

BJ said, "Today we saw her talking to someone that wasn't there."

"She was sitting on her bed talking up a storm, and we swear that we saw her bed move like someone got up," Carlos said.

"Maybe she was talking to Goldie?"

The boys shook their heads. "A goldfish doesn't make a butt sized dent in a bed," said Carlos.

Rhonda remembered some of the strange things Bailey has been saying lately about her new friend with the red hair. "She's five years old, boys. Kids her age often have imaginary friends." She placed one hand on each boy's shoulder—god, they were almost as tall as she was. "Bailey hasn't made many friends since we moved here. As far as I know she has only two friends, and I'd barely call them that." She sighed. "She's the new kid and feeling lonely."

"What about her bed moving?" Carlos asked. "It had a dent in it like from someone's ass—then it didn't"

"Watch your language, please."

BJ nodded vigorously and pulled a paper from his pocket. He handed it to Rhonda.

"What is this?" Rhonda studied the drawing. It was a complex picture of the carriage house and obviously much beyond her daughter's artistic abilities. Above the house, a crow was sketched in, its feathers realistic and detailed. Below the picture was a name written in what she recognized as Bailey's printing: PAUL, in all capital letters.

She remembered the day Grandma Elise brought her donuts. *There was a little red-headed boy that disappeared one day, his name was Paul Wilson.*

"Is this why you two asked me about The Omen?"

The boys nodded.

"So you think your sister is the devil."

They nodded again.

"Pizza okay for dinner?"

They nodded once more.

At the end of May the Antelope Reservoir project began. It would take six weeks for the water to leave the reservoir and begin its trek to the neighboring state. The waterline slowly lowered during the week, the shoreline becoming increasingly shallow and muddy. Secrets began to be exposed as the waterfront shrank inch by inch, most of them long-lost boat oars and the occasional shoe. The water gurgled into the formerly dry Antelope Canal, splashing past its banks as it made its way to the Regent River and then on to Kansas. The hope was that Colorado would have a snowy enough winter next year to fill it up again, but you could never tell. Colorado weather was finicky, and the drought had been horrendous for the last seven years; still, people were hopeful. Antelope had been a beloved camping, fishing, and boating spot since 1964 when the Platte River flooded, and the reservoir was built soon after. Families had been enjoying it since its completion in 1966.

"There's a whole lot of muck down there," Norman said, as he and his partner Dave watched the water pour into the canal. They stood atop the dam that was exactly forty-two feet above the mouth of the ongoing draining. "I knew it was going to stink, but this is something."

"It's going to be smelly for some time," Dave said, checking the speed of the water flow, "It'll dry out by next August, I imagine." He hopped into the state park truck, and Norman followed. "We'll clean out the grates to the outlet pipes tomorrow. It looks as if it's doing fine on its own at the moment." He turned toward Norman. "Let's grab a beer on the way home, my treat."

As the day went on, more pieces of the past were exposed to the sunshine for the first time in over fifty years. It would take a while for the water to give up all its mysteries, but inch by inch the ground would be uncovered. The catalog of objects from the past grew—snagged fishing bobbers, lost shoes, and dead trees that once grew strong and tall.

Some secrets were the remnants of good times gone by: toys and picnic gear, beer coolers, and swim fins. Other secrets were meant to stay forgotten and hidden. Across Antelope Reservoir to the south, not far from the outlet pipe, where the grates protected the canal from becoming clogged with various refuse, the earth quivered, and a herd of startled deer fled into the brush.

Chapter Fourteen

Stinky Cages of Poisonous Snakes!

RHONDA PUT THE PICTURE of the carriage house and the crow into her back pocket and lightly knocked on Bailey's door.

"Come in."

Rhonda sat on Bailey's bed. "Sweetheart, what's this?" Rhonda unfolded the drawing paper and smoothed it down. "Who's Paul?"

Bailey touched the paper with her fingers, moving over the letters that spelled out his name. "He's my friend. He drew this. He's a really, really good artist, isn't he?"

Rhonda wanted Bailey to open up to her. If she voiced her doubts or asked too many questions, it could suppress her daughter's responses. "How did you meet him?" she asked. "And where did you meet him?"

"I met him right here in my room."

Rhonda felt a chill slide slick and cold up her spine but did her best to remain outwardly unfazed. "Is he here now?"

Bailey shook her head, "No, he had to go to sleep. His father gets angry when he visits me." Bailey's lower lip trembled. "His father is so mean, Mama."

"Have you seen his father too?"

"One time," she began, and buried her face in Rhonda's shoulder, "he tapped on the window." Bailey stood and demonstrated against the glass: *tap tap tap*.

Rhonda didn't believe in ghosts, and she grew concerned thinking that an adult man could be tormenting her daughter. Was he also a figment of her imagination?

"What did his father look like?"

"I didn't actually see him, just a dark shape outside the window. I just heard tapping. Tap tap tap, like with a fingernail. Rhonda pulled her close. "Then Paul got really afraid and left in a hurry." Bailey wiped her eyes and bit her lip. "I don't know if his dad can come in the house. I think Paul keeps him out. Paul says I remind him of his sister."

Rhonda swallowed down a morsel of panic. She nodded and touched the signature on the drawing. "But sweetie, isn't this your handwriting?"

"Yes," Bailey said. "He's not very good with letters and spelling—he gets things mixed up. I helped him with that. He drew the picture, though." She turned to her mother, her expression serious and unusually childlike. "Mommy? I promise I'm not making this up. Am I in trouble?"

Rhonda stroked her hair and pulled her close. "I believe you, sweetpea, and no, you're not in trouble. I'm only trying to understand." Rhonda lifted her daughter's chin and looked into her deep brown eyes. "Why don't you tell me everything that you know. Everything that Paul has told you." Rhonda kissed the top of her head; sometimes, not often, she still got a subtle whiff of the infant Bailey had been. Now was one of those times. She could swear she smelled baby shampoo.

"I know that Paul is very sad," Bailey said. "I know that he misses his sister and his best friend." She began to cry. "I know he's scared of his father and wants me to help him."

This seems all too real.

"Help him do what exactly, Bailey?" Rhonda asked, "and what is he afraid of?"

"Help him find his sister and his friends," she said, swallowing hard. "And to get out of the dark. He's afraid of the dark, Mama."

"How do we do that? How do we help him?"

"We need to find him and keep him safe, and find his sister and his friends." Bailey swallowed a sob. "His father is so angry, that's what he's most afraid of. I think that's what's in the dark."

"What's in the dark, honey?"

"His father." Bailey struggled to pull herself together. "We have to help him, Mama. Please believe me. His father is a very, very bad man."

Rhonda began to wonder if Paul could be a real boy with real fears of his parents. Should she call the police? "Do you think it would help if we call the police?"

"The police can't help him, they've already tried." Bailey wiped her nose with the back of her hand, and Rhonda pulled a tissue from her jeans pocket and handed it to her. "The police can't *see* him."

Bailey's pink curtains fluttered, and Rhonda jumped and held her close. "Then that's what we'll do," Rhonda said. "We'll do everything we can to help him"

"Everything?"

"All that we can, yes, but I need you to be completely honest with me."

"I will be, Mommy."

"Good girl." Rhonda handed the picture back to her daughter. "Let's go make a salad to go with the pizza. You can help me."

"Okay." They slipped from the edge of her bed and Rhonda took her hand. The indent from where she was sitting slowly disappeared as they stood, just as the boys said it had earlier this afternoon.

It looks as if I'm going to have to get more facts about this house from Grandma Elise at the next pickleball game.

The idea of a young boy so terrified of his father made the hairs on Rhonda's neck stand up. Imaginary friend or not, they'd get to the bottom of it.

Am I chasing ghosts or an abusive man and a scared little boy?

It was 9:00 A.M. sharp when Anita knocked on Rhonda's front door. She was holding a plastic crystal potluck platter she had found while looking for the keys at Ethan's house, and she'd washed it before using it. *That was big of me.*

On top of the platter was a cake from the grocery store—chocolate, chocolate, and more chocolate. Anita glanced over at Henry and Edna's unit and saw movement behind the up-stairs curtain. Good, Kenny had found his way inside.

Rhonda answered the door. "Hello Anita! What a surprise. Come on in." She was in yoga clothes, and she was sweaty and breathing hard.

"Did I get you away from something?"

"Nothing important, don't worry."

Anita handed her the platter with the cake. It sat proudly in the middle in all its gooey chocolate glory.

"You didn't have to do that," Rhonda said as she took the plate.

"Oh, I wanted to, you've been so friendly. It's the least I could do." Anita eyed the entryway. She didn't see a dish or a peg board that held keys, although Rhonda's purse was draped across the newel post. Purses held keys.

"Would you like some coffee or tea?" Rhonda asked.

"Sure."

"Espresso, or regular coffee?"

"Regular is just dandy," she said as her eyes took in the kitchen and the breakfast bar. It was neat and tidy. There was a bowl, but all it held was fruit. She checked out the refrigerator for hooks on magnets. Nope, just kids' pictures, one of which was a crayon sketch of the carriage house and some crows. No keys.

"I like your house," Anita said, strolling into the living room. "Ours is just like it, but our window faces out back." There was a long cream-colored sofa, tidy end tables with lamps, and a coffee table. No basket of keys in sight.

Anita walked over to the fireplace. The coffee machine hissed in the kitchen behind her. The photos on the mantle were of her family and friends, with knick-knacks in between, but still no damn keys. Anita leaned against the kitchen counter without taking a seat.

Rhonda brought over slices of cake and mugs of coffee; Mild Breakfast Blend for them both.

"What a dreadful tragedy the other night," Anita said, giving herself a pat on the back for adding in 'dreadful tragedy'. She'd googled other words for "fucked up mess" on her phone until she found an app called a Thesaurus and downloaded it. Handy!

"Is there any word from the police? Ethan was a nice man, I can't believe anyone would want to harm him."

Anita took a big bite of cake, "I hear he had some sketchy friends." Oh shit. What had she said? Kenny was one of the sketchy friends. "At least that's what I've heard." Through another mouthful of cake she asked Rhonda, "Where are your kiddos today?"

"They're over with my sister Carla. They might drive to Denver and go to the zoo. Carla has a son Carlos's age."

Hot diggity damn, thought Anita. She'd be able to make an excuse to go upstairs and check out the main bedroom.

"Where are your girls?" Rhonda asked her.

"They're home in front of the TV. Thank god for TV, cable is the best babysitter." Rhonda nodded, but her raised eyebrow gave her away. *Fancy schmancy coffee lady thinks she's better than me.*

"The cake is wonderful, I'm so glad you stopped by." Rhonda said, as her yoga class still played in the background on the television.

Anita put a hand on her round belly and grimaced. "There must be eggs in this cake. Do you mind if I use your bathroom? I can't do eggs." She thought she saw Rhonda cringe.

"Of course, it's right here on the other side of the stairs."

Anita walked over to the powder room and peeked inside—no sign of keys.

"I hate to ask this of you, but do you mind if I use the main bathroom?" She did her best to look embarrassed. "Powder rooms are a little cramped for ladies with voluptuous derrieres like mine." She'd looked up "fat ass" with her new thesaurus too.

"No problem, it's up the stairs and at the end of the hall."

Anita plodded up the stairs, one hand on the rail, one hand on her belly. "Eggs just about do me in."

Anita looked over the stair railing and saw that Rhonda had busied herself putting the cake plates into the dishwasher and rinsing out mugs. Anita deftly backtracked, lifted Rhonda's purse and took it with her. *I'm as stealthy as Catwoman when I wanna be.*

What Anita saw at the top of the landing was familiar. Three bedrooms and a bath; all the doors were closed, and the floor looked freshly vacuumed.

She peeked into the first door. Posters and action figures, a basketball in one corner, a desk with a computer, and an overflowing hamper. She silently closed it. Tiptoeing to the next door, she could see it belonged to the little girl that lived here. A few dolls, a goldfish in a bowl, a drawing table, a desk. Not as much pink as her girls had. She silently clicked the door closed. On to what hopefully would be pay dirt.

Anita stood by Rhonda and Tate's bed and emptied out Rhonda's purse she had snagged on the way up. She picked up a key ring. Car keys and house keys, a few others, but none with the eight-sided head Kenny had told her to look for. Standard ladies' purse stuff, a wallet (with fifty-seven dollars in it—now forty-seven), hand lotion, a pack of tissues, lip balm, mints, a bottle of Advil, and not much else. She shoved everything back inside. "Well, hell."

On to the main bath. She peeked around looking under cosmetic bottles and baskets of lotions and creams. Nothing. Anita thought that bathrooms and kids' rooms were unlikely places to hide keys. On to the nightstand drawers. She checked them thoroughly and came up with nada, zilch, zip, nothin'.

"Anita? Are you okay up there?" Rhonda's voice met Anita at the moment she was leaving her bedroom. She hurried over to the bathroom, went in, flushed the toilet and walked out just as Rhonda hit the top of the stairs. "You've been up here awhile, do you still feel sick? Do you want me to call someone?"

Anita hid Rhonda's bag behind her back and followed her down to the main level, silently draping the purse back over the newel post.

"Would you like another cup of coffee? Maybe some ginger tea?"

Anita grabbed her handbag. "Nope, I'm good." She thought for a moment. "I would take the rest of the cake though, the kids will eat it later."

Rhonda cut a piece of plastic wrap and covered the rest of the cake, handing back the platter. "Thanks so much for dropping by."

Anita let herself out, closed the door, and shot off a text to Kenny. "Empty fucking handed." She patted her pocket with Rhonda's ten spot. *Well, not totally empty handed.*

Atop the refrigerator, forgotten for a moment, sat a cute red ceramic jalapeno shaped like a dachshund. Its long, sharp tail held a ring of keys, one with an octagonal head.

At the same time Rhonda was cutting the chocolate cake, Kenny was rummaging through the Hansens' kitchen. Since Edna and Henry weren't home, Kenny could be more thorough than Anita had been at the new lady's house.

He found their junk drawer. That would be a good place for keys! Unfortunately, other than screwdrivers, a hammer, and a few million orphan nails, there didn't seem to be much else. He pocketed a Bic lighter and a couple of quarters then shut the drawer. Opened it again, swiped an ancient roll of pennies, then slammed it closed.

Kenny opened the refrigerator; no one put keys in the fridge, but he was hungry so he made himself a sandwich.

Munching on leftover roast beef and cheese, he began to scout out the rest of the Hansens' house. There was a pegboard by the front door which held various keys and rings, but none of the damn things were for the strange little stinky cocaine room. He wished he could just cut the blasted lock off, but then the muscle would know there was a problem and that they weren't doing the job they were being paid to do. What if they didn't fork over the cocaine babysitting money? He had to find those keys!

For the life of him he couldn't understand the need to check on drugs every day. Maybe it wasn't drugs? Maybe there was a hostage in there that Ethan had been feeding every day, or some kind of exotic animal? What about the smell? It could be a dead hostage! Or some stinky cages of poisonous snakes!

Kenny shook himself out of his daydream and got back to the task at hand. Whatever was in the basement, it was pissing him right the fuck off, and he needed to keep his wits about him.

He searched the lower level to the best of his ability, and, sandwich in hand (this was sandwich number two), he headed to the stairs and the upper level.

Two bedrooms and one bath. He peeked into the bathroom first. Herm..pink fluffy rugs and toilet seat cover, pink tile and sink. How do you pee around a rug that grips the bottom of the toilet? He couldn't help himself, he gave it a try. Anita would fucking kill him.

After he had the good manners to flush, he gave the bathroom a quick look around. The medicine cabinet held all the things you'd expect in a house full of old people. Kenny sniffed Edna's perfume. It reminded him of his nana, so he sprayed a little on his shirt. *Whatever, nobody puts keys in the bathroom, that's stupid.* He closed the door to the geriatric Barbie bathroom and continued his search.

He opened the door to Henry and Edna's bedroom. "Every room smells like my nana and pop-pop," Kenny muttered, giving his shirt a sniff and wiping his eyes. He'd loved his grandparents. He started to think of his grandma, and the great roasts and pies she used to make. Maybe he'd stop on his way out for sandwich number three, Edna's roast was almost as good as his nana's—maybe better. *Sorry, Nana.*

The second bedroom puzzled him. While the rest of the house looked like Leave it to Beaver exploded, this bedroom paid homage to his own teenage years. It was set up in the way you'd set up a room for a teenager. As far as he was aware, there were no teenagers in the quad. A bunch of rotten little kids, including his own, but no teens. Yet in this bedroom there was a desk, a plaid bedspread, posters of bands that he hadn't thought about in decades. Except for one, but it wasn't his type of music and damn, didn't they break up in the 90s?

There was a Walkman on the desk. Kenny picked it up. "I haven't seen one of these in twenty-five years," he murmured reverently. An ancient computer that used floppy disks, and a partially dismantled hard drive sat nearby.

There was also a terrarium with a petrified and very dead snake inside. Kenny shivered. "I fucking knew there'd be snakes." He was not a big fan of legless reptiles, the creepy little alien freaks of nature made his skin crawl. There were probably snakes in the cocaine room.

Stop it! Stop thinking so much!

But what if there were? What if there were buckets full of snakes doing all kinds of gross snake stuff and stinking up the basement? Maybe they're poisonous snakes, and one would bite him and he'd die? What if it bit him right in the dick and he had to have it amputated?! Anita would suck the poison out if it...*Shit, now I'm getting hard... Nana always said that there's a silver lining to everything... mmm Nana's roast beef...I wonder if there's enough for another sandwich?*

STOP IT STOP IT STOP IT! Kenny looked down at his tight pants. "STOP IT!" He shook his head and brought himself and his dick back to the present and the task at hand.

The keys. He had to find the keys.

He searched through the closet. Jeans, more jeans, shirts, shoes—a backpack on the top shelf. Bingo!

Kenny sat down inside of the closet and dumped out the contents of the backpack. Notebooks fell to the floor, there must have been ten of them. With his back against the closet wall, he casually flipped through them; they were all handwritten by someone named James. "This Journal Belongs to James Hansen, February 10th, 1997," he read, his lips forming the words.

What keys? Ever since he was a child, it was hard for Kenny to stay focused.

He read a small section of one of the notebooks.

I didn't clearly know how to feel after this encounter. Should I be flattered that she sought me out? Should I be annoyed that she barged in without asking? Should I have screamed, reached across the table, grabbed her by the throat, yanked that damn tooth from her mouth and dropped it into her soda like another piece of ice?

Kenny pulled himself back to current events and dropped the journal like it was on fire. Whoever wrote this was one crazy fuck! Spooked, Kenny had the overpowering feeling that he needed to make like a tree and leave. He began to frantically shove the notebooks back into the pack. Nothing could seem out of place, or the Hansens would know there had been an intruder.

Something small and white had dropped to the floor from within one of James Hansen's ledgers, and Kenny stopped short of grabbing it. It was a tooth. A human tooth by the looks of it. Its roots were long, claw-like and the color of warm ivory. Kenny, who was easily distracted, also had a whopper of an imagination. He could see the tooth slowly get up, its long roots turning to fangs. He could imagine it turning, somehow seeing him and dashing at him in small, quick steps on sharp, slender white legs. He dropped the backpack as if it were filled with C-4 and scootched on his backside across the closet floor.

The tooth lay there, unmoving. Christ Jesus! He had to clean up, it couldn't look like he broke in. Whimpering, he shoved the incisor—'*Should I have screamed, reached across the table, grabbed her by the throat, yanked that damn tooth from her mouth and dropped it into her soda like another piece of ice?*'—back into the backpack with one of the stray notebooks. He wasn't touching that thing! He threw the pack and its contents into the closet where it landed upside down and the contents shifted and spilled. Beyond caring, Kenny slammed the closet door, ran down the stairs, forgot all about the key and the extra roast beef sandwich that was better than his nana's, and climbed back out the downstairs powder room window.

In James Hansen's old bedroom, a single tooth had lazily rolled from its canvas home of twenty-five years, tinkled onto the hardwood floor and landed artfully next to a Polaroid picture; head down, roots up, like carefully placed, bitter enamel claws.

Chapter Fifteen

Limp Dinks and Margaritas

1997

This Journal Belongs to James Hansen

I can barely breathe as I relive tonight's events. My heart feels as if it may grind its way out of my chest in an attempt to get away from me. I knew it would happen someday. I knew I couldn't control it forever, but I didn't think today would be the day, although I suspected that Kimberly White would be the person.

I sometimes take my father's fishing truck and head to Antelope Reservoir. It's quiet there if I stay away from the public campgrounds and go after dark. I enjoy listening to music on my Walkman; sometimes I smoke a little pot, and often I let my mind wander off on its own, enjoying my own company, lying on my back and contemplating the stars. There are times when I bring a lantern and write in my journal. That's what I was doing right then, sitting on an outcropping of rocks that dangle at the summit of the dam and to the south.

I had the lantern on, which was a big mistake because who do I see walk up? I couldn't quite believe it: Kimberly White. She told me she was camping with her family down the hill, saw the lantern and decided to check it out. Am I some kind of beacon for mental abuse when it comes to that person? She sat down next to me, pulled out a pack of gum and offered me a piece. I declined. She put a square of the pink stuff in her mouth and took a seat next to me. I could feel her arm brush mine when she asked what I was doing on the dam. I showed her my Walkman and pulled out a joint from my pocket. I asked her if she wanted some. She said no, thank god. I would have had to have thrown it away after she sucked on it and it tasted like her wintergreen bubble gum.

Without warning she turned and kissed me. I pulled away and stared at her. Her gum was now in *my* mouth. I panicked. I spit. I grabbed her by the throat and squeezed, and her necklace snapped off and fell to the rock. <u>It had been in my mouth.</u> Her feet kicked, and the lantern fell into the water.

I learned that day that it is not easy to strangle a full sized human being, but I persisted. My mind spun at the adrenaline rush. Dear sweet Jesus, her gum had been in my <u>mouth</u>.

It took a good three minutes for her to still. The whites of her open eyes were red with broken blood vessels. The stars reflected in her irises. Her mouth hung open, and that damn tooth mocked me. I went to my dad's truck, searched his tools and found some pliers, grabbed his Polaroid camera, and proceeded to rid her of that unsightly deformation and capture it on celluloid. I placed her left incisor into the small change pocket of my Levis then carried her to the top of the dam, filled her jacket with stones, put the chewed gum back into her mouth, and dropped her over the edge. My heart flip-flopped in my chest as she sank into the black depths of Antelope Reservoir. The last piece of her I recall seeing is a swirl of unnaturally blond, honey-colored hair.

I sat for a brief while in my father's truck with the dome light on writing about the experience while it was fresh in my mind. I pictured Kimberly lying in the deepest part of Antelope Reservoir, curious fish nibbling at her open, blue eyes as she sinks deeper into the silt, blond hair swirling about her face; a golden interment shroud.

I reached into my pocket and stroked her tooth for a moment, an action that calmed me. I'd confiscated her broken necklace and hung it on a branch close to the trail, about one mile from water. I still had her tooth in my hand, and as I sat there studying it—the sharp, bloody roots, the smooth enamel surface—I noticed that her tooth had lost its anxiety-inducing effect on me, now it was no longer inside of Miss White. I marked my place in my notebook with the Polaroid picture I'd taken, turned my father's truck around, and left Antelope Reservoir and Kimberly White behind—just beneath the sand.

"We clobbered you fellas!"

Grandma Elise waved her pickleball racquet at Mario and Ben. The Limp Dinks had been thoroughly thrashed, eviscerated, and left for dead by the Sideout Seniors. Grandma put an arm around her partner, Sylvia Mejia. "Two little old ladies clobbered your whiny toddler asses and handed them to you on a plate." Grandma cackled, "Margaritas are on you two losers." She made an L with her thumb and forefinger and slapped it to her forehead.

"Maybe we let you win," Ben whined some more.

Sylvia flexed her arm. Beneath the crepey skin was one fine-looking muscle. "Bullshit," she said. "We were on fire—and it's your job to buy the drinks to put it out." She licked her finger, touched her bicep and made a hissing sound.

Mario headed toward the bar. "We're not going to win this argument, Ben."

"Great!" Grandma yelled after him. "Get some nachos too. Extra guacamole and sour cream!" She paused then yelled, "Please."

Rhonda and Carla joined them at the outdoor table on the patio of La Casa de los Frijoles. The bright orange umbrella kept their plastic chairs in the shade.

"You did great for your first time, sis," Carla told Rhonda, patting her on the back.

Rhonda was red-faced and sweating. "Ya'll play for blood!" She was justly proud of herself for making it through the round without being totally humiliated, having a heart attack, or falling on her face. "I need water before booze," she said. She had brought her own water bottle, but that bitch was empty half an hour ago. "With ice. Preferably intravenously."

"We'll whip you into shape, you play us next week. Tell them what that's like, Ben," Grandma sing-songed.

"Elise, you and Sylvia are brutal, guitar-smashing rockstars."

Grandma beamed. "I'm glad you've come to your collective senses. Like I always tell my grandkids: being a sore loser is a bad look."

Mario sat the platter of nachos and a pitcher of margaritas down on the table that now held six people: The Limp Dinks, The Designated Dinkers, and the Sideout Seniors. The Pickle Ticklers and the Spin Doctors sat one table over, already halfway home to Margaritaville. The Net Ninjas had headed home; Carol Wiesmann had a sore hip. Grandma had pointed out that she didn't drink with her hip, but the party pooper left anyway.

Carla filled Rhonda, Grandma, Sylvia, Ben, Mario and then her own glass. "We're going to need two more of these."

"Three," said Rhonda.

"That's the spirit!" said Grandma.

Rhonda turned to Grandma. "Speaking of spirits…I've been wondering if sometime I could ask you a few more questions about the history of my house."

"Are you seeing spooks?"

Rhonda hesitated. "Well, I'm not seeing anything, but my five-year-old daughter has an imaginary friend, and he's seeming all too…real lately."

"Oh! I know all about imaginary friends, my grandson had one of those. We all thought he was losing his marbles." Grandma took her first drink of margarita. "Ahhhh. Makes all the pain and sweat of pickleball worth it—not that I'm in pain, nor do I sweat that much." Grandma continued, "Anyway, what you need to do is call our friend Egypt December."

Sylvia nodded enthusiastically in agreement. "She's amazing!"

"Egypt December?" asked Rhonda. "That's a real person?"

"Yep, she told Sylvia right where to find her lost remote."

"Egypt lives across town in a small cottage. She's our resident medium."

"Medium what?" said Rhonda.

"Not a *size*, silly woman," Grandma said, giving the salt on her margarita a lick, "a medium, as in she talks to spooks and haunts and dead folks."

"She told me where to find my remote, and there it was," Sylvia said, dipping a chip.

"She told me where to find my Seductive Pink lipstick," Grandma added. "It was right there behind the toilet." She reached over and dabbed at a spot of guacamole on Sylvia's chin. "We thought we had ghosts, but it ended up being our punk-ass neighbor. That story is for another time though, right now you have a spook problem to deal with."

"I don't need to find anything, I just want to know more about the house and the little boy that went missing with his father in the fifties. And I don't think I have spooks. Just a daughter with an overactive imagination, or privy to some information I don't know about."

"Well," said Grandma, gesturing to Mario that they needed another pitcher, "I've heard Egypt's been practicing and can do a lot more than find things now."

Mario got up dutifully and headed to the bar. There were sweat stains under the arms of his pink polo shirt.

"I think I'll do some computer research before I call a medium," said Rhonda.

"Or a large," said Grandma. Both she and her pickleball partner cackled.

"I'll think about it though," said Rhonda.

Grandma picked up her purse And shuffled through it. It looked to weigh about fifty pounds. "I have her card," she said.

Rhonda took the card and placed it into her backpack. Carla kicked her sister under the table.

Mario returned with two pitchers of margaritas.

"Now that's what I'm talking about!" said Grandma.

"¡Me encanta La Casa de los Frijoles!" said Sylvia.

"¡Me encanta Mario and Ben paying!" said Grandma. "Losers."

Sylivia and Grandma clinked glasses. "Mario! You forgot the blasted queso dip."

"Jesus. How much can one old lady eat?" he mumbled.

"Fuck around and find out," Grandma said, giving him the stink eye. "And watch that 'old lady' shit."

Anita took a road trip to Denver. Kenny had been scared out of his mind when he came home from searching the Hansens' house. Some bullshit story about a walking tooth. That man had the most overactive imagination of anyone she'd ever met. He did look a little like Brad Pitt. Well, maybe if you bought Brad Pitt on Temu.

Anita knew just what would cheer her man up and bring him out of his funk.

She pulled into the parking lot of Great Big Expectations in Northglenn, a suburb of Denver. Great Big Expectations was a plus-size lingerie store which specialized in sexy clothing for women with luscious curves like hers. They also had a wide array of fun items and toys. Some of the toys were actually remote controlled—what a world!

Anita searched through the racks of lacy things that were in her size. Ohhh, a red teddy! She held it up to herself and looked into the mirror. This would reset Kenny's attitude in a heartbeat. Well, more than just a heartbeat, he wasn't *that* quick. Anita chuckled to herself. The saleswoman gave her a knowing look.

"I'll take this," she told the woman, "and by the way, how much are those remote controlled dildos?"

The woman told her.

"I'll take the pink one in the Traveling Titillator style."

Anita thought about Brad Pitt in Thelma and Louise. *Yeeha! Ride 'em, cowboy!*

Todd and Not Todd sat in the best room in the shittiest hotel in the ass end of Denver. It had two bedrooms, a sitting area, and a kitchen. Calling it the penthouse was pushing it, but Todd would take it. There was important work to be done.

"I don't know why we had to include a middleman," said Not Todd. "It just complicates things."

"It's what Mr. Holyworth wanted."

"Did we pick the right people?" Not Todd asked. "Ethan seemed okay, but the rest of them, I dunno. They're like a ticker-tape parade of extra stupid."

"Now that, my friend, is a question that has not yet been answered." Todd stood by the window that overlooked the front range of The Rocky Mountains. "Time will tell." He was getting a bit nervous about the exchange of goods that was about to go down. Every time he passed by the garage there was something idiotic happening.

"Only Ethan knew what's really in that basement room. He damn well better have filled someone in on how to take care of it."

"You think the other assholes still think it's cocaine?" said Todd, lighting up a smoke in the non-smoking hotel room.

"I certainly hope not, because Formaggio con Amici is a delicate commodity that needs to be tended to daily to keep the little larvae that live inside alive." Not Todd grimaced. "Who'd eat that shit anyway?"

"People with more money than brains, I suppose."

Not Todd nodded and joined him at the window. The view was stunning, the mountains still capped with snow into the beginning of June. "Has Holyworth said anything about Ethan and Aaron? Their cut was small but substantial enough. Twenty-five thousand is a ton of money to dipshits like them."

"He said if Kenny and Ishmael do a good enough job, to let them have it," Todd replied, as they both took in the impressive view.

"What if Kenny *doesn't* do a good job?" Not Todd said. "This is a distinct possibility, that guy is a knuckle-dragging paste eater."

Todd turned and met his gaze. "Then we off him."

"And that big woman he lives with."

Todd chuckled. "You get bonus points for the big ones."

"That's a lot of bonus points my friend," said Not Todd.

Secretly, he thought she was damn sexy.

Five-year-old Bailey Ramos Benson stood in the living room of her home in a Pinecone Pioneers uniform, white socks, and black shoes. She had a look on her face that would rival Wednesday Addams.

Rhonda fussed with her daughter's hair. "Cheer up, it'll be fun!"

"This is gonna suck giant donkey balls."

"Bailey! Where in god's name did you hear that?"

Bailey shrugged her shoulders and continued to look irritated.

"You'll make friends and do fun things," Rhonda told her. "Do you want a ponytail or braids?"

Bailey gave her mom a sideward glance without moving a muscle. "Braids."

"How about I make you a deal," Rhonda said. "If you go to three meetings, only three, and you hate it, you can quit. But give it a chance, you may like it a lot."

"Fine."

Outside a horn honked. "They're here, grab your water bottle and let's go. Next week I'm driving the carpool." If there's a next week, Rhonda thought.

Bailey marched to the front door, opened it, stepped out, and slammed it behind her.

"Good grief," Rhonda muttered, watching out the living room window as her little Wednesday climbed into the station wagon.

While Bailey was gone for the afternoon, Rhonda came upon three boxes she had left to unpack. The first held a set of her parents' Funk & Wagnalls encyclopedias which had come free with a purchase from the grocery store in the 1970s. Her mother had collected them diligently over the years. *Think of how many boxes of laundry soap she had to buy to have a full collection. What kind of daughter could part with something like this?*

Rhonda decided to not unpack it but store it, although she was running out of storage space in the main house. *That's what the basement is for—storage. Someday Carlos and Bailey can throw them out. Problem solved.* She pushed the heavy box back into the closet where it came from. She'd think about moving it later; it was too heavy to carry downstairs on her own. She'd wait for Tate to move it or get Carlos and BJ to help.

The next box held Halloween decorations and old costumes that her mother had sewn from when the kids were younger. She lifted Carlos's devil costume. God, it was so tiny. *Where does the time go?* She really should donate them to the thrift store. Someone would surely be happy to have a complete devil costume courtesy of Nana for next Halloween. She brought it to her face and inhaled. Flashes of good memories bolted through her senses. She couldn't do it. She stacked that box on top of the other for later. She'd *think* about it. Nope. She couldn't do it. It would go into storage as well. Maybe someday she and Tate will have grandchildren?

Feeling justified by this idea, Rhonda opened the third box. A rush of memories greeted her. Great-grandma's china, topped off with something that warmed Rhonda's heart: Great-Grandma's mantilla—the veil she wore on her head to mass every Sunday. Rhonda blew the dust from it, gently folded it, and laid it back in the box along with the dishes. Such cherished keepsakes, but three boxes in the bedroom closet equaled a full closet. She was going to have to force herself to make a trip to the basement.

Maybe she'd wear the mantilla when she worked up the courage to go down there. Couldn't hurt.

Chapter Sixteen

Can I Have a Donkey?

PAUL HUDDLED IN THE CORNER of his bedroom, his body rocking, tears flowing, and whimpering sounds escaping his lips.

His father, all six feet four inches of him, was a looming presence. "Drawing on the walls is unacceptable. It doesn't matter that it was in the carriage house—this has put me in an impossible situation, Paul." Edgar paced the length of Paul's bedroom, his boots thumping out a steady, booming beat.

He stopped and confronted his cowering son. "I have two options. One," Edgar said, counting off on his fingers, "I can take off my belt and be done with you now."

Paul made mewling noises, and Rose appeared at the door, "No! Don't touch him!"

Edgar gave her a push, and she fell onto her bottom between Paul's bed and his dresser.

"Or, two," Edgar continued, his voice thundering through the house, "I can put you in the basement, and you can sit in the attitude adjustment room." He grabbed his son by one thin arm and pulled him close to his face. "Which do you think is a more appropriate punishment, son?"

Paul looked away, his body shaking so hard that his teeth could be heard chattering from across the room. Rose covered her ears.

"I hate you! Leave him alone!" Rose got to her feet and rushed toward her father.

Once again, he pushed her aside as easily as if she were made of spider's silk. "I'll deal with you later." This time Rose fell and hit her head on the nightstand. She sat dazed, a tiny trickle of blood running down her temple. Edgar jerked Paul to his feet and dragged him from the room.

Staggering to an upright position, Rose ran after them. Her father was halfway down the stairs, carrying a screaming Paul over his shoulder with effortless ease. Rose slipped around him and stood blocking his way with outstretched arms. Blood trickled from her temple to her jaw and dripped onto her white cardigan. "Put him down, you're hurting him!"

Edgar placed his free hand on her chest and gave her a hearty shove, toppling her from the landing and down the rest of the stairs. This time she stayed down.

Her father stepped casually over her unconscious body and made his way toward the basement to deal with his disobedient son.

Bailey rarely remembered her dreams. Usually, they were filled with abstract odds and ends which filtered into her subconscious mind and then flitted away in a heartbeat. This one was different. She tossed and turned in her sleep, her dream a bright vision of reality.

Bailey clutched her pillow as she woke, her eyes wide, not in terror but in resolution. "I'll do that. I promise," she whispered. "I'll find them and bring them here." She rolled to her side and watched Goldie swim back and forth by the soft glow of her night light until she drifted back to sleep.

"Mom?" Bailey asked, "I need to go into the carriage house."

Rhonda closed her computer and gave her daughter her full attention. "Is there something you need from there? The only things in there are rusty tools and lawn equipment."

Bailey shook her head and looked down. "I don't need anything, I need to inspect it."

Rhonda pushed her chair back. and stood, thinking "inspect" was a big word for a five-year-old. "I don't understand. Make me understand, sweet girl," she said, and gathered Bailey in her arms.

"Is there a ladder?"

"Yes, I believe there are a few of them. Why?"

"You're not going to believe me."

"Try me, you might be surprised."

"Paul wants us to go into the loft," Bailey said, her brown eyes meeting her mother's.

Rhonda suppressed a frown. "Paul does? He told you this?"

"Uh huh, he said it would explain some things. I'm getting better at understanding him."

Rhonda pushed in her chair; it screeched on the hardwood. She never wanted her fierce daughter to think her wants and needs were unheard or unimportant, even if she didn't understand completely.

"Let's go find a ladder then, babygirl." Rhonda plucked the keyring from the tail of the ceramic dachshund atop the refrigerator, pocketed it, and took her daughter's hand. On the way out, she grabbed her phone and one of Carlos's baseball bats.

"I'm not a ..." Bailey closed her mouth and gave Rhonda's hand a squeeze.

Rhonda opened the carriage house door with a very old-looking key which had a perfectly round head. Dust swirled as fresh air replaced the stale. Bailey lingered at the doorway until her mother flipped on the lights. Once the light scattered the shadows, she followed Rhonda in, her little black shoes clacking on the concrete. Tools hung from the walls and rafters, sharp and ancient as dragon teeth, dripping rust and cobwebs. A tarp which covered lawn equipment stirred to life caught in the draft of the open door, dry, crisp grass clippings raining down around them in a brittle scatter which made Rhonda sneeze.

"There's a big ladder," Bailey whispered, pointing. Her voice was as meek as if they were in some holy place, like church at Christmas time.

Rhonda rubbed her nose, retrieved the ladder and placed it against the platform that held the loft. "I'm going up first to make sure it's safe."

Rhonda examined the ladder for stability then tentatively climbed one rung at a time, evaluating each for steadiness. At the top she turned on her phone flashlight. She was up to her shoulders in darkness but said nothing as the light swept from wall to wall. Climbing the rest of the way up, Rhonda hoisted herself up onto the loft's platform and stood.

She tested the floor with a few good stomps. Dust scattered and wood creaked. Rhonda pinched her nose to keep from sneezing again. The boards felt a little mushy in places. A few forgotten and very sharp-looking nails pierced the surface of the floor's surface.

"I don't want you up here, dollface," Rhonda said. "It could be very dangerous. Actually, it *is* very dangerous, so stay put, please."

As Rhonda snapped pictures, the flash on her phone sparked, illuminating the loft in skippy bursts. She caught glimpses of old toys on the floor and faded artwork on the walls. The strobe of the flash was making her a bit dizzy so these few dozen photographs would have to do—for now. There was no way she was letting her daughter climb into this unsteady space.

Rhonda slid her phone into her back pocket and climbed down the stairs, the metal rungs clanging as she went.

"What's up there, Mama?"

"It looks like a play area, I think." Rhonda stashed the ladder back where it had come from and flipped off the lights. She locked the door, took her daughter's hand, and headed back to the house.

The instant they stepped into the house, Bailey asked to see the photos. Rhonda held her off and said she had to lighten them somewhat so they would be sharp. She hated fibbing to her own child, but she wanted to see what was on them first.

Tate had a three-day weekend, and Rhonda and the kids couldn't have been more excited to see him. Bailey clung to his leg as he walked stiffly into the living room dragging her with him. Carlos grinned happily, and Tate threw an arm around him.

"What did you bring us?" asked Bailey.

"Bailey!" Rhonda said, "at least let him put down his suitcase and take off his jacket." She laughed and threw her arms around him. "My turn," she said, and Tate's arms encircled his wife's waist and he pulled her to him, kissing her long and hard.

"Get a room," Bailey giggled, still clinging to his leg.

Rhonda laughed. "Where in the world did you hear that phrase?"

Bailey shrugged. "On TV, I guess."

Well, Rhonda thought, *better to have your kids see you kiss and love on one another than listen to you fight.*

After a few moments of hugs, kisses, and squeals of "Oh, how we've missed you," Tate kicked his dress shoes off and flopped on the couch. "I have never been so happy to hear this much noise."

"Don't get too comfortable, Daddy. What did you bring us?"

"Well, I brought you…me." He laughed as Bailey pounced him. "I brought good news, that's what I brought," he told them. "I'll be home two weeks early. I don't have to go back."

The hugs, kisses, and squeals of "Oh, how we've missed you" started all over again. Tate didn't mention that the fact there'd been a suspicious death only yards from where his family slept had made him step down. "Now, let's see what I brought the two of you!"

Carlos and Bailey gathered around.

"This is for my darling daughter," Tate said, and brought out a junior archeology kit. "You dig and hammer through the rock and sand and find real fossils." He handed it to her, adding, "we'll do it together."

Bailey grabbed it as if her father had brought her the Hope Diamond. "Thanks, Daddy! I love it!" She stopped a moment, turning the box over in her hands. "How much can I get for fossils on eBay?"

Tate chuckled and handed Carlos an envelope. "I couldn't fit the real thing in my suitcase, so we'll go to the hardware store tomorrow and get one."

Carlos ripped open the envelope. "My own metal detector? Thanks dad!"

"Someone named Mom told me you wanted one."

"I'm gonna call BJ right now! We'll find that buried treasure, I know we will! Then we'll be rich!"

"Tomorrow night," Tate said, "campout and treasure hunt on the back property line. Now let me see this treasure map!"

That evening, after the kids were asleep and their clothes were scattered across the main bedroom like confetti, Rhonda curled into the crook of her husband's arm and told him about her week. "The police are saying either suicide or an accident," she said, cuddling in. "The strange thing is, the gun went missing." Rhonda frowned. They think maybe his friend Aaron was there at the time and took it with him. It was worth some money, it belonged to Elvis."

"Elvis Presley?"

"The one and only." Rhonda sighed, propped herself on one elbow, and looked down at him. "You should have seen it Tate, there was blood and brains everywhere."

Tate tucked a strand of dark hair behind his wife's ear and trailed his finger over her jawline to her lips. "You really suck at post coital pillow talk."

Rhonda chuckled, "I just wanted you to know about this in case you have second thoughts about stepping down." She threw a leg over him. "And if you ever want 'post coital pillow talk' again, you won't critique me."

"Guess what, Rhonnie?"

"What?"

"I already stepped down."

Rhonda threw her arms around his shoulders. "Oh my god, Tater, seriously?"

"Yep." Tate laughed and flipped her over like a pancake. "And no critiquing from me, I'm just happy to be home." He gave her a smirk and pressed into her. "Real happy."

"I can see that," she said. "We'll talk murder later."

He kissed her again. "I'm that obvious, huh?"

"Six inches of obvious."

"Come on, at least eight inches."

"In man inches?"

Tate laughed and pinched her bottom. "What would that be in actual inches?"

"Just right...it would be just right."

Tate and Rhonda were up before the kids. Rhonda had her computer open and was looking at the photos from the carriage house loft she had hastily taken yesterday. "Take a look at these, Tater."

He walked over, stood behind her, and put his hands on her shoulders, "Where did you get these?" He looked honestly concerned. "This isn't in *our* house, is it?"

"Bailey insisted we check out the loft in the carriage house; she was adamant about it. I went up with my camera. I didn't want to take her up there before checking it out myself, and I'm glad I didn't: it felt as if some of the boards had dry rot, and there were a bunch of exposed nails."

In the photos, crumpled dolls and children's toys littered the dusty wooden floor. There was a table in one corner, and what looked to be an assortment of drawing and painting equipment suitable for a child. The walls were covered in sketches of childlike scenes. Always a group of two or four stick figure children holding hands, two black, two white. Three large, one small. The dark-skinned boy was approximately half the size of his sister. The other two children had orange hair, one boy and one girl. Each was signed, in childlike cursive, Rosie and Paul, Leyta and Johnathan.

The west wall had to have been drawn by someone with much more talent than a child. An enormous crow, with details that rivaled any adult professional artist, covered the wall. Its feathers were elaborately drawn in black crayon or chalk, its eyes glistened with a realistic intensity. The rafters had leaked at one time, and the ensuing water drops had cut the crow directly in half from top to bottom. In its realistically-rendered talons it held a man with a dark suit and hat. Under the painting in bold, black block letters it said, "Carrying Father to hell."

The holey old tent had bought the farm, so before the campout treasure hunt could commence, a trip to Patton Hardware had been in order.

Equipped with a spanking new, hole-free tent, Tate, BJ, Carlos, and Bailey set up at the far western side of the five acres belonging to the house at 291 Chestnut Street. Cottonwoods and aspens grew along the bank of a shallow creek which cut through the tail end of the property, obscuring the view of the house and giving the illusion of unpopulated wilderness.

Bailey had a pan and was sifting for gold in the creek. "Daddy?" she said, "if the treasure map leads us to a bunch of money, can I have a donkey?"

"If we find a bunch of money, you can have a herd of donkeys."

"If we find a bunch of money," Carlos said, "I want a media room." BJ readily agreed to this idea and bobbed his head. "And a 'no girls allowed' sign."

"Be nice, Carlos." Tate opened Beatrice Wilson's hand-drawn map and examined it, frequently glancing up to compare it to the landscape. "The X on this map sits at the bottom of the largest cottonwood behind the carriage house." He handed the metal detector to his son. "You do the honors, Carlos, this belongs to you. But first, let me tell you how this gadget works. Metal detectors detect different kinds of metals by generating an electromagnetic field. When this field encounters a metal object, this light"—Tate pointed to a button on the detector—"will flash red indicating the presence of a buried metal object…"

Bailey yawned.

"Sorry, kids. I can't help myself, I'm an engineer."

BJ and Carlos examined the digital display on the handle and flipped it on.

"I should really shut up, you two are aces at electronics."

The three children nodded, and Carlos began a slow sweep at the base of the cottonwood tree, gradually increasing his search field.

The hunt for Beatrice Wilson's treasure was on.

One hour, three soda cans, two Chuck E. Cheese tokens, and a handful of nails later, Carlos powered down the metal detector. "Maybe she dug the box up?" he said, taking a drink from his water bottle.

"If she'd dug it up she wouldn't have left the map and key under the basement stairs," BJ said. "She'd need the key to open the box."

"Let's do another sweep around the base," Tate said, and the kids agreed.

Bailey, obviously bored, opened the flap of the tent and left the boys to their business. She flopped down on her Barbie sleeping bag. She'd brought Goldie and her bowl along for the action.

Bailey sighed. "I'm never gonna get a donkey."

Goldie bubbled in apparent agreement.

Chapter Seventeen

Nana Took Me to the Bar

Rose, Leyta and Johnathan lived in separate areas of what Bailey Benson had mistakenly called Harpoony Hills.

Harmony Hills Village Senior Living Facility was a new and ambitious approach to elder care. Built on the bones of what was once a two-story mall in North Denver, it was an experimental trial run for what could be a replacement to your traditional-style nursing home. Replacing the antiseptic and hospital-like structures of the past, Harmony Hills Village was a small town created within a mall which had lost its purpose to online shopping. The mall had been gutted, and within its walls were realistic-looking streets and tiny houses with windows overlooking an outdoor facade.

Each home had a porch with outdoor furniture. Some of the residents planted flowers or herbs in pots and took great pride in tending to them. The faux cobblestone streets—vinyl and nonslip, but completely realistic-looking—along which the homes sat were about ten feet wide. Ornate black lamp posts dotted the sidewalks, and as the days grew late, the lamps would turn on, adding to the illusion of being out of doors. Residents could sit on their porches and talk with their neighbors. Strolling the grounds was encouraged with or without help.

The dome that covered Harmony Hills mimicked the outdoors—and the time of day. When it was daytime outside, it was daytime in Harmony Hills. When it was night, stars twinkled, and a full moon helped light the streets along with the old-fashioned ironwork lanterns. Gracing the vinyl-cobbled village were a town square, a pub, a cinema, cafés, a library, a beauty/barber shop, and a few small stores which sold essentials. The nurses' stations dotted the streets and were made to look like clinics which blended in easily with the small-town feel of Harmony Hills Village.

Leyta, along with everyone she knew, loved this place.

Trees, parks, and walking trails graced what was once a fifteen-acre parking lot, and some of the indoor homes had windows overlooking the green space. In the parkland was a gazebo for guest musicians—bands, choirs, and solo artists—to perform in the summer, and close by stood a children's playground and picnic area. It was truly a unique endeavor that seemed to be working and which brought joy to both residents and employees.

Schoolchildren of all ages became involved in Harmony Hills. The older ones tended gardens and greenhouses, whose crops would be split between the school and the village's cafeterias and restaurants. Some worked in the cafés and eateries, and the teenagers went home feeling good about themselves and their talent, and earned credits for the classes they took. The smaller children visited the bonus grandmas and grandpas, played in the playground, and participated in craft projects and programs. The project seemed to work for everyone involved and was being seriously looked upon as the way of the future.

The upper level of Harmony Hills was reserved for those who were in need of memory care. While these residents still enjoyed the quiet streets, tiny houses, and hometown facade, they also benefited from staff trained specifically for the care of those with memory issues.

This is where Rose Wilson was spending her later years, and Leyta and her brother Johnathan thought this a phenomenal success.

Rose had a one-room upper unit where she received proper care, while the siblings lived in a two-bedroom on the first floor of the village. Leyta and Johnathan could visit every day and take Rosie for excursions in the park, where they'd sit by the lake; sometimes they'd be followed by a line of elementary school kids wearing hats they'd made themselves at craft time.

Today was a bit rainy, so the siblings accompanied Rose to the café for tea. Rose was having an exceptionally good day, and it was a delight to see. A teenage waitress from the nearby high school set tea and pastries on the faux alfresco patio table. As luck would have it, it never rained inside Harmony Hills.

"I feel him close today, Leyta," Rose told her lifelong friend. "I feel Paul close by."

Leyta nodded, and Johnathan squeezed his sister's hand under the table. Leyta squeezed back. She appreciated the support of her brother, who knew these types of conversations were difficult for her.

Rose's eyes met Leyta's with stone cold clarity. "We have to find a girl named Bailey," said Rose.

"Bailey?" Leyta gave her shoulder a wee shake. "Stay with me, Rosie."

"Yes, Bailey is the key to setting everything right with Paul." Rose's face was serious as she locked eyes with her friend of seventy years. "And I think Bailey might be in significant danger." Rose took a sip of tea, clear enough today to drink on her own.

"Bailey?" asked Johnathan, "what's her last name? Where does she live?"

"She's not far, and Paul is close to her."

"In Patton? In the old house?"

"I'm not..." Rose sat her cup down. "I think..."

Leyta steadied the teacup on the saucer as Rose's moments of clarity slipped away as if on a gentle but cruel breeze. In mere seconds, she sank back into her own world: you could see the fog settle in.

As Rose drifted, Johnathan's hand tightened on Leyta's. "Bailey?" he asked, placing his napkin on the café table.

Leyta sipped her tea, sure that Rose's mind had been clear today and the task was apparent. "Rose has always been...sensitive. If she thinks we need to find someone named Bailey in Patton, we need to do just that."

A line of schoolchildren marched by singing songs and clapping their hands. The teacher leading them wore a yellow hat and sang loud and a bit off key.

The teenage waitress appeared and asked if they'd be needing anything else.

The siblings declined her gracious offer. It wasn't tea they needed, but a bit of detective work and a whole lot of luck. Leyta was sure that Bailey—whoever she may be—was looking for Rose as well.

"I say we cut it off," Anita said.

"What?" Kenny had been lost in thought.

"I *said,*" Anita told him, her hand on her generous hip, "I think we should just cut the damn lock off."

"If we do that, we'll have to do it right before the switch and be careful nobody sees us. I saw the new lady taking boxes down there yesterday, and Henry was down there today bringing up a couple of jars of who-knows-what that Edna had canned last year."

"I hope it wasn't peaches," Anita said, "I like those a lot."

"You steal an old lady's peaches?"

"They won't notice, they're old."

"They're old but not stupid, Anita. Being old doesn't make you stupid—never underestimate old folks." Kenny looked at her.. "Didn't you have a nana?"

"Yes, I had a nana. She used to take me to the bar with her."

"Your nana took you to the bar with her?"

"Yep. Didn't yours?"

"My nana took me to the park." Talking about nanas made Kenny think of his own nana and her totally boss Sunday beef roasts. Roast beef made him think of Edna's roast beef that he'd made into sandwiches—which led him straight to the fanged tooth in the psycho kid's backpack. He shivered.

"The spaghetti sauce she cans ain't bad either," Anita went on, obviously wanting to get a rise out of him. "See my jar fulla quarters for The Pines Laundorama?" She smirked. "Jar courtesy of Edna Hansen and her kick-ass tomato sauce."

"Jesus Christ, Anita!" Kenny said, covering his face with his hands. "Can we get back to the damn lock? It's keeping me up at night."

Anita placed her hands on his shoulders. "Speaking of keeping you up at night…"

This got Kenny's attention.

"I made a trip to Great Big Expectations today…."
What lock?

"..and I bought a few lacy things and a few surprises."
Lock, cocaine, walking teeth, possible death…
Anita, mmm…

She bent and kissed him. "And the kids are going to my brother's tonight."

Kenny's mind became as empty as the romaine lettuce section of the supermarket after a salmonella outbreak.

All thoughts of what could, in three days, end up being a bloodbath or conceivably time in prison, evaporated. Kenny placed his hands behind his head, leaned back, smiled, and thought about Anita's sweet, sweet peaches.

June 23rd, 1997

Patton Gazette

Kimberly White, seventeen, daughter of Jane and Phillip White, was last seen at Jumping Trout campground adjacent to Antelope Reservoir on Tuesday night, June twentieth at approximately 10:15 PM. Miss White's belongings were accounted for, and there were no witnesses to her leaving the campsite. Her necklace was found two miles north of the reservoir on the Shadybrook Trail. Abduction has not been ruled out in this case, and ground searches continue. This is an ongoing story.

1957

Rose awoke at the bottom of the stairway, her brother and father nowhere in sight. The blood on her forehead had dried, making Rose think that she might have been lying there for quite some time. Once on her feet, she did a quick scan of her body to check for injuries from the fall. Her ankle was sore, her head was pounding, and a goose egg had formed on the back of her skull.

Rose stumbled toward the basement door. She did not want to run into her father. She listened from the top of the basement stairs, and, after finding the dark void quiet, she flipped on the light. She hurried down the wooden staircase, slid down the concrete wall and sat before the locked room.

She knocked quietly. "Paul?" There was no answer. Rose jangled the intricate lock, knowing her father kept the octagonal-head key on a ring in the pocket of his trousers. She shook the lock louder and raised her voice, "Paul, answer me."

From inside the basement room came a whimper and a small voice filled with fear. "Help me, Rosie."

Paul rarely spoke.

"I'll stay here with you until he lets you out," Rose said through angry, gritted teeth. "I hate him."

Paul whimpered but said nothing more.

Rose switched off the light and fumbled in the dark until she felt a wall. She didn't want father to come down, see lights on and know she or her mother had been down there. In the dark, she felt her way back to the room where her brother was held captive. "I'll stay here with you, Paul. When the door from upstairs opens I'll hide under the stairs and then meet you in your room."

Rose placed her palm on the old door and leaned her head against it; the cool metal felt good on her throbbing skull. "I wish he were dead."

With conviction, she added, "I could kill him myself."

Anita wiggled into her new red teddy and ran her freshly manicured hands over her curvy body. She'd gone for the whole package—a pedi too. Her punch card at "You Get Boyfren Nail" was full, and it was free, so why not? She made her long red nails into claws and inspected her reflection in the full length mirror. "Rawwwwr," she purred at her sultry image.

She stood in the doorway to the bedroom, one hand on the door jamb, the other on her hip. "Hi, Babe," she said, touching her backside, then blowing out a smokin' finger. "I'm on fire and you're my fire hose."

Kenny was lying in bed in nothing but his tighty-whities. From the looks of things, red was now his favorite color.

"I brought my good boy some toys too. One is called the Traveling Titillator, it's remote controlled" she said, crawling onto the bed and making the mattress springs squeal in dissent.

Kenny reached for her and put her hand on his now even tighty-er tighty-whities. "Looks like your good boy is about to go bad…"

She rolled on top of him, pinned his arms above his head, and grinned. Her size 52 H breasts enveloped him like a sweet, warm titty tsunami, washing away every brain cell he professed to have with it.

Nacho the chihuahua sat in the doorway and watched, whimpered, and tilted his head a little, as if he were hearing the faraway sounds of air squeaking out of a balloon.

Kenny's muffled, "Yeah, baby," came from somewhere beneath a big, beautiful, bodacious Anita.

"Yeehaw!" said Anita.

"Mrmmph!" said Kenny

Nacho whined and high-tailed it under the living room couch.

"Fuck this shit," said the bedsprings.

Chapter Eighteen

Used Tacos

1997

This Journal Belongs to James Hansen

I'm considering recreating the event with Kimberly. It's been half a year, and law enforcement is convinced she either ran away—it's been said she's done it before—in the middle of the night or was abducted and taken north of Antelope toward Denver. Leaving her necklace on the outer reaches of the park, amid broken branches that resembled the sight of a struggle, worked very well in my favor. Her parents have posters with their daughter's face on every lamp post in Patton. I'm quite sure they're all over Denver as well.

I watch my king snake with his prey, and it makes me relive that night. The fear, the anticipation. Of course, it's nowhere near the intensity of that summer evening, but on a small scale it has sufficed for now. The actual act was an unmitigated rush that I've not been able to duplicate by any means. I felt as if every thought and sensation I have, and ever have had, imploded into a single laser beam of being and understanding. All that I've questioned folded in upon itself into a tiny dot that weighed a billion tons, like the material of a neutron star. I don't quite know how to explain it. Each time I see a poster or a news article about that night, I feel it again. Not to the extreme of the action, of course, but a tiny fragment of it.

I want to experience that again. I need to revisit that moment again. Another trip to Jumping Trout campground might be in order.

I'm thinking about the baby birds in the plastic bag when I was a child. I'm thinking about grandma having her stroke, the light winking out of her eyes, and her skittery spider hands attempting to escape her circumstance. I'm thinking about Kimberly White and her open mouth, chewing chewing chewing. I'm thinking about how kids from school gather at the reservoir on Friday and Saturday nights and, two by two, wander off into the woods. I'm thinking about Kimberly's pink bubble gum that lies in what's left of her jaw at the bottom of the reservoir. Of course I think about the tooth that resides at the bottom of my backpack. Sometimes I ground myself by keeping it in my pocket and rubbing it between my fingers.

I have a lot of introspective thinking to do.

"See? Being a Pinecone Pioneer isn't that terrible," Rhonda said to Bailey as she hung up her uniform and laid out a set of shorts and a shirt to change into.

"We went to the bug museum!" Bailey was all but bouncing off the walls. "There was a walking stick that had to be *this* big!" Bailey held her arms wide apart to demonstrate.

Rhonda shuddered inwardly. "That's amazing, honey!"

"It had really long legs, and they let us hold it. They said her name was Gladys. She crawled up my arm and sat on my shoulder, it was great!" Bailey pulled on her tennis shoes and buckled the velcro. "There was a tarantula named Kevin, too—we could pet him but not hold him, they said maybe next time. Can we go back to the bug museum, Mom? I want to see the big glass box of daddy longlegs again. There must have been a million of them!"

"I tell you what, you go wash your hands and I'll get you a snack. I made chocolate chip cookies while you were gone."

Where's the full body hand sanitizer? Is it against the law to spray your kid with Lysol?

Rhonda did not like long-legged insects. She made a mental note that taking the kids to this museum of all things creepy crawly would be Tate's job.

Bailey skipped off toward the bathroom. "I made two new friends today." The water started running. "A girl named Sarah and a girl named McJennifer."

"McJennifer?"

"Yes, her parents think it's unique."

"Okay…" Rhonda cringed harder than when Bailey told her about touching the walking stick. "Maybe you can have Sarah and McJennifer over some time."

Bailey showed her mother her clean hands. "Okay!" But, Mom?"

"Yes?"

"Everybody calls Sarah by her middle name, Khaleesi Renée."

Rhonda stifled a snort. "Who else did you meet?"

"One kid named Scott, he's pretty nice."

"What does he like to be called?"

"Scott." Bailey twirled in circles.

"Next week we're going to the place where they keep all the old people."

"A senior community?"

"Yes!" Bailey said. "It's called Harpoony Hills. We're going to do crafts and have a parade and eat cookies and push old people around in the park."

"Push them around in wheelchairs?"

"Yes, the ones that can't walk." Bailey looked at her mother as if she'd grown two heads. "They can walk if they want to, it's not like we're going to push them if they're standing up. I guess there's a playground too!" She sprinkled a few flakes of fish food into Goldie's bowl; Goldie swam to the surface and gobbled them down. "Good girl."

Goldie blew a bubble in response.

Bailey was momentarily serious. "Some of the other Pinecone Pioneers don't have grandmas and grandpas, like we do." She looked up at Rhonda. "I bet those kids have the most fun of all. It'll be like they have grandmas and grandpas like me and Carlos—except they don't buy them stuff when they spend the night."

Bailey was smiling again, her brain visibly shifting back into happy mode. She babbled cheerfully as she hopped down the stairs, then turned as she reached the landing. "Mom?"

"Yes, honey?" Rhonda was ecstatic to see her daughter having a fun time appropriate for a five-year-old.

"I'll wear a ponytail next week, instead of braids." *Goodbye Wednesday Addams.*

"Mom?"

"Yes?"

"Can I call Grandma and Grandpa after dinner?"

"Of course! We'll video chat."

"Mom?"

"Yes, sweetie?"

"Can I have a walking stick?"

"No, but you can have a cookie."

"Kay!"

Kenny came into the garage whistling. "Hi-di-ho, Izzy!"

"Well, well, somebody got some last night." Ishmael grinned.

"You have no idea. My girl is a machine. A big, sexy, juicy machine."

Izzy laughed. "You go for it, my man," he said, leaning against the workbench. "Hey, by the way, when are you gonna move this piece of shit cow truck?"

"I'm working on the engine today." Kenny patted his truck right beneath the cow's happy dancing backside.

"And, Kenny my man, you gotta give it a second coat of paint. 'Dan's Used Furniture and Supreme Meats' still shows through, and you have the word 'TACO' right under 'used'. I told you that before."

"I gotta get it running first. Then I'll repaint, get my cow friend here a new sombrero, and gut the inside so that it's the best rolling kitchen ever." Kenny lifted the hood. "We gotta get our money first, not too long now." *If I can open the damn cocaine or whatever-is-in that room door.*

Izzy patted his friend on the back. "You're right, not too long now, just two days."

Kenny cringed as Todd and Not Todd strolled by. *Fucking "little person."*

Not Todd stared a hole in him. Hopefully not deep enough to read his thoughts.

The Antelope Reservoir continued to drain. Little by little the shore line receded, giving up secret after secret, and as it did, mysteries of various sizes were exposed. Today it would expose its greatest enigma of all.

"Norman," said Dave, "I think you need to see this." Dave took off his cap and pushed back his sweaty hair. "And bring your phone, we're going to have to call the authorities."

Norman jogged over.

"Sweet baby Jesus, no, I didn't need to see that." He dialed 911, and the two of them went back to the work truck to wait for the police.

"Edna?"

Henry's wife was sitting on their late son's bed. She looked up at him with red, swollen eyes; she'd obviously been crying for some time.

"Aww, Honey, talk to me. What's the matter?" Henry said, as if it wasn't crystal clear.

Edna pointed toward the closet, her knobby hands shaking.

James's backpack was upended inside the closet door. Henry was stricken. "Why in the world did you get it down, sweetheart?"

Edna shook her head. "No, Henry, it was that way when I came in."

Henry knew that Edna often spent time in James's old room. It was like a museum that she'd refused to change for thirty-five years. It worried him, but he understood— he understood much too well.

"Are you sure you didn't spill his backpack?" he asked. "Maybe when you were vacuuming?"

Edna shook her head, the tears streaming down her face. A few had dripped onto her green house dress.

Henry took his wife's hand and kissed it. A crooked tooth dropped from it onto his lap.

"Oh, good Lord." Henry took the tooth, went to the closet, and dropped it back into the pack that held their son's journals. He closed the latch with shaking hands and set it back onto the shelf.

Henry sat back down by his wife of fifty years and held her as she wept.

After helping his wife prepare for bed, Henry had Edna tucked in and settled. She was in clean night clothes, and a cup of chamomile tea had calmed her a bit. The hefty shot of whiskey he'd added hadn't hurt either. He'd had one too–truth be told, he'd had three. He was as upset as Edna was.

He sat by her bedside and stroked her hair as she began to drift off. It was three in the afternoon, but Henry was fairly sure she was down for the night. He'd turned on James's old cassette player and put one of his own tapes into it, and a collection of Elvis's love songs hummed softly from across their bedroom. Edna liked it when there was a bit of background noise while she slept.

Henry kept watch until he knew his wife was safely nestled into the safety of slumber. Her breath was finally calm and steady as Henry bent and kissed her forehead. He left the room, leaving the door open a crack in case she woke and called for him.

The past had made a reemergence this afternoon, and the reawakening terrified him.

Kenny broke down, went to Patton Hardware and bought a pair of bolt cutters that he fully intended to return for a refund after Friday night. He also purchased a lock with a combination. No more of this lost key bullshit. On his way out of the store, he noticed Todd and Not Todd parked one row up and two spaces down from where he'd parked the cow truck. Yep! The cow truck was running.

Kenny sauntered over to their car and rapped on the glass. Not Todd, wearing sunglasses, pressed slacks, and a black fedora, rolled down the window. *Where the hell does this little fella shop?*

"Are you two assholes following me?" said Kenny. "I mean… are you one and a half assholes following me?" He could be a cocky bastard.

Not Todd's short stature had the top of his head resting halfway up the front passenger seat. Not Todd slid his shades halfway down his nose, looked at Kenny, and smiled. His right front tooth was gold.

Todd stared straight ahead, his hands at two and ten, his face expressionless, a gun on his lap. Turning only his head and wearing a mask of indifference, he picked up the gun and pointed it straight at Kenny's dumb mug.

At the sight of the gun, Kenny backed up, clutched his hardware store purchase to his chest, and sprinted back to his pending taco truck, thinking, *Mexico is looking better and better.*

It took three tries to unlock the piece of shit (bought and paid for piece of shit) cowmobile.

Bailey was playing in a turtle-shaped sandbox with Anita's younger daughter, Sophia. Rhonda had bought it and filled it that morning.

"We need more sand toys," Bailey said to Sophia. "Do you have any sand toys in your house?"

Sophia looked up from the cave she was constructing. "I do, but my Daddy is here and the door's locked."

"Why is your door locked?"

"I think they're practicing singing, I could hear them through the window."

"Do they sing a lot?"

"Almost every day."

"I bet they're really good singers with all that practice."

Sophia said nothing and continued the excavation of what could be the largest turtle sandbox cave of all time. Nacho the chihuahua was her assistant, digging furiously right next to her, sending sand flying from the confines of the turtle sandbox onto the grass.

Bailey surveyed the yard. It looked a lot better since Dad was home. He'd pulled weeds, mowed the grass, and thrown away years of junk, papers, and rotten lumber.

"I have an idea," she said, noticing the lock to the carriage house hanging open. Bailey dusted the sand off her hands and brushed away the grains that stuck to the back of her shorts. "Be right back. I know where there's a few shovels."

She sprinted toward the carriage house door and cracked it open. Daylight intruded into the dark interior of the dwelling, and the tools on the walls seemed to twitch in the shadows; they looked menacing and sharp. Bailey reached for the light switch, and the carriage house became just that again; a dusty, cobweb-filled space.

Bailey stepped in, not having been inside since the day she and her mother had taken photos of the loft. The ladder was still propped against the edge of the upper story, exactly as they'd left it. Dust motes floated like tiny living things, hovering and adrift, as if they were minute seaborne beings buoyant in something thicker than air. All thoughts of shovels and sand toys were forgotten as Bailey stood at the bottom of the ladder looking up. She and her mother had examined the photographs they took that day together. There had been an enormous crow drawn on one wall with what had to have been crayon. The rest of the pictures seemed either harmless or out of focus to Bailey, distorted not just from age, but from her mother's lack of photographic prowess.

Bailey walked to the ladder and shook it. It seemed sturdy enough, even though the wood and hardware were obviously the victim of time and weather. She put one tennis shoe on the first rung, followed by another and another, until her body was high enough to peek over the top.

What had shown on her mother's photographs as an enormous crow was replaced by a tree filled with crows—hundreds of crows. With closer inspection, Bailey could see the trunk and limbs of the tree were also made of crows. Swirling crows, bent and deformed into unnatural shapes to mimic the bark and limbs of an old cottonwood. On its branches, luminous birds sat, each detailed feather so sharp that it could have been drawn yesterday, their black heads turned every which way as if they were sentinels looking for an enemy that could approach from any direction. Their eyes were shiny-bright as they sat watch over their keep.

Bailey took another step up and lifted herself onto the platform of the loft.

"Paul?" she whispered." Is this where cyou live?"

One of the drawings fluttered to the floor, and Bailey picked it up, the tape that had held it for so many years crumbling in her hands. She folded it gently, taking care not to crack the aged paper, and slid the picture into her back pocket.

"Paul? Are you here?" She could feel him here, his long ago, once solid substance a mere wisp of crystalline molecules.

"Paul?" Her heart skittered in her chest like a small animal frantically wanting to free itself from its confines.

A roar of beating wings filled the loft space, sending the air into motion. Bailey covered her face and fell to the floor. The ladder shook behind her and clattered onto the cement. She spun and watched it crash, sending up a cloud of dust. Bailey shrieked and peered over the edge of the loft.

"*Paul?*"

"Paul is *dead*," a deep male voice whispered in her ear.

She heard scurrying off in the dark, akin to so many spiders, then louder, the rustling of hundreds of wings dragging the malevolent voice with them back into the gloom.

Bailey screamed as she fell to the ground, her elbows scraping the splintered wood. One hand slipped from the rickety floor of the loft into the blackness, and she just barely steadied herself as she came close to toppling off onto the concrete below. She felt the flutter of wings on her fingertips and jerked herself back.

Bailey screamed. She screamed until her throat was raw, and the quivering of distant wings stilled to a whisper and dissolved.

Chapter Nineteen

Bailey, McJennifer, Khaleesi-Renée, & Scott

Rhonda had made a meatloaf for dinner. Or, as Carlos called it, "Mom's famous ball of grease".

It wasn't that fatty! She'd used lean beef, for crying out loud. Tate loved meatloaf mixed with oatmeal as a filler instead of cracker or breadcrumbs: he said it reminded him of the hamburgers they used to get in the lunchroom when he was in middle school.

The baked potatoes dinged in the microwave, and the green beans in the steamer on top of the stove were finished. "Carlos!" said Rhonda," Please go get Bailey, it's time for dinner."

Carlos yanked out his ear buds. "What?"

"Get your sister, we're going to eat," Rhonda repeated.

Carlos put down his game, headed to the front door, and made his way around the house. Last thing he knew, Bailey had been playing with Sophia in the new sandbox. Why didn't these quads have back doors?

The sandbox was empty, no Sophia or Bailey in sight. "Bailey!" he yelled through cupped hands, "dinner!"

He heard a voice call from inside the carriage house.

"Carlos! Get Mom and Dad, I'm stuck in the loft! Please, please hurry!"

Carlos peeked his head into the carriage house to see Bailey peering over the edge of the loft, the ladder lying flat on the ground. Bailey's face was smeared with tears and black chalk.

"Don't move, I'll be right back." Carlos didn't want to put the ladder up himself, knowing she'd come down on her own and probably break a leg. Man, his little sister got herself into some mundo-tremendous shit.

Dinner was cold.

The meatloaf sat congealed in its own fat, and the beans were wrinkled like so many green fingers which had stayed too long in the bathtub. The potatoes sat shriveled and forgotten in the microwave.

"What were you thinking, dolly?" Rhonda asked her. "You could have cracked your head open. There are rusty nails everywhere and the wood is rotting!" Rhonda ran her hands over her daughter's body, checking for injuries. "You could have been seriously hurt!"

Bailey noticed that her mother was visibly shaking, and she felt a pang of guilt.

Tate picked Bailey up and placed her on his lap. "That was a very dangerous thing you did, sweet pea." He hugged her to him.

"What a little moron," said Carlos.

Tate and Rhonda simultaneously pointed toward the stairs and his bedroom.

"Fine." Carlos clomped up the stairs.

Rhonda dabbed at her daughter's skinned elbows with a wet cloth followed by antibiotic ointment and two hot pink band aids.

"The crow on the wall was different," Bailey said, her head on her dad's shoulder. "It changed, it's not like the picture Mommy took."

A concerned look passed between her parents, and Bailey knew just what they were thinking. Then they said it aloud.

"Baby, that's not possible."

Bailey started to cry again, "It is! I saw it!" She pulled a black feather from her long dark hair. "See?"

Bailey watched a look of concern travel between her parents.

"Let's go check it again, what do you say?" said Tate. "It's dark in the carriage house, maybe you imagined it."

"I didn't!"

"Then it won't hurt to check."

Holding hands, Rhonda and Bailey followed Tate to the small brick outbuilding in the backyard.

Tate leaned the ladder back against the edge of the loft and climbed up.

"One big, very impressive crow," he said.

"Then it changed back!" Bailey insisted.

Tate came down the ladder. "Let me hold the ladder, and you climb up and peek. Don't you dare go up there, just peek."

Bailey climbed the rungs and squinted into the dark loft. Her father was right. There was one big crow. Where had the tree made from hundreds of birds gone off to?

She came back down the ladder and said nothing. She wasn't about to tell her parents about the scary man's voice that had breathed in her ear, *Paul is dead.* She knew Paul was dead—he'd told her as much. Bailey thought that the man she'd encountered probably was as well. She was certain Paul had summoned the crows to protect her. To protect her from whatever evil spoke to her in the dark.

Her bedroom would seem unnaturally cold that night.

Anita stood guard at the top of the basement stairs while Kenny screwed around with the lock to the cocaine room.

"It's not working!" he complained. The bolt cutters clattered to the ground, making a sound exactly like what you'd expect bolt cutters clattering onto the ground would sound like. Just like that.

"It smells like The Stock Show down here."

"You gotta hurry, Kenny!" Anita yelled down to him. "The new lady could be home any minute."

"Don't let nobody down here, babe!"

"They'll have to go straight through me, lover," said Anita.

"That's my girl." He picked up the bolt cutters and jammed them into the hasp of the lock. Kenny wasn't a muscular man, but he was strong and wiry and gave it his all. His teeth clenched, his biceps rippled, his back and legs were tense with exertion. The lock clinked to the floor. "I got it! It's off!" Kenny held his nose, "Christ, it reeks down here!"

"Great! Hurry up and get the other lock on, and let's get the hell outta here." Anita's backside blocked the door, eclipsing the sun, and her head swiveled as she kept a close eye out for any interlopers.

Kenny couldn't help himself—he had to take a peek inside, and what he saw made him stagger backwards. There was no cocaine in the cocaine room, only piles of what looked like cheese. Rotten, melting cheese swarming with buzzing flies. Cheese that was *moving*. It was crawling with fly babies—maggots, they called them, he guessed. The sight made him gag, and he all but puked on his shoes.

"Anita, it's not cocaine!" Kenny pulled his t-shirt up and over his nose and tried not to vomit.

"Then what the hell is it?"

"I think it's super rotten parmesan," he said through the fabric of his shirt.

"Like the stuff in the green can?"

"No cans. Great big wheels of the things, there must be a hundred of them." He gagged again. "And there's flies and bugs everywhere!"

"Are you sure it's not a body? A body would stink and have bugs. Maybe it's Aaron. Nobody's seen him since Ethan got his head shot off."

"No, it's not Aaron! Unless he's the fucking man in the moon made outta cheese!"

"Cheese, huh?" said Anita. "Can you bring me some up? I was gonna make spaghetti for dinner tonight."

"Oh, for fuck's sake…"

"And grab some of Edna's peaches, I like those things."

Kenny, stumbling from the intensity of the smell, took a quick look around the rest of the cheese room. On the wall opposite the contraband queso was a jail cell with bars, an old mattress, a small chair that faced the corner, a few ratty blankets, and a bucket which could only have been used as a toilet. The walls were covered in sketches which looked as if they were drawn in black chalk: dark birds with black glistening eyes.

Kenny creaked open the cell door for a better look-see. The figures—people, trees, houses—were craftily drawn pictures of misshapen crows or ravens…some kind of big black birds, what did he know about birds? They swirled into the shapes of trunks and bark, the walls of houses—and, worst of all, a tall, looming figure, also made from crows, which dominated the space. Its outstretched arms made it look like some type of dark Christlike figure; its black mouth hung open as if mid-scream; raven talons made up its teeth.

The cell and its contents, including the lock, looked as if it had been hanging there since Moses was a baby.

A fly landed on Kenny's face, and he yelped and backed out of the cell like a dumb lady in a horror movie. Curtains of cobwebs wavered and grasped at him with slender silk fingers. Kenny let out a cry and took off toward the main door.

This was more terrifying than cocaine. This delved deep into WTF territory. He should take Anita and the brats, load up the cow truck and head to Mexico. How would they get across the border? They could head to New Mexico—that was almost the same thing, right?

"The new lady just pulled up!" Anita yelled. "You've got about thirty seconds before she busts us!"

Kenny stared at the black figure drawn on the cell wall. It loomed over him in judgment. He looked across the room at the rolls of bug-infested cheese. *Fuck it.*

In his haste to escape, he almost forgot the new lock and the bolt cutters. He shouldered the cutters, snapped the combination lock onto the hasp, and hightailed it for the stairs.

Kenny and Anita ran from the basement, Kenny behind her, pushing her along to speed her up. They crashed through the door of quad number three and slammed and locked the door.

"Holy shit, babe, it's a nightmare in there! I've never seen anything like it! I'm like totally…"

"What's the combination to the new lock?

"Well, shit," said Kenny. He hadn't a clue.

Anita did a slow slide down the wall onto her ample backside. "Fuck. Me." she said, huffing for breath.

"Right now?"

Anita punched him.

Henry was right: Edna did sleep through the night.

He crawled in next to her about ten, careful not to wake her. Henry wasn't feeling very well; for the last few weeks he'd felt as if he were coming down with a cold. He suppressed a cough so as not to disturb his sleeping darling.

Edna had clung to the past for a very long time, and Henry thought that it was high time to begin letting a bit of it go. He fell into a fitful sleep and dreamed of his wedding day over fifty years ago. Edna was beautiful in white lace, her gauze bridal veil muting her youthful face and blonde waves. Even through it he could see the twinkle in her eyes. In his dream, the minister proclaimed that he could kiss his bride. Just like so many, many years ago, he lifted the veil, and his new wife smiled at him.

She was missing her right incisor.

Henry bolted straight up in bed. As his heart raced in his chest and the sweat dried on his skin, he resolved that it was definitely time to lay the horrors of the past to rest.

Disturbing dreams plagued Henry throughout the night. He woke before Edna, went downstairs, and started the coffee. Still in his pajamas and robe, he fetched the newspaper from the front stoop. He liked being able to read a hard copy of the paper; it was a lifelong habit, and it's just what you do when you drink coffee. You read the newspaper.

The headline screamed at him: "Body Found in Antelope Reservoir".

Henry sucked in a breath and read the article. Twenty-five years. It was bound to happen someday, and before long the body would be identified. Before Edna could see it, he took the newspaper outside and to the trash bin. Fearful with anticipation of what was to come, he resolved to take his late son's backpack to the basement and burn it. Unfortunately, he never got that chance.

The Pinecone Pioneers were suited up and ready to go. It was Rhonda's turn to be assistant troop leader and carpool coordinator. McJennifer's mom was driving the remaining kids.

McJennifer's mom was named Summer, and looked just like you'd expect someone who would name their kid something that uNiQuE would look like. Yoga pants, a shirt that could almost pass as a crop top but had the decency to hit her perfect belly button, sneakers that probably cost more than a month's worth of groceries. Summer's blonde hair was pulled up in a purposefully messy bun, and those *had* to be eyelash extensions.

Pinecone Pioneers ran around Rhonda's living room, bumping into things like a bunch of wasps trapped in a jar—but cuter.

Summer clapped her hands together, "Okay, Pioneers!" she hollered in a voice that screamed, "I used to be a cheerleader and still think I am, even though I'm a forty-something mom." She gestured. "Everyone out to the cars, we're off to Harmony Hills to visit some grandmas and grandpas!"

Clap-clap-clap pom-pom waggling motion, kick! It was going to be a long, long day.

Eight little brown uniforms in sixteen black clacky shoes dashed for the door.

"Harpoony Hills!" Bailey was the first Pinecone outside.

McJennifer's mom whispered to Rhonda, "I hope they're not like my kid's grandparents, or all we'll be doing is looking at pictures from their latest cruise to the Bahamas and being told not to sit on the furniture."

The kids piled into the minivans and off they went, singing the Pinecone Pioneers theme song.

Twenty minutes, and thirty million verses of "We are Pinecone Pioneers!" Later, Rhonda and McJennifer's mom pulled into the parking area at Harmony Hills.

"Do you have any weed?" Summer asked her as they herded the kids toward the playground.

Rhonda laughed, unsure if the woman who gave birth to a McJennifer was serious or not.

The exterior of Harmony Hills was beautiful. The landscaping was like a park, and there was even a small pond with a fountain in the center. Benches and pathways wound their way around the green. The playground and plaza were surrounded by manicured lawn, and many residents were already there, waiting to push kids on swings and catch them as they came down the slides.

All senior living areas should be this way, thought Rhonda. It seemed to work so well.

Several craft tents were set up around the perimeter of the play area. One tent offered face painting, one was cut-and-paste craft hats that would be used later in the parade, and one was filled with cookies, which could be purchased with tickets earned for good behavior during the day.

Bailey, McJennifer, Khaleesi-Renée, and Scott were at the face painting tent waiting as patiently as five-year olds-could for their turn. McJennifer ran up to show her mother her makeup: she had a bright, rainbow-colored unicorn on one cheek and yellow glitter stars falling down the other. Scott had a mighty fine rendition of Spiderman crawling down his nose, and a web across his forehead.

It was Bailey's turn, and the woman in charge of the painting was whispering to her. Bailey was shaking her head. Rhonda could see the face painter nod and begin work on her daughter.

Five minutes later Bailey appeared, a black crow covering both of her cheeks; her nose was the body.

"That's…different," said McJennifer's mom.

"Paul wanted to be here, but he can't leave the house. I did it for him."

Leyta and Johnathan held Rosie by her arms and directed her to the elevator. Leyta keyed in the code which would allow them to leave the memory care unit. Today, there were a few field trips planned by local elementary aged kids, and they thought Rose might enjoy an outing. Although Rose's mind was sometimes lost in the unknown, her body worked perfectly most days. Leyta and Johnathan sat Rose down at a picnic table by the playground, and the three of them smiled as they watched the children run and laugh; some of them wore brown Pinecone Pioneer uniforms.

Bailey galloped toward the playground heading straight to the horses on springs, "I get the green one!" As she was about to throw her leg over the little green horse, she stopped in her tracks. Rose sat across from the jumble of slides, swings, and happy screaming children in the shade by a picnic table. Bailey lowered her leg, met Rose's eyes, and walked purposefully across the pebbled playground.

Rose's moments of clarity came in spurts. Her reality wavered from the present time to the past, and sometimes in between or beyond. The little girl who stood silently before her had a crow drawn across her face.

Bailey and Rose locked eyes for a moment of heartbeats. Rose stood, and Leyta and Johnathan looked on bewildered as Rose took Bailey into her arms and both began to cry. Black paint trickled down the child's face leaving rivulets of pink skin through the pigment. They held one another and wept.

Rhonda ran over to where her daughter stood clinging to a red-haired older resident. Bailey sobbed onto the elderly woman's chest, her face paint smeared on her lilac blouse.

"I'm so sorry ma'am!" said Rhonda. "Baby, what are you…"

Leyta looked at Rhonda and put a finger to her lips. "Shhhh."

Rhonda nodded warily, stepped back, and observed, stricken by the explosive show of emotion on both of their parts. "What's happening?" she asked Johnathan, who also had tears in his eyes.

"Is your daughter named Bailey?" Leyta asked her.

"Yes, how did you know that?"

"Rose has been waiting for her."

Rhonda stood silent and dumbfounded.

"Is Paul alright?" Rose asked Bailey.

Bailey pulled back, her face a mess of streaks and smears. "No, he wants to see"—Bailey looked at Johnathan— "you, but he *needs* to see *you*," she continued, staring into Leyta's deep brown eyes. "It's the only way he can climb out of the dark, he needs to see Leyta."

Leyta nodded as if she understood perfectly. "I need to see him too. It's time to set it right."

Rose hugged Bailey to her once more. "Tell him I love him."

"I will, but he already knows that. He knows you all do."

It was decided that Saturday, Rhonda would drive back to Harmony Hills, pick up Johnathan, Leyta and Rose and bring them to 291 Chestnut Street for a visit.

Chapter Twenty

King of the Planet of Dead Guys

This Journal Belongs to James Hansen

I'm uncertain, but I believe her name was Tiffany. Actually, I'm fairly certain, because I'd checked her driver's license. She'd stood out to me because of her extremely long false nails. They were a garish shade of pink and studded with gaudy fake jewels that flickered unnaturally in the light of the bonfire. She'd been easy to lure away from the party to the south of the campground at Antelope. All it took was a few smiles, the promise of pot, and a proper smack to the head with the claw end of a hammer. Not hard enough to kill her, but a good enough strike to put her out; I didn't want her unconscious forever.

I had thought through my actions more thoroughly than I had with Kimberly's spur-of-the-moment termination. I took Tiffany to the spot where Kimberly took her last swimming lesson, waited for her to awaken, and then, using my hands and the weight of my body, strangled her. Before I pushed her into the water, I watched her unmoving body for a long while, taking in the peace and stillness of it all. Her eyes stared into the night sky, a reflection of stars and moonlight that spoke straight to the center of me through those wide, glassy eyes. It bordered on romantic. What did they see now, I remember wondering. Where was the essence of her? I believed that she winked from existence, but could she somehow be in another place and be sharing in the tranquility of the moment? I honestly hoped so.

I needed a few minutes to sit and think. To understand. As I reluctantly rolled her into the blackness of Antelope, I remember thinking how otherworldly the water looked at night. How, as soon as the sun rose, the water would transform to a less malevolent space.

Once she was safely in the reservoir, I took her purse two miles north along the trail and scattered the contents on the floor of the forest. Before I left, I dropped nine of her long pink nails a few feet from her macraméd handbag. The last I placed safely into my pocket.

Rest well, Tiffany. Perhaps someday you and Kimberly will have company.

Henry knew that Edna would find out about the bodies discovered in Antelope Reservoir.

He sat down at the kitchen table and took a sip of his coffee. It had gone cold, and he pushed it away. Henry decided it would be wise to tell Edna about the discovery before she heard it from someone else. Seeing the newspaper would be a big shock for her, so he'd wait till she came downstairs and had a bit of coffee herself. He'd let her sleep another few minutes and then check on her; she'd been sleeping an awfully long time.

Since James was a child, Henry and Edna had known that he was a different sort of boy. It was only in his later teenage years that they discovered exactly how different. The couple had done everything in their power to keep him—and all those around him—safe. Therapy, family activities, more therapy. It had been a long and difficult journey.

Henry picked up his phone and looked at his lockscreen. It was a photo of a two-year-old James, all smiles and dimples. He glanced at the fireplace mantle where his only son's ashes took center stage. Henry scrubbed his face with both hands; life had become so complicated and stressful.

He heard Edna on the stairs and stood to meet her and help steady her. It was becoming harder and harder for Edna. They may have to think very soon about finding a place to live that didn't have as many stairs. The idea of a stair lift was a good one, but for that money and the sale of their fourth of the quad they could certainly afford a first-floor condo close by.

Henry stuck his phone in his pocket and stood. Pain raced through his chest like a car had hit him, and he fell to his knees gasping, taking the table and his chair with him. He had the presence of mind, even though the world was a spear of white-hot pain, to fumble with his phone, push and hold the right-hand button, and gasp, "Siri, call an ambulance."

As Henry's vision grew dark, his phone clattered to the floor. "I'm sorry," said Siri, "I didn't catch that, can you repeat?"

"Henry?" Edna called from the top of the staircase. "Henry, are you alright?" She'd heard the commotion in the kitchen and stopped at the top of the landing. "Henry? Answer me?"

In her rush to get to Henry, Edna missed the last step coming down. Her arthritic ankle bowed and snapped, and as she attempted to grab the banister she felt her wrist fracture. Edna screamed out in pain as she fell onto the orange and brown tiles that covered the landing before the front door.

Edna dragged herself across the living room carpet and into the kitchen. Her husband of fifty-two years lay crumpled on the floor. "Henry!" Edna grabbed his phone, opened it, and called for help. She also called Rhonda and asked her to unlock the front door. Thank god she knew a thing or two about smartphones. The pain in her ankle and wrist should have been all encompassing - but all she could think about was her Henry, who appeared not to be breathing.

The sound of sirens wailed in the distance as Rhonda unlocked the Hansens' front door and jogged in.

"Edna!"

"In here, in the kitchen!"

Rhonda dropped to her knees, put her ear to Henry's mouth, said a little prayer, and began CPR. The paramedics arrived within minutes and took over for her. Henry was placed on a gurney and rushed away. Two firemen were working on Edna and lifted her on to a gurney of her own. The stretcher ratcheted up with a snap, and Rhonda saw Edna cringe. The older woman grabbed Rhonda's arm with her good hand. "Go to James's room, get his backpack from the closet, and take it with you." Edna began to drift in and out of consciousness but her grasp on Rhonda's arm did not. "Promise me."

"I promise." What an odd request. "I promise I will."

The paramedics left the Hansens' house, taking with them all sounds except for the ticking kitchen wall clock. Rhonda had never been upstairs in their home but figured it would be easy enough to see which room had been James's.

It ended up not only being easy, but obvious. The bedroom looked as if an older teenager had just walked out of it. Rhonda opened the closet and looked around. All of Edna and Henry's only son's clothing still hung on hangers or were folded in neat piles. On the top shelf she saw a canvas tote. She took it down, slung it over her shoulder, the heft reminding her of her own backpack filled with books from her days in school. As she made her way down the stairs the contents in the bag shifted. *What an odd thing to ask for while your husband is on his way to the hospital, not knowing if he's alive or dead.* Rhonda locked up the house and took the backpack home as requested. She placed the satchel in the hall closet. Edna had requested she take it, not open it.

That night at 9:12 PM Henry Hansen, husband to Edna and father to James, passed away.

1997

This Journal belongs to James Hansen

The white mouse is nowhere in sight—save for a bulge in the reptile's midsection. My pet lies curled in the corner of the terrarium sated, still, and at peace. Friday I will visit Antelope Reservoir and find my own serenity.

Ishmael Martinez borrowed his sister's piece of shit gray 2001 Toyota Corolla and discreetly followed Todd and Not Todd to a hotel outside of Denver. A gray 2001 Toyota Corolla was about as invisible as a car could get, and he was in stealth mode.

Izzy knew something was off with this whole deal: it just smelled wrong, and he'd learned early in his life to trust his instincts. Ishmael was not a dumb man, but he was kicking his own dumb ass for agreeing to drive his van for illegal purposes with people as stupid as Kenny, Aaron, and Ethan. What the holy hell had he been thinking?

Ethan was dead. Aaron was either a murderer, on the run, or dead too. Kenny. Oh, boy, Kenny. What a dimwit. Continuing to go along with this deal did not seem worth the money. Izzy knew in his gut that if he continued with the plan as it stood, he'd most likely end up as King of The Planet of Dead Guys. *Uh oh, here comes Todd and Not Todd.*

Damn, Not Todd really was a shorty. They were both wearing black suits and sunglasses. Out of the blue, Izzy wondered where the hell Not Todd found suits that fit. Shit. He was starting to think like Kenny. All they needed to complete their outfits were a couple of memory neuralyzers from that movie about forgetting there were aliens.

Izzy scrunched down in his seat and kept watch. He cracked the window, hoping they were talking loud enough for him to hear, even though they were two spaces away. Ishmael couldn't tell which of the Todds was talking. Not Todd's voice was bigger than his body.

"...Holyworth said just to off them when we get the goods. They're too stupid to keep their mouths shut, and I agree."

"This whole deal has been one gigantic clusterfuck from start to finish. I don't care if things go smoothly on Friday, I volunteer to be the one to drop them where they stand."

Izzy watched Todd slip into the driver's seat. That was not a memory neuralyzer in the holster on his hip. Izzy's insides turned to chocolate pudding, and he squeezed his butt cheeks together. I'm out, he thought. The instant The Todds left the parking lot, Izzy backed out of the parking space, squealed out of the parking lot, and headed toward the highway. He decided to accidentally borrow his sister's inconspicuous piece of shit 2001 Toyota Corolla and point it straight toward his cousin's house in Pasadena—but first he'd need to stop at Walmart and buy new underpants.

Henry Hansen's funeral was a small affair. They had no family to speak of, and most of the attendants were friends of Henry's from the years when he was working at the post office. The rest were friends of Edna's that she'd made over time from her book club. Rhonda, Tate, Carlos, and Bailey were all in attendance.

After the service, Tate pushed Edna's wheelchair back to the van. She was staying in rehab for the time being until her broken ankle and wrist were healed; it would be a long, slow road to recovery. The rehab van lowered its ramp and Tate gently rolled her inside, setting the brakes and securing the straps.

"We'll meet you back at the rehab facility," he told her, and kissed her on the cheek. She smiled and nodded at him. Tate turned to his wife; the kids were already buckling themselves into their seats in the family car.

"Rhonda?" Tate said, "Edna asked me to tell you to bring the backpack to her today, she wants to talk to you. Alone."

Rhonda knocked on Edna's door at rehab. A very soft, "Come in," came from inside.

Edna was sitting at the window looking out onto the grounds, her wrist in a white cast, her leg also in a cast and elevated. She motioned for Rhonda to close the door and have a seat across from her. Rhonda sat and placed her purse and James's backpack on the floor next to them.

"I always thought I'd go first, you know." Edna said, her hands in her lap. "I never worried about being alone, I didn't think I needed to, I was the one with the health problems."

Rhonda nodded and listened.

"Henry never had any heart issues before this." Edna sighed. "Maybe that's a good thing, no worries, just, poof. One day he's gone." Edna looked at Rhonda for the first time. "You know what makes this easier?"

Rhonda shook her head.

"He loved me. I loved him. We both knew it, and things were good. We didn't have any unanswered questions or guilt between us, except"—Edna paused and pointed at the backpack—"Except for that." Rhonda could see she was silently crying. "And it's time," Edna went on, "for that bag filled with all of our guilt to come to light."

Edna put a hand over Rhonda's. "This could take awhile, do you have time?"

Rhonda sent Tate a text and asked if he would take the kids home. "I do now," she said. "I'll take a Lyft home."

Edna slipped what appeared to be a stack of notebooks from the canvas satchel. She put the notebooks in chronological order, one through six and handed Rhonda the first one. Rhonda sat back to read.

The first thing Rhonda noticed was that the handwriting was neat and precise. The second thing she discerned was these were not the musings of a normal teenager. The first of the journals documented James, and how he felt about the world. It was obviously written by a brilliant boy with very serious mental health issues, nothing like the postpartum depression that she'd struggled with and come through with lots of therapy, the support of her family, and carefully monitored medication. This was something different. Something violent.

Rhonda closed the journal. Edna was ready with journal number two, and handed it to her.

Two hours later, Rhonda set the last of James Hansen's journals on the table. "I don't know what to say. Did you take these to the authorities?"

Edna shook her head. "The journals are only half the story." She fidgeted with her fingers and took a big breath. "I want to tell you the other half, and then let you decide what to do with the information." She wiped her eyes. "He really was a good boy most of the time, and I loved him. I still love him. A mother will do just about anything to protect their child." She shook her head. "But this…how could I protect others from…him? How could I protect him from himself?"

Rhonda nodded, horrified.

"Let me tell you the rest," Edna said, slipping the books back into the maw of bag. It swallowed them whole.

Chapter Twenty-one

Cows Love Westerns

The Hansen House, 1997

Edna kept a tidy house. She prided herself in that. She always made the beds, always cleaned the bathrooms, and the kitchen was usually (unless she canned homemade spaghetti sauce) spotless. Edna wiped down the bathrooms once a day, and every Tuesday and Friday were vacuum days. Wall-to-wall carpet covered most of the floors in the Hansens' home, except for the kitchen, the bathrooms, and the entryway. There was a method to Edna's madness; she'd start at the top, end at the bottom, and then dust the entire house.

She knew that Henry didn't mind if she missed a few cleaning days, and he never complained; but being brought up in the household that she had been, with a mother like hers, having a clean house and a hot meal on the table were two things that were required. Her mother had said a smile and heels were required as well, but Edna didn't take things that far—Henry would think she'd lost her fool mind. Her housework started in the bedroom she shared with Henry, and she worked her way out, leaving those lovely, clean vacuum streaks in its wake. She pushed the vacuum down the hallway and into James's room. His room was never as tidy as the rest of the house, but she gave the boy some space. Teenagers needed space and privacy.

Gosh, how she wished he had a few friends. He told her that he had friends at school, but none of them had ever been to Hansens' home. Now that he was driving, he went out at night sometimes and claimed to be meeting these school friends. Edna hoped he was, it would be so good for him. Since he was six years old he'd been going to therapy regularly. His new therapist, Dr. Shelliker, seemed to be doing him some good. James was almost an adult, and Edna was uncomfortable thinking about what his life would be like when he was a grown man and out on his own. She and Henry had always been there to keep him safe and to protect him.

Edna moved his laundry basket out of the way, avoiding the terrarium that housed his pet snake. James was in charge of his own laundry, and it looked as if it needed done desperately; she'd speak to him when he returned home from school. She lifted the basket onto the bed, and his backpack tumbled to the floor.

What she did next was something she would struggle with the rest of her life—she read the journals and the horror that splattered out of them.

When Henry came home, James was still nowhere in sight. He found Edna sitting on their son's bed, her head in her hands, journals spilled around her. It looked as if she'd been sitting there a long time.

"Sweetheart," Henry said, "what's happening? What's wrong?"

Edna handed him the first journal, clasped her hands in her lap, and stared at a blank spot in the wall as if it would give her the answers.

She didn't move while Henry read their only child's psychotic musings. His face had the glassy, wide-eyed look of a man going into shock. He gathered up the journals, upended the backpack, and one crooked tooth and a long glittery fingernail fell to the bedspread. The nail had been pulled from the quick of the skin and still held tissue and a bit of blood. And then there were the Polaroids.

Edna leaned against her husband as if she would faint. Henry gasped and placed his body in front of his wife's in an automatic move of protection. He scraped the objects back into the bag.

"We need to talk long and hard about how to proceed."

Edna nodded, took the satchel, put it back onto the bed where they had found it, and left the vacuum in the hallway by James's bedroom door.

For the next three days, there was a quiet storm cloud over the Hansen home. Henry and Edna would talk secretly after the house was settled and James was either gone or in his room.

"We have to do something, Edna," Henry said. His face looked older and drawn.

"He's our child!" Edna protested. "He's almost an adult. He'll spend the rest of his life in prison! They could execute him!"

"The two young women who he murdered were also someone's children. We need to call the police."

Edna nodded, looking out the bedroom door. The vacuum still stood in the hallway. "You're right," she whispered, "and from what we just read, he plans on doing it again." Edna began to sob, and Henry held her until she was stable enough to leave their son's room and close the door.

Despite Henry's protests and his insistence that the authorities should be contacted, Edna would not allow her only child, *her brilliant boy*, to rot in prison.

Seventy-two hours later, Edna busied herself in the kitchen. The house smelled of spices and grilled meat. The pot on the stove was one her mother had given her and was filled to the brim with bubbling chili. Edna got herself a bowlful and sat down at the kitchen table to eat. She hadn't eaten much in the last few days, and surprised herself to find she had an appetite. She finished the bowl, filled another, put it onto a tray with two tortillas, and walked up the stairs to her son's room. Edna could hear the music from ten feet away.

"I've brought you dinner, my love," she said, setting the tray by his nightstand. "I think your dad and I may go out tonight to dinner and a movie."

James gave her half a smile, nodded, but didn't make eye contact. "Thanks, Mom, I probably won't be home when you get back from dinner. Don't wait up, I'll most likely be late."

Edna sat on the edge of his bed and stroked his hair. He flinched and reflexively jerked away a bit.

"I love you more than anything in this world," she told him.

James picked up the bowl of chili made from Jeanie Garcia's recipe and took a spoonful. "It's great."

Edna walked to his doorway, blew him a kiss that she thought he probably didn't notice, closed the door, hooked the handle of the vacuum under the doorknob, and walked down the stairs. There was no way in God's green earth that her son would die in prison, to be remembered as a monster. He'd die where he was the most comfortable and loved.

She went to the kitchen, threw out the rest of Jeanie's chili with her secret ingredient, and washed all the dishes. She'd get James's bowl and spoon later and wash those too.

Later that evening, when Henry returned from his fishing trip, she would call the police and proceed from there. If they assumed it was an accident, fine. If she spent her remaining days in prison, she didn't care. All she cared about was James. James would not suffer.

"Now that Henry is gone, I really don't care what happens to me," Edna said, meeting Rhonda's eyes. "All these years he kept my secret; all these years he protected me." She sighed. "All these years he was an accomplice by doing so."

Edna's eyes were clear now, and she said, "I'd do it again to keep James out of prison. He was what the world would see as a devil, but to me he was just my boy. The sweet boy in the Spiderman outfit at Halloween. The boy who made me a ceramic ashtray in elementary school, even though I've never smoked a day in my life." She sighed again. "The boy his father taught to fish. All these years his urn sat on our fireplace mantle—and I put him there."

Rhonda was stunned by Edna's admission. She'd murdered her own son.

Her son was a monster. He would have killed again. It was a nightmare that Henry and Edna had carried with them for twenty-five years.

Rhonda knew what she needed to do. She gathered the journals and put them into the bag.

"Will you be going to the police?" Edna asked her. Her eyes were stony, clear, resigned.

"No Edna," Rhonda said, "I'll be burning all of this."

Edna nodded.

Rhonda left the room and shut the door, reasonably sure she'd never see Edna again.

Kenny punched in Ishmael's phone number for the sixth time, and for the sixth time it went straight to voicemail. "What the actual fuck? Pick up the phone, douchebag." Kenny tried a seventh time. "Listen up, asshole," he said to voicemail, "I can't do this on my own. We need your fucking van, and it's sitting outside of the shop illegally parked. Last night the cops put a boot on it." Kenny took a deep, shuddering breath. "At least let me know where you keep the keys,"—he gritted his teeth— "please."

Well, fuck.

On a whim, Kenny asked Alexa, "Alexa, dial the nearest U-Haul."

A young woman picked up on the second ring. *At least somebody answers their damn phone.*

"Patton U-Haul, how may I help you?"

"Uh, hi, I'm looking to rent a truck. A small one."

"May I ask how many pounds you'll be moving, what the contents are, and how far you'll be driving?"

"Uh…I'm not sure how much it weighs, but it's about nineteen million dollars worth of…" He added, "Just to the city line."

Click.

Kenny frantically dialed Izzy's phone one more time. Somewhere south of Patton, in a cow pasture, Ishmael Martinez's discarded phone rang. Three cows stood in a circle and stared at it as it jangled the default ringtone. One of them poked it with her nose. YouTube came up; *Bonanza* was playing and there was a cow stampede going on.

"Hey," said Clarabelle, "I know that guy!"

Chapter Twenty-Two

I Was Cleaning it and it Went Off!

Bailey took the drawing that she had taken from her time trapped in the loft and spread it gently on the table.

It was another image of the carriage house. The carriage house was a recurring theme. This time, it was the inside of the dwelling. The loft and walls of tools were prominently drawn with amazing details. Not much had changed. The floor was covered in a carefully drawn yellow flecked pattern, which looked to Bailey as if it were what used to cover the bottom of her hamster's cage (God rest his soul). The carriage house floor was entirely covered—except for a clean-swept circle.

Bailey snatched up the drawing and scrutinized it. Her eyes went wide, and a new certainty formed in her mind.

"The sisturd…" she whispered, touching it with a fingertip. A rush of air flew through her room, and the chair where Paul would sit with her to draw toppled to the floor. Startled, Goldie dashed around in her bowl.

At that instant the old, seeded glass windows on the carriage house rattled in protest, sending a flock of starlings out of the cottonwoods and into the crystal blue afternoon.

Bailey took a glue stick and attached Paul's drawing to her bedroom wall.

"The sisturd…"

Tap tap tap. The distinct sound of a single fingernail upon her bedroom window.

Johnathan, Leyta, and Rose sat on patio chairs on the siblings' private porch in Harmony Hills. Each tiny house was just that; three hundred square feet for a one bedroom, and the two bedrooms barely took up four hundred square feet. Rose's studio was on the secure second level. It was very small with only a bed, two armchairs, and a bathroom. Each home had a front porch, and neighbors would wave and visit as if they were on an actual street in a small town. Of course, the streets weren't wide enough for traffic; the only traffic the well-tended streets did get was people strolling.

Rose was having a gray day. Her gaze went from one end of the street to the other, her head turning but her eyes obviously not registering what she was seeing. Leyta looked on with concern.

"Once Rhonda and Bailey get here she'll clear a bit, I reckon," Johnathan said.

Leyta thought it sounded as if he was trying to reassure himself. She, on the other hand, was sure Rose would be more lucid the instant she saw her old home at 291 Chestnut Street.

Leyta saw Rhonda and her daughter turn the corner toward their tiny house. "There they are!"

The three were waiting for them as Rhonda and Bailey arrived at Leyta and Jonathan's tiny townhouse. Rhonda greeted each of them in turn, and Leyta grabbed her for a big hug. Bailey rushed to Rose, and the older woman wrapped her arms around her.

"Would you like to see the inside of our home first?" Leyta asked Rhonda, as she stepped around a very large, very healthy-looking potted geranium.

Rhonda readily agreed, and Johnathan opened the front door. Leyta took Rose's hand as Bailey took the other and followed along.

"This is amazing!" Rhonda said, and meant it sincerely. The Harmony Hills cottages were truly that: cottages. A cozy living area was adjoined by a breakfast nook and a very simple kitchen which consisted of a small refrigerator, a bit of counter space with a sink, and a two-burner stove topped by a compact microwave. Leyta explained that the memory units didn't have the kitchen feature, but most of the time she and Johnathan cooked at least one meal for themselves. Johnathan would escort Rose down from memory care to join them.

"We live in one of the few two-bedroom units," Leyta said. "I believe there are only three available in the entire village."

She showed Rhonda her bedroom, which had older furniture and walls filled with photographs. "This is our mom and dad," she said, pointing at a photo of a smiling couple accompanied by what could only be Leyta at around eight and Johnathan as a toddler. "I think this was taken not long before Rose's brother Paul disappeared."

There was also a photograph of Leyta and Rose as children, sitting in what appeared to be a young girl's room, filled with dolls and toys. "That's Rosie and me." The girls were laughing and had their pinky fingers hooked. "We used to say we were bread and butter and butter and bread." Leyta swallowed hard. "And we have been for seventy years."

"I wasn't allowed into Leyta's room much," said Johnathan.

"You were a bratty little three-year-old that got into our things."

Johnathan just shrugged and grinned. "And now we live together, and I stay out of your things."

"Unless those 'things' are in the refrigerator," she said, scolding him good-naturedly. "Come see the bath and his room."

"This is Paul, Mama," Bailey said, pointing out another picture. "Paul and Rosie."

Rose took the picture down so that Bailey could see it up close. Rose touched his face in the photograph, and Bailey did the same. The pair beamed at one another.

The bathroom looked like any other bathroom, but had a walk-in shower, a shower chair, and a red emergency button hanging on a string. Leyta had it decorated in shades of lilac with matching rugs straight from the sixties.

Johnathan's room was similar in size to Leyta's, but he had a smaller bed, leaving room for a TV and a reclining chair. "We need two television sets," he said to Rhonda, "all my sister watches are reality shows and soaps."

"Oh, no I do not!"

"Oh, yes you do!"

Rhonda was charmed. It was like a standalone home, just smaller, safer, and in close proximity to healthcare. She chuckled to herself. *Johnathan and Leyta argue exactly like Carlos and Bailey. I guess you never grow out of some things.* She thought about her own relationship with her sisters and smiled. "Harmony Hills Village is the most inventive endeavor I think I've ever seen. With all the large malls that are dying, this could be the wave of the future." She looked out the kitchen window which overlooked the green.

"The inside cottages have windows like this as well, but they have realistic scenery that changes with the season and time of day," said Johnathan. "Rosie's unit is very similar but built in a way that keeps her safe and makes it impossible to wander, even though it gives the illusion of independence. We'll show you sometime. But now, I think we should be going, we don't want to use up your entire day."

The five of them strolled unhurried to the front entrance, Bailey holding Rose and Johnathan's hands.

"It's as if they've known each other forever," Leyta said.

Rhonda nodded. "I don't usually bite into supernatural things, but Rose and Bailey are not strangers."

The five of them headed out of Harmony Hills and toward Rhonda's van.

"I'm just gonna go with them to the basement," said Kenny, "give them the bolt cutters, tell them the truth about what happened with the first lock, and press how Aaron might have swiped it the night he disappeared." He was wearing a hole in the carpet from pacing. "Then I'm gonna get our cut, come back up here, get you and the little demons, and we're heading out. Make sure you have a suitcase packed and in the cow truck."

"I can't believe we're disappearing into the sunset in that piece of shit cow truck."

"It's the only vehicle we own right now. It's either the cow truck, or stay here and hope they don't kill us all." He thought for a minute. "Izzy didn't come to work today, Damn I hope he doesn't fuck this up, we need his van to load the goods."

Anita wasn't feeling any of it. "I have to tell you babe; I'm worried as all get out." Her voice trailed off for a moment, then brightened. "I just had an idea that might keep us out of the morgue!"

"Do you really think this'll work?" Kenny was carrying the bolt cutters, the broken old lock, and a bottle of super glue.

"I do, as long as *you're* the one that unlocks the door for them," said Anita. "Just make sure they can't see, use any key, and bust the lock apart again."

"You're the brains, babe, let's give it a try."

Anita stood watch at the top of the stairs, and Kenny crept down them. "I feel like I'm in one of those action movies where they crack a safe and it has a big pile of gold bars in it—but this is only buggy cheese." He turned and looked up at Anita. "Maybe there are gold bars *in* the cheese!"

"Stop daydreaming, James Bond, and hurry up, you're giving me an attention headache."

Kenny stopped midstep, bit his lip, and for once had the good sense to say nothing about her butchering of the English language. He took the bolt cutters and easily cut off the new Patton Hardware lock. "They don't make um like they used to," he said. He hooked the old lock onto the hasp, took the super glue, put a bit on the sides that had been cut, and held it.

"What's taking you so long?"

"I gotta hold this till it dries."

"How long's that gonna take? I need to use the little girls' room."

Once again, Kenny had the sound judgment to not say a word about the "little girls" portion of that sentence. "I think I almost got it."

"Thank god," Anita said. "I'm dancing up here, Kenny."

"Shit!"

"What?"

"I glued my fingers to the lock."

"Goddammit Kenny! Just yank them off," she hissed at him.

"My fingers??"

"It'll just take the top layer of skin off, the new lady is out back taking out her trash!"

"It hurts, babe!" Kenny whimpered, "It's gonna rip my fingerprints off, and I'll leave my DEA all over it."

"I think the new lady is coming this way! Yank it off like a bandaid, babe!"

Kenny gritted his teeth, jerked his hand from the lock, screamed, and ran up the stairs, his fingers bleeding. Three of the other fingers on the other hand were glued together like a crab claw.

They made a dash back to their quad. "I didn't see the new lady."

Anita shrugged and grinned at him. "I knew if I said I saw her it would hustle your ass up."

"You owe me big time, babe."

Anita kissed his hand-claw.

"It'll be okay…maybe," Kenny reassured her. "Do me a favor though, since you owe me."

"What?"

"You know that pink Traveling Titillator that you bought when you bought that sexy teddy?"

"Yeah?"

"Be sure you're wearing it before we head out of town." Kenny took the remote out of his pocket and gave it a try. From the next room something squealed like a baby piggy.

Kenny waggled his eyebrows. "Fresh batteries."

Anita kissed him. "You think of everything, lover."

After a bit of research on his phone, Kenny figured out that acetone will dissolve super glue. Anita took a cotton swab and carefully dabbed his claw. Slowly but surely, his fingers separated, and the crustacean that was his hand now had five digits. He also smelled as if he'd just come out of You Need Boyfren' Nails. Acetone was some stinky stuff.

"I'm gonna take a shower, babe," he said, and kissed her. She waved at him seductively. Kenny waved back, a drop of acetone falling onto the raw skin of his other hand. He yelped and did a little dance. "Jesus Christ that stings!" he whimpered and dragged himself to the bathroom as if he'd just had both arms amputated. Stripping off his acetone-scented clothes, he bent into the shower and tested the temperature. Stepping in under the hot stream was heavenly: he leaned back, letting the warm water burble into his mouth. Ahhh.

Kenny's mind began to wander. He thought of the money they'd have not long from now. He thought about how they could make a stop in Vegas after leaving town. Maybe he'd buy a wedding ring, and they'd tie the knot; wedding rings were cheap at Walmart, right? He thought about Anita in her new red teddy rolling around in the payout money on a California king-sized bed, the green bills crinkling under her big, luscious backside. Ah, Anita, his beautiful, beautiful goddess. Kenny's soapy hands began to wander as he thought of it all. He pictured Anita on her hands and knees amidst the money, looking over her shoulder at him, her red teddy swallowed by her luscious round, dimpled beach balls.

Mmmm…Anita…mmm money…(don't think about the cheese, don't think about the tooth)…mmm Tantalizing Titillator…

"What in the holy fucking hell are you doing?"

Kenny jerked back into reality; the soap fell to the floor, he caught himself on the shower rack, and the washcloth fell over his erection, making it look like a happy little pink ghost. Kenny sputtered trying to find his words, then blurted out, "I can wash as fast as I want!"

"You're not getting any tonight," Anita said, rolled her eyes, and slammed the door.

The happy little pink ghost dropped to the floor.

"I was cleaning it and it went off!"

Rhonda pulled the van into the driveway at 291 Chestnut Street.

Bailey was out like a shot to open the doors for Leyta and Rose, then took Rose's hand. Rhonda unlocked the front door to quad number one, and the five of them entered into the foyer.

The three older folks and Bailey looked up to the second floor as though rooted in place. Rhonda watched them closely. It was as if her daughter had merged effortlessly with the trio, making them a seamless quartet who shared an enormous secret.

Bailey looked up at Rose and said, "Do you want me to show you where I see Paul?" Any trace of Rose's fog had lifted; she was as present as Leyta and Johnathan.

"Yes please," Rose answered.

Leyta shivered, looking up at the house that had once been a source of both joy and unspeakable heartache.

In the carriage house, the air grew thick with turbulence, and the ground trembled.

Edgar Wilson had left Paul in the basement to sit in the attitude adjustment room for two days. Rose spent most of her time in the basement with him, unless mother or father called for her. She couldn't let father know she was down here with her brother. Rose knew that to punish her- *to hurt her* - he'd most likely leave Paul there longer. This would cause her more misery than any type of physical or emotional punishment. She heard his heavy footfalls on the basement stairs and ran to hide under the staircase in the dark.

"Are you ready to come out and behave yourself?" Her father boomed.

Rose covered her mouth so that he couldn't hear her breathing.

"I said," father bellowed, "are you ready to come out and behave, you disobedient little retard?"

Rose heard a small whimper, and then the turning of the key in the lock.

"Christ it reeks in here," Rose heard the sounds of father's boot kicking something metal which she knew could only be the bucket that was to be used as a toilet. "You're covered in filth. Get up." Rose heard nothing. "I *said*, get up and get up now."

Rose could hear shuffling and peeked out from her hiding place. She watched as her father dragged Paul from the room; he had to be so thirsty and hungry. He looked barely conscious. She heard her father swear and then throw Paul over his shoulder and huff his way up the basement stairs.

Rose waited until she knew that she wouldn't be seen, ran up the staircase, then up to the second floor and to Paul's room. He was lying on his bed, his lips cracked, his body trembling. "I'll get you some water."

Paul gulped greedily, whimpering and unable to talk, Rose gave him an apple that she'd taken from the kitchen, she stripped him out of his soiled clothes, put him into the bathtub and gently scrubbed him down. Once she had him in clean pajamas, she brought him a sandwich that her mother had passed to her when father wasn't looking, and he ate it carefully avoiding the crust. Paul stared at the wall, his mind somewhere far away. She filled his water glass and tucked him in, stroking his still damp hair.

Paul looked up at her, meeting her eyes. Rose could count on one hand the number of times that had happened. Rose crawled in next to him and held him until he drifted off to sleep.

"I'll never, ever let him do this again Paul. I promise."

Today

Rhonda stood on the tiled landing as Rose began to climb the stairs. She obviously knew the layout of the house even though it had gone through a major remodel. "Paul?" she whispered, clutching Bailey's hand. She took another step. Rose looked behind her and motioned for Leyta and Johnathan to follow. Rhonda followed a few steps behind wringing her hands and keeping a close watch on her daughter. She felt as if she were out of place in her own home and would happily have stayed on the landing but for Bailey. She was not about to let her daughter out of her sight.

Rose took the last step and once again called for her brother. "Paul? Are you here?" She stood before Bailey's bedroom door, cocked her head as if to hear clearly, reached for the knob and turned it. Silence encompassed the top floor. The kind of enveloping silence that made Rhonda's ears feel as if they might pop. *The air feels different.* Tiny hairs on the nape of her neck stood up at attention.

Bailey entered first, walked to her bedroom wall and took down Paul's picture she'd found in the loft of the carriage house. "Is this what you wanted me to show them?"

Rose's voice wavered as she took the drawing into her hands, "he's here, isn't he?" she said, examining Paul's artwork.

Bailey nodded, "he is. But he's not alone."

The water in Goldie's bowl was vibrating, sending Bailey's pet swimming in tight, frantic circles.

Bailey laid a hand on the glass sphere and the ripples ceased.

"Is this the sisturd?" Bailey asked, pointing to the circular area of Paul's long forgotten drawing.

"Yes, that's the cistern."

Paul's artwork dropped from Rose's hands and fluttered to the floor like a dry, dead leaf.

Chapter Twenty-three

Is Goldie Okay?

1957

Edgar Wilson arrived home early from work, and he called for his wife.

"Beatrice!" Where was that infuriating woman? Probably out with her colored friend, Sheila. Edgar knew that Beatrice saw Sheila behind his back. How could he not know? People in this town *talk*.

Walking out the back door, he heard laughter coming from behind the carriage house. He walked around the brick building to see what was happening on his property.

Paul was sitting with that little colored girl's brother on his lap; they were laughing together, and it outraged Edgar. Why could he be a pleasant, happy child in the company of this black boy? Why was he always so contrary in his own home, around his own family?

Edgar stepped around the corner, and Johnathan stood swiftly and ran back toward the trees. Edgar grabbed Paul by the front of his shirt and lifted him to his toes. The childish laughter that had rung out just heartbeats before stopped instantly, replaced by terrified whimpers. Paul was shaking, his head rocking back and forth.

Edgar screamed into his face, spittle flying, "I never want to see those colored kids on my property again!" he yelled. "Never again, do you understand me, boy? I'm finished with this nonsense!"

Paul only moaned. A string of drool dripped from his lips, his eyes squeezed tightly closed. Then Paul did something that set Edgar on fire. He began to scream and kick.

Edgar threw him over his shoulder. "Time to pay a visit to the attitude adjustment room."

Today

Rose closed her eyes, a faint smile on her lips, her open hands held out at her sides. "He is here, I can feel him. Oh Paul, I'm so sorry." Tears melted down her cheeks. "I'm so very, very sorry. I only wanted to protect you. I'm so sorry! To this day, I still want to protect you. Please, please Paul," she begged, "show me how I can do that."

"He doesn't blame you, Rose," Bailey said.

"Of course he doesn't," Leyta said, sobbing, "It's all my fault." She scrubbed at her face with her hands and leaned into Johnathan. "He's actually here?"

"Yes," said Rose and Bailey together as the air in the bedroom became charged with static. It sparked as if it were filled with microscopic pieces of charged metallic particles.

"What's happening?" asked Johnathan.

"You were much too young to remember," Leyta said, and took his hand. "This has nothing at all to do with you, please know that."

In the carriage house, the concrete floor buckled and then shattered, cement flying up and then raining down in sharp-edged, angry fragments.

Rhonda jumped at the sound and ran to the window. She saw a single crow land in the branches of the long dead cottonwood that stood thirty yards or so from Bailey's bedroom window. It appeared to be looking directly at her.

1957

Upon hearing the commotion, Rose and Leyta hurried down the ladder from the loft and out the carriage house back door. Paul was melting down in a tantrum that she'd never seen the likes of. Johnathan was cowering just behind the tree line.

Rose threw herself at her father; he stumbled, caught himself, and shoved her. She landed on her backside, got back up, and collided headlong into the back of his knees. Edger's legs gave way, and he dropped Paul to the ground where his head connected with a protruding stone.

Instantly, Paul's cries went still. Edgar got up, looked down at his daughter and kicked her in the back with his hard-toed boots.

Paul remained quiet. So quiet. So very quiet.

Dead quiet.

Today

Bailey ran to her window in time to see the panes of seeded glass shatter in the carriage house. She turned and met Leyta's eyes. "The bad one, he's here too." Bailey inhaled sharply. "Leyta? Paul says it's you he wants."

Leyta nodded but said nothing.

Rhonda grabbed her daughter and pulled her back from the window. "What in the name of god is happening?"

Dark smoke oozed from the empty black holes that were once the carriage house windows. It emerged from the shattered glass like fingers tentatively testing their unfamiliar surroundings. Spilling into the daylight and across the ground, it slithered like a living thing, a malevolent force creeping toward the house, feeling its way blindly along, a subterranean creature freed into the light. The mass of sooty darkness seeped over the grass, devouring it with slow, measured assurance, picking up speed and confidence. The house seemed to call to it. Tendrils of menacing, acrid smoke tipped with deep luminous green reached for the brick home in a sightless but steady crawl. The viscosity left a smoldering black simmer in its wake;

the scent of burning grass and something akin to tar filled the air as the advancing black mass throbbed and pulsed.

Bailey and Rose took a step back. They stood there, watching in shocked silence as the fingers of thick, shining black mucus began their ominous crawl up the outside walls. Seared leaves of ivy fell like fiery black snow.

1957

Leyta shrieked as Paul and Rose hit the ground. Rose groaned, and her eyes fluttered open then closed again. Edgar looked at Leyta, his dark eyes raging. He kicked his daughter again, never breaking eye contact with Leyta as she continued to scream. Rose moaned and rolled onto her belly.

Edgar picked up Paul as he lay unmoving on the ground, slung him over his broad shoulder, and headed into the carriage house, muttering, "Worthless, ungrateful children." He dropped Paul onto the sawdust floor, got a crowbar down from his tools, and lifted the lid of the long abandoned cistern. It creaked open from years of rusty closure.

When Leyta realized what he was about to do, she ran after them, pleading for Rose's father to stop. "You can't do this! You're a monster! You've killed him, you've killed him! Oh god, Paul!" she shrieked after him.

Edgar turned to her, growling, "You're next, you meddlesome little black bitch."

Rose staggered into the carriage house, her eight-year-old body hunched in pain, her hand clutching the spot where Edgar's boot had hit soft flesh. She charged at him, and once again he pushed her hard enough to make her stumble and fall.

Edgar picked up his son's corpse as if he weighed nothing, Paul's head lolling back, his body limp.

Rose was back on her feet, and she and Leyta tugged at the monster's back as he dropped Paul's lifeless body into the old cistern like a sack of garbage.

Today

Dense black smoke engulfed Bailey's bedroom window, leaving the space in a whorl of darkness. The silver shimmer that had filled the room and was the essence of Paul fell to the ground in a solid wave; its incandescence scattered and disappeared beneath the baseboards.

Rhonda took Bailey by the shoulders, pulling her away from Rose, and placed herself between her daughter and the darkened window. The thick, gelatinous presence outside the window sucked and pushed at the glass until the window looked as if it were breathing. The glass and its wooden pane bucked and groaned until it splintered onto Bailey's bed in a fall of razor-sharp ice. Goldie's fishbowl exploded in a shower of water and glass. Bailey screamed and scooped up her thrashing pet, dropping her into last night's plastic rainbow water cup that sat on her dresser. Bailey's face creased in anger.

As the inky, viscous ropes crept into the jagged opening, blue sky showed through the top half of the window. Rhonda saw that there were now three crows perched in the old cottonwood.

A silver glimmer timidly ascended from the floor and encompassed her daughter in a shroud of luminescence. Rhonda crossed herself, and a thought ripped through her—one she knew was right. Seeing her daughter cloaked in silver gave Rhonda the courage to do what she needed to do; she sprang for the stairs and headed toward the basement. "Do what you can to keep it at bay!" she called back, "I'll hurry! Keep Bailey safe. Do whatever you need to do to keep my baby safe!"

She's. Not. A. Baby.

1957

Rose cried out as Paul's body disappeared into the cistern. She pounded on her father's back, and he turned toward her. He grabbed her by the arm, dragging her with force toward the hole in the ground. Rose screamed as her sneakers plowed the sawdust-covered floor.

By now beyond words Edgar grunted and huffed, pulling his daughter along as she attempted to twist from his grasp. His fingers bit into her flesh.

The wet *thwack!* of what sounded like a blunt object hitting a ripe melon pierced the air, and his steel-vice grasp released his daughter. Edgar fell to the ground moaning.

Leyta hit him again with the crowbar. As he lay semi-conscious and groaning, she fell to her bottom, braced herself on the wall, and used both feet to push him into the open black maw of the old water storage tank.

In the corner of the carriage house, Johnathan covered his ears and curled into a whimpering ball.

Today

A high-pitched hum filled the room, and the black slime rose and formed into a vaguely human shape. The presence slid past Bailey and Rose and stood looming before Leyta. Its mouth opened impossibly wide; viscous black droplets acrid as tar mimicked hundreds of thin, razor-edged teeth.

"It's me he wants," Leyta said. "I'm the one who trapped him." She stood a bit taller. "I'm the one that *killed* him, and to this day, I'm not one bit sorry that I did!" She spat on the ground, and her saliva sizzled at the thing's feet. A roar shook the house.

"And now, I'm the one that will send him to hell!"

Bailey let go of Rose's hand and placed herself between Leyta and what had once been Edgar Wilson. The bits of silver particles surrounded Bailey, and as the blackness reached out to grab her, it flinched and retracted as if from something searing hot. The gelatinous mass lost its human shape; its face melted back into a shapeless blob, and the thing bubbled back a few steps. The stench of charred meat filled the room as it retreated, but the sensation of threat still thickened the air with unmistakable menace.

"Paul kept him trapped for all these years!" Rose said, wringing her hands, her gaze never leaving the bubbling mass that lurked in the corners. "My brother was able to filter through the minute openings of the cistern because he didn't deserve to be there, but my father couldn't completely." Rose cried out as smoke swirled around her ankles. She stomped her feet, and it receded with a hiss. "Sometimes his anger would allow tiny bits of him to seep through the barrier, but never all of him. He rightfully belongs in the dark!"

"Leyta being this close gave him the strength to break free," Bailey said, then cocked her head as if listening to someone speak, "Paul says to tell you that there's a lot of power in revenge-fueled hatred."

The perimeter of the room sparked and crackled with renewed energy. Spidery black probes tinged with fire blistered their way tentatively from the nooks and crannies of Bailey's bedroom, feeling their way back to life.

"Then there's a lot of power in me," said Leyta. "And in Rosie." She took Rose's trembling fingers in her own, "more power than he could possibly imagine."

As if in furious challenge, the essence of what was once Edgar Wilson roared back to life.

Outside, Rhonda saw the old barren cottonwood was filled with crows. Hundreds and hundreds of crows, each looking in a slightly different direction, their heads cocked, their black feathers glistening.

She flung open the basement door and ran down the stairs. "Please keep Bailey safe!"

1957

A moan came from inside the cistern. "Rose…" Her father's voice sounded wounded and weak but still held the threatening malice she'd come to fear for all these years. "Rose, you'll be sitting in the basement room until you dry up and turn to dust."

Rose and Leyta peeked down.

Paul was still, his eyes open and unseeing. Edgar obviously had a broken leg, and his head wound was a gaping gash that streamed with blood. The girls looked at one another, and, using their combined strength, pushed the heavy metal door to the cistern shut. Edgar's voice was captured as the cover clanged closed. Together, they locked the opening and swept the sawdust back over it. They rolled the old ore bucket that had sat atop it for years back into place and gathered up a weeping Johnathan.

Johnathan held tight to his sister's shoulders as she carried him from the carriage house and closed the door. Rose and Leyta held each other, sobbing.

Rose was bruised and inconsolable. "Bread and Butter," Rose whispered into her best friend's shoulder as she clung to her.

"Butter and Bread," Leyta replied, and kissed Rose's cheek.

Leyta took Johnathan home, and the events of the day were not mentioned again for seventy-five years.

Today

In the basement, Rhonda headed swiftly to the three boxes she'd placed under the steps a few days ago. She ripped open the top one and grabbed Great-grandma's mantilla which had been blessed so many years ago.

Will it do any good? I have to try!

She sprinted up the stairs and toward her daughter's bedroom. Maybe she read too many horror novels, maybe she did have a bit of buried faith…maybe, just, it would work. She grasped the only blessed thing she owned tight in her fist.

Deep, raspy growling came from Bailey's bedroom, and as Rhonda entered she saw that the human-like figure was now a threatening oily carpet. Multitudes of long fingers on slender arms formed from beneath the baseboards and crept toward Leyta. It was regrouping, malevolent and lethal.

A voice that seemed to seep from the walls whispered, "I've waited a long time for today, I've dreamed of this day…" The voice went from deep to trilling. "Did you think I'd forget you?" Dozens of arms with crawling fingers spidered toward Leyta, but she didn't waiver. Rhonda placed the mantilla in Leyta's hand and gathered Bailey to her chest. The essence of Paul prickled on Rhonda's skin.

Leyta held up the mantilla and thrust it out toward the shapes that once were Rose's father. The onslaught stopped for a moment, then a loud laugh bellowed through the house; the pictures on the wall shook, and Goldie teetered precariously on the edge of Bailey's dresser. The water in the glass vibrated.

The protective silver motes that surrounded Bailey slipped away and entwined themselves in the black lace of the mantilla. The inky tentacles shrank back a few inches and twitched, as if momentarily confused.

Outside the shattered window, Rhonda saw the mass of crows' heads turn. Where they once seemed haphazard, they now, as a unit, stared directly at the house. All of them, their shining black eyes zeroed in on the events transpiring inside Bailey's bedroom.

Leyta thrust the mantilla, lustrous with glittering silver specks, at the manifestation. It backed up farther, its tendrils retreating toward the window, long fingers skittering. It stalled a moment in indecision or, *please god!* fear; it shuddered, then attempted to gather itself back into its humanesque form. Less strong and pronounced than before, it sagged onto itself, folding over and over like slimy black taffy. The menacing wave growled in its multi-octave voice and came for Leyta.

She stared it down. Bailey buried her face in her screaming mother's chest as they backed toward the door.

Rhonda saw the flock of crows in the cottonwood take flight, darkening the sky, hammering into the side of the house with a sound that shook the rafters. Feathers flew as the room filled with a mass of gleaming black wings.

Inch by inch, the pitch-black figure was pulled toward the window, its multitude of fingers screeching on the hardwood floor. Little by little it retreated, the talons of the crows pulling it outward in a flurry of frenzied flight. What was once Edgar Wilson howled as it was pulled from 291 Chestnut Street, lifted into the air above the ruins of the carriage house to crumble in a gray rain of ash that evaporated as it hit the ground.

The room stilled, the silence solid and all-encompassing. A single crow flew into the room and sat on the windowsill, its head tilted, its eyes focused on Rose. As its black beak opened, the pearly bits, the silver molecules that were the embodiment of Paul, swirled to life, flying directly into the big bird's mouth. Its eyes glowed silver as it cocked its head, nodded, and took flight, disappearing into the copse of cottonwoods.

"Is Goldie okay?" came a small voice.

Rhonda burst into tears and clung to her baby.

Chapter Twenty-four

A Day of Cheese and Pickleball

Rhonda stayed at her sister Carla's house for a week before she felt comfortable enough to go out of the house on her own. Carlos had been treasure hunting with Tate when the carriage house exploded, and it was now surrounded by police tape. Carlos seemed fine staying with BJ, since he knew little of what had happened that day. Bailey, on the other hand, wanted to go home.

"I made Paul a promise, Mama. I promised to make it a happy place," she said, pointing to the house she had drawn in all her five-year-old innocence. The sun was big and yellow, the front of the house had only one door, and a porch wrapped around it. Smiling stick figures of what had to be her and Tate and both kids stood in green grass. A crow sat in a tree. At least Rhonda thought it was a crow; Bailey was only five, and sometimes it was hard to decipher what she'd drawn.

Rhonda pointed to the crow, "is this Paul, baby?"

"No, it's just a bird."

"Where is Paul now?"

"I don't know, but I know he can't come back, and that's a good thing." Bailey looked up at her mother. "The bad one can't come back either, he's gone forever."

Rhonda looked skeptical.

"I promise, Mama."

"Why is there only one door, and what's this here?" Rhonda pointed at the porch.

"That's the way the house is supposed to look." Bailey smiled.

Rhonda remembered the blueprints of the original house that hung in Edna and Henry's living room.

"Oh, and Mama?"

"Yes?"

"I'm not a baby."

She most certainly was not.

"I never thought this old mystery would be solved," said Sheriff Cruz.

"Can't believe it," Deputy Lerner said. "I remember my parents talking about how a father and son went missing from this place, but I was just a kid, I didn't pay much attention."

"The CBI think it was a gas leak that blew this place apart," Sheriff Cruz said, surveying the damage, caved-in roof and all. "They're gonna bulldoze the rest, fill in the cistern, and most likely plant over it."

"Have they ID'd the bodies yet?" asked the deputy.

Sheriff Cruz shook his head. "As of now, the remains are still at the morgue. You know how it is when the Feds get involved. We get only the basic information at first. They siphon off just enough info to keep us appeased."

Deputy Lerner bent and picked up a handful of black feathers. "What the hell?" He dropped them and let them flutter to the ground, then wiped his hands on his uniform slacks.

"And," Sherrif Cruz continued, "I heard through the grapevine that Beatrice Wilson's will stated that if her husband's body was ever found, it was to be buried in a different cemetery than the one with her family plot. The son, however, was to be buried next to her. There's also a space for his twin sister when her time comes, she's still living."

Deputy Lerner removed his cap and scratched his head. "Do they have any idea what happened? How they ended up in that old cistern?"

"No clue. The Feds are looking at it as a homicide, at least as far as the child that was involved. His skull was crushed."

"I heard the father was a sonofabitch," said Deputy Lerner.

"I heard that too."

Crime scene tape flapped in the wind as Anita walked out of her condo. "Hey Andy, hey Barney."

Sheriff Cruz cringed—he hated being called Andy.

Deputy Lerner grinned; he loved every moment of being Barney to the population of Patton. He had a Barney Fife shrine in his basement.

"Are the dead guys gone?" Anita asked. A little chihuahua barked at Andy's shined shoes. "Nacho! Hush, don't bite the police!" she said, scooping him up.

"Yes, Anita, they've been gone for a few days now," Andy said, keeping a keen eye on Nacho. His Aunt Juanita had one of those little chihuahua monsters when he was a kid, and every time he bent over the damn thing bit him in the ass. In Jimmy Cruz's mind, chihuahuas should come with a trigger warning. He'd rather deal with bank robbers and drug dealers and rottweilers. He was two hundred and sixty pounds and afraid of five-pound dogs.

"Great," said Anita, and headed back to her quad. Nacho looked over her shoulder, stared directly at Andy, and silently lifted his upper lip.

The next week, Paul was buried in the Patton cemetery alongside his mother. His sister and a few friends attended, among them the Ramos Benson family.

Edgar Wilson was buried twenty miles away, close to the Nebraska border between Antelope Reservoir, a field of abandoned oil rigs, and a wildlife preserve. Animal and bird life were abundant. The trees were filled with watchful birds with glossy black feathers.

Carla was not going to take no for an answer. "You're coming today, you need to get out."

Rhonda looked at the ground.

"There'll be margaritas…"

"Hrmm.. tempting." Rhonda thought about the conversation she'd had last night with Tate. He was worried about her, and thought therapy might be a good option. She wasn't against the idea, and the more time that went by, the better an idea she thought it might be. But first she wanted to talk to Grandma Elise about her friend Egypt December, the psychic medium and Finder of Things. And Grandma would be at pickleball if she went today. Rhonda sighed.

"Okay, I'm in."

The Designated Dinkers were slaughtered by The Limp Dinks. Mario patted Rhonda on the shoulder. "It's been a tough week for you, sweetheart. Let's split the cost of adult beverages and junk food today."

"It's fine, Mario," Rhonda reassured him as she dug out her credit card. "I will let you go and order though, I'm pooped!"

Grandma took her seat at the outdoor umbrella table. "Losing will do that to you!"

Mario kissed Rhonda on the cheek and went off for snacks.

"Grandma Elise," Rhonda began, "since I have you alone for a moment, can I ask a favor?"

"Sure, honey," Grandma said, "anything for you. It's gotta be a real pisser to find dead people in your yard."

Rhonda grimaced. "Yes, it's been a week." She continued, "Could I have the number for your friend

Egypt December?" Grandma visibly brightened. "I have your number on my fridge, but I don't have hers." Maybe because Rhonda had tossed the medium's card into the trash before she left La Case de los Frijoles that day.

Grandma dug in her purse and pulled out a business card that said, "Egypt December, Medium and Finder of Lost Items". "I thought I gave you one?"

"Sometimes I lose things." *Yeah, like my damn mind.*

Rhonda put her finger to her lips as Ben sat down. Grandma nodded and made a zip it motion with her fingers.

Ben looked from one woman to the next and raised a well-plucked eyebrow. Secrets were in the air.

After a couple of very strong margaritas, a bowl of guacamole, and two platters of nachos, Rhonda sat in her car staring at Egypt's card. Would she do this if she wasn't two margaritas into a nap? What the hell.

Rhonda punched Egypt's number into her phone, and the call picked up on the first ring.

"Hello Rhonda," said Egypt.

"Oh, good god! you *are* psychic!"

Egypt laughed. "Actually, Elise Brown phoned me and said you might call. How may I help you?"

This is nuts, she thought. "I'm wondering if you could meet me at my house sometime soon, I'm sure you heard we've had an…incident."

"Yes, I did hear about that."

"I want to make sure the house is safe for us to move back into," Rhonda said. "Whenever you have time."

"How about half an hour from now?"

Rhonda swallowed hard, thinking about stepping foot again into 291 Chestnut Street. "I'll be there."

Thanks liquid courage, she thought, left her car, and walked home.

Twenty-eight minutes and thirty-seven seconds later, Rhonda was opening the door to 291 Chestnut Street quad number one. Behind her was an older woman, possibly Grandma Elise's age but very petite, with long gray hair tied in a bun. She wore colorful clothing, black and white checked slip-on sneakers, and bracelets too numerous to count. Rhonda opened the door and gestured her in, not only out of respect and politeness, but also because she was scared shitless to go in first.

Egypt headed directly upstairs. "This way, yes?"

Rhonda nodded but said nothing, allowing the older woman to find her own path.

"I've brought sage to cleanse the house, but so far I feel nothing at all." She turned into Bailey's bedroom where the shattered window had been boarded up. "There was a very dark presence here at one point, but it's gone, it's completely gone." Egypt stood in the center of the room and held her hands out. "There was also a very protective entity." She took a deep breath. "It's gone too, and it feels justified."

Egypt saw Great-grandma's mantilla on the floor and smiled. "I'm unsure if this helped at all, but I'd keep it in a place of reverence. Do you have a basement?" she said, stepping into the hallway.

"Yes. Yes, we do."

"There's a room there that needs to be saged. Nothing dangerous is in there, but it needs to be cleansed and allowed to be turned into something more positive." She handed Rhonda the sage. "You can do this later on your own with no problem. You'll know when."

Rhonda saw Egypt to the front door. "Thank you so much for coming, I really appreciate it. How much do I owe you?"

"No problem, and no charge," Egypt said. "Oh! One more thing. Please tell your son and husband that they're searching in the wrong place."

Rhonda raised an eyebrow.

"The protective entity in this home had dyslexia, along with other issues. His mother was also dyslexic." She paused a moment, then added, "Oh, and when you go down to sage the basement room…take a bat. It's in your son's room in his closet, behind his hamper of dirty clothes. Remember to tell your husband what I said."

"I will, I'll tell him."

"Thank you, please do. Finding things is my specialty." Egypt smiled and showed herself out.

A bat?

Tate and Carlos spread the picture of the carriage house out on the table. The now dead cottonwood took its place of honor on the left side of the map Beatrice Wilson had drawn so long ago.

"I don't get it, Dad," said Carlos. "We've dug and searched everywhere around that tree, there are literal trenches."

Tate nodded. "Mom's friend Egypt said we're digging in the wrong place, but it specifically says, 'beneath the cottonwood on the south side of the carriage house'." He thought for a moment. "Carlos? You're old enough to know what dyslexia is." Carlos nodded and Tate continued, "You know those old photos of the house that Mom brought over and was going to take to Edna the next time she visits?"

"The one with the floor plans?"

"No, the black-and-white picture of the house and property." Tate pushed the drawing to the center of the table. "Run and get me that one. On second thought, bring them all, please."

Carlos returned five minutes later with a stack of old framed photographs. He set them out one by one on the table.

Tate picked up an eight-by-ten. "Here. This is an old cottonwood, on the property, by the carriage house. Notice anything odd?"

"It's not there anymore."

Tate took Paul's picture and held it backwards against the light. The tree shone through on the north side of the carriage house.

"Bingo! Grab the gear and call BJ. I'll get the tent. It looks like it's gonna be an all-nighter."

Bailey begged to go home. Carlos was about done with having to share a bed with BJ. Tate was insistent that they needed to get back into a routine, and that he and Carlos had camping plans for that night and would be close by. Rhonda could tell he didn't quite believe everything they told him had happened.

"How close by?" asked Rhonda.

"Only at the edge of the property line, so about three hundred and fifty-three feet from the house," he said. "I'll keep my phone with me at all times."

"You're such an engineer, Tater. That's damn specific."

"It's why I get...*got*...paid the big bucks."

Her daughter tugged on her t-shirt to get her attention. "It's safe now, Mama," Bailey whispered, but Rhonda wasn't so sure.

"We need to get your window fixed."

"It's boarded up for now," Tate said, "but I can do that in the morning." He placed his hands on Rhonda's shoulders and turned her to face him. "I've cleaned up the glass, and she can sleep with us tonight." He kissed his wife on the forehead. "It's time to let Carla and BJ have their house back."

This, Rhonda couldn't argue with. Egypt said it was safe to live in— except... "There's one thing I want to do first." She thought about the sage bundle in her purse. "I'll go, on one condition."

Eager eyes were all on her.

"That you and Carlos take Bailey with you tonight, at least for a little while," she concluded.

Carlos was obviously not pleased. "Do we have to?"

"Only for a little while. Then I'll walk out and get her."

"What do you have planned, Rhonda?" Tate asked. "You have that look in your eyes like when you painted the living room goose turd green."

"No geese, and no turds, I promise."

"Well then," said Tate.

Carlos groaned. Bailey cheered.

"Oh, I'm supposed to tell you you're digging in the wrong place."

Carlos and Tate spoke as one, "We figured that out."

Grandma and Sylvia Mejia were in the pickleball finals. The Senior Slammers were playing the Limp Dinks once more for the whole enchilada. Grandpa Brown was on the sidelines rooting his wife on.

"Is this almost over?" said Grandpa Brown, "I'm missing my show." Ben was also on the sidelines as Grandma and Mario hammered it out on the court.

"What's your show?" Ben asked.

"Wheel of Fortune, and I'm missing it."

"You can watch it on demand, you know."

"I can?"

"Yep, Mario and I can show you how."

"Okay, I feel better, you're on." Grandpa looked at Ben and asked, "Are you and Mario married?"

"Not yet," said Ben, showing him the ring he wore on his left hand, "next year."

"Are Elise and I invited?"

"Absolutely."

"Great, because I gotta see this. I'll probably ask a bunch of dumb questions, but I've never been to a gay wedding before."

"Ask me anything."

"Who's catering?"

Ben laughed. "The venue, we're having it at Starling Castle."

"Is there coconut shrimp on the menu? I love that stuff."

"It is!"

Grandpa grinned. "Let me know the date and we'll be there. I'll let you know about a time to show us how to use the on demand feature for Wheel."

Ben put his rainbow visor on Grandpa's head. "You're getting sunburned."

"Thanks," Grandpa said, adjusting it. He had to admit Elise looked cute in her culottes. "Pickle the shit outta them, Honeybunches!" Grandpa yelled.

Maybe he'd stay for Margaritas. Maybe.

Tate, Carlos, BJ, and Bailey set up the tent at the far side of the five acre property, approximately where the long-gone cottonwood once stood.

"If you find treasure, what are you going to do with it?" Bailey asked.

"It doesn't matter," said Carlos, "it's the hunt that's the fun part."

"I feel like a pirate!" Bailey said.

"Arrrrgggggg," said Tate, "let's go find us the booty." He tapped his daughter on the nose.

Bailey covered one eye with her hand, "Arrrrg!"

"I wish I had a pegleg," said BJ.

Carlos agreed, "That'd be so cool. I'd love a hook for a hand."

"Why do all pirates have missing body parts?" asked BJ.

"Because they're cool as FUCK," said Bailey, and skipped ahead.

"I can't imagine what you'll be like as a teenager," Tate said, dropping the supplies in the predesignated spot. "Let the treasure hunt commence!"

"Arrrggg!!!"

Rhonda dropped her purse on the table at 291 Chestnut Street number one. She opened the bag and pulled out the bundle of sage. The scent reminded her of New Mexico after the rain.

After rummaging around the kitchen junk drawer for a bit, she found a lighter and shoved it into her pocket. Standing on the step stool, she reached on top of the fridge and grabbed her ceramic dachshund, whose tail held the key that had given Kenny nightmares. She shoved the keys and the dachshund into her pocket, headed toward the front door, stopped, dashed up the stairs, and grabbed Carlos's bat from his bedroom. Yep, it was right there behind his stinky socks and underpants.

"Better safe than sorry. Thanks, Egypt."

Chapter Twenty-five

1,000 Cabbage Farts

Kenny had to pee for the third time in half an hour. His nerves were jangling like a cartoon fire truck.

"Remember," Anita said, talking with her hands, "act like you're unlocking the room, give the lock a big tug, and it should come right apart."

Kenny nodded, and put a finger to his left eye, which was twitching. "I got it, babe," he said. "Are you all packed?"

"Yep."

"Are Opps and her sister ready to go?"

"Stop that Kenny, it's just mean."

"All the suitcases in the cow truck?"

"Yes!" Anita was obviously getting annoyed at his questioning. "Let's just get this over with, take your cut, and get out. You're making me so nervous! Look at my hands shaking"—she held them out for him to see— "I'm afraid I'm gonna have a pancake attack."

"Just gotta cross all my Is and dot all my Ts." Kenny patted his pocket for the fake key. "Wait ten minutes, then head out to the truck, load the kids, and wait for me."

Anita was all but pushing him out the door. "I love you, babe."

"I love you too." He bounced on the balls of his feet. "If we're not all dead in an hour, will you marry me in Vegas?"

"Yes! If you don't fuck this up!"

Kenny grinned, "Don't forget to wear the Traveling Titillator." He opened the door to 291 Chestnut Street number 3. "It's party time."

The stench that encompassed the cellar had grown stronger since Rhonda's last venture into the basement. Maybe that's why Egypt had suggested sage? To counteract the stink? Rhonda took the bundle and lit the tip with the lighter; it blazed for a moment, she blew out the flame, and fragrant smoke filled the air.

Feeling rather foolish, Rhonda waved the bundle into all the corners of the storage room, under the stairs, up and around Edna's canned goods, and went twice over the evil washer and dryer. What could it hurt? The damn washing machine made the basement sound like a bowling alley. Maybe Egypt was right? She'd known where the bat would be.

"Okay," she said, not quite sure of the proper words she should recite while cleansing a basement of spooks.

She felt like an idiot but said aloud, "If there are evil ghostly entities down here—*begone!*"

The washing machine made a random thump. She tightened up on the baseball bat.

"I knew it!" Rhonda frantically waved smoke over the Whirlpool for good measure. "It's gonna take more than burning turkey seasoning.."

Rhonda stood before the little locked room. "Let's get this over with." She removed the key ring from her pocket and found the octagonal key head, but...but the lock was lying broken on the floor. *How odd.*

She cautiously opened the door.

Tate, BJ, and Carlos had the tent set up and the metal detectors out. So far, they'd found a few cans and a screwdriver. They also found the remnants of what had to have been an enormous cottonwood concealed by weeds and sagebrush. The stump was as big around as a VW bug, and her dad and the boys were busy weed whacking around its perimeter.

Bailey was sprawled out on her brother's sleeping bag, her head propped up on her hands. She was bored out of her mind. She wanted to be in her room, or watching TV. She was hungry, and sick of pretending to like BJ's baloney and cheese sandwiches. She peeked out of the tent; her brother, cousin, and father were preoccupied playing treasure hunters. Bailey very quietly crept from the tent and headed back toward the house.

Margarita late afternoon time had turned into Margarita evening time and there was yellow nacho cheese in Grandma's hair. Grandpa and Ben were talking baseball, and she and Mario were talking canapés.

"I like the little flaky ones with spinach and cheese inside," said Grandma.

"Spanakopita?"

"You can say it in any fancy language you want, Mario, they're still little spinach sandwiches"—she pointed a finger at him—"and delicious."

"Agreed. Fancy little spinach sandwiches are on the menu for the reception."

"Will there be a band?"

"A DJ, I think."

"Great," she said, finally noticing there was nacho cheese in her hair, and dabbing it with a napkin. "I hope neither of you Limp Dinks pick crappy music. Nothing ruins a wedding reception like crappy music. I was at a wedding once where they had a string quartet. I thought I was going to fall asleep right in my quiche. Now I have to figure out what to wear, I don't want to upstage—"

Grandma's phone rang and she answered it. "Hello, you've reached Elise Brown's unwanted advice service, how may—"

On the other end of the line she heard Bailey say, "Grandma Elise Brown? This is Bailey Ramos Benson. I found your number stuck with a magnet on the kitchen fridge. I can't find my mom."

"Don't open the door for anyone but me," said Grandma, "and stay on the line, I'm on my way."

She turned and waggled a finger in Grandpa's direction. "Keep an eye on that one."

Rhonda was no expert, but she could tell the source of the smell that had permeated the basement was right inside the now-open doorway, and damn, was it rank.

She relit the sage bundle until it flamed and thrust it into the darkness; the lights clicked on, and she about jumped out of her skin when she saw two men standing inside. One tall, one very short, both in black suits. Behind them was what looked to be a jail cell with a mattress, and on the other wall were stacks upon stacks of what had to be wheels of cheese.

Rhonda let out a frightened cry, dropped the burning sage and the baseball bat. She was trying to back away when the taller of the two—who was holding a gun—grabbed her, pulling one arm behind her back, and yanked her inside.

"What the actual hell!" she cried, keeping one eye on the bat. "Jesus!"

"Yes," said the shorter of the two, "cheeses."

The larger man hit her on the head with the pistol butt and she went down, the bat rolling across the small room.

"Lots of cheeses, very expensive—and ruined cheeses."

Kenny silently opened the basement door and was hit with a wall of stink that smelled like a thousand cabbage farts shot straight from Satan's asshole. He pulled his t-shirt over his nose and slowly edged down the stairs. "Hello? Todd? Not Todd?" He looked around. "Where are you, you evil little fucker?"

No answer. Kenny assumed he was the first one here. Great, that may just give him the upper hand. Everything seemed still. He knew what he'd do. He'd unlock the door, stand by it, and wait for Todd and Not Todd. He wouldn't even need to try to pull a fast one with the fake key—Eureka! He'd be out of here with pockets full of money before you knew it.

Kenny heard a muffled groan from behind the door. Shit, maybe he wasn't alone. He reached for the lock to yank it free, and whatcha know? No lock.

The door flew open, and a big hand pulled Kenny inside the room of funk and smacked him upside the melon with what could only have been the butt of a gun. What did he know? Just like Ethan, Kenny knew jack shit about guns, and we all know how that little fiasco turned out.

Grandma grabbed her straw purse, downed the remainder of her margarita, and stuck her visor back on her head. "Let me stress again, you boys keep an eye on this drunk old geezer," she told Mario and Ben, "and I'll be back shortly."

After turning to leave, she thought twice about it and grabbed her pickleball racquet, giving it a swing.

Grandpa filled his glass. "Take your time Elise." There was a sound from the TV over the bar of a bat hitting a ball.

"Yeah!" said Grandpa and Ben together, and fist bumped each other.

Mario looked at the two of them and rolled his eyes. He put his hand to the side of his mouth and stage whispered to Grandma, "Hurry please, darling."

Chapter Twenty-six

Mr. Coffee Saves the Day

RHONDA OPENED HER EYES, and there were three of everything. Three large men in black suits, three small men in black suits, and three frumpy-looking Brad Pitts. Argh! She must have been hit harder than she initially thought. It wasn't Brad Pitt, it was Kenny. Kenny-Brad was on his knees, and the taller man had a gun pointed at his face. Rhonda, being a connoisseur of fine yet shitty mystery and horror fiction, knew enough to play dead.

"It's pretty obvious that the goods haven't been checked since Ethan dropped dead," said Todd.

"We lost the key!" Kenny whimpered as a stream of blood dripped into his eye and he wiped it away. "How was I to know there was gonna be forbidden cheese in here? They told us it was cocaine, that shit don't go bad!" Kenny looked at his fingers and noticed the blood. "I'm fucking bleeding!" He looked as if he might faint. Rhonda opened one eye a bit wider as the world finally came into focus.

"You've cost us a lot of money, Kenny. You have no idea how much this product goes for. To the appropriate customer with fine tastes in wine and exotic foods, of course," said Todd, his voice low, steady, lethal.

"He looks more like a tater tot and Mountain Dew kind of guy to me," said Not Todd.

"But they're covered in bugs! I'm so sorry! Was Ethan picking off the bugs? Was he on some weird fucked up bug patrol?"

"They're maggots, and that's not the point," Todd walked around him, keeping the gun pointed at his head. "They have to be *live* maggots for us to sell this formaggio, and you killed them, so it's no good to us now."

Kenny was crying now. "Shit, man, I'll get you some more bugs, just tell me what I need to do!" Kenny was on his knees all but begging. "They sell them for turtle food at the pet store...I..." even on his knees he could look Not Todd straight in the eyes, and, having a squirrel's brain, he blurted out, "Christ, Mr. Fun-sized, what are you, about four foot three?"

Todd chambered a round.

Not Todd pulled his gun out as well, pointing it at Kenny's big fat mouth. "Play stupid games, win stupid prizes." He smiled slowly, the light glinting off his gold tooth as he racked the slide.

Rhonda inched her hand into her pocket and pulled out the ceramic jalapeno-shaped wiener dog which had held the keys. She fingered its sharp tail.

"You can't shoot me!"

"We're *gonna* shoot you," the Todds said in unison.

"Say howdy to Ethan for us, asshole," Todd said.

Kenny squeezed his eyes closed and whimpered.

Rhonda hauled back and jabbed the wiener dog tail into Todd's calf with the mighty strength of a woman who's read too many thrillers and seemed to be living in one right now.

Todd screamed in pain. The gun went off. The bullet ricocheted off of a metal jail cell bar and hit Not Todd right between the eyeballs. Todd hollered as he fell to the floor, his gun skittering away, the little jalapeno dachshund stuck from his leg like it was taking a blood red leak on his pants. Not Todd hit the ground like a quarter of a sack full of potatoes, taking three putrid wheels of Formaggio con Amici with him, deceased maggots and all. A carafe from an old Mr. Coffee maker rolled off a shelf and onto the floor.

Kenny screamed like a little girl and went down faster than a twenty-dollar whore in a room full of sailors.

Rhonda yelled at him, "Kenny, get up! Take the bat and break his fingers!"

"We have maggots *and* bats?"

"Not that kind of bat, you idiot, the baseball bat! It's right behind you in the corner."

Kenny picked up the bat and stared at it as if he were holding a live cobra. He was obviously in shock. Todd lay on the floor clutching his leg, his bloody fingers creepy-crawling toward his gun.

"Jesus Christ, Brad!" Rhonda grabbed the baseball bat from his grip and smashed the hand Todd was using to grab his gun. He roared as Rhonda jumped over him, took the bat and gave him a matching pair of catchers mitts. *Broken fingers grab no ankles, motherfucker!*

Todd roared in pain.

Rhonda snatched the glass Mr. Coffee pot and smacked him across the face for good measure; it shattered into sharp shards, some of which stuck from his cheeks at awkward angles. She grabbed Kenny by the arm, turned, kicked Todd again, and then ran for the stairs, dragging Kenny behind her. Sirens wailed in the distance.

"Who the hell's Brad?"

"Shut up, Kenny." Rhonda said dragging him toward the stairs. She made a mental note to buy a Mr. Coffee and toss out her fancy espresso machine.

Anita sat in the passenger's side of the cow truck, her leg nervously tappity-tapping as if it had a mind of its own. Up down, up down, tappity tappity tap. The kids were in the back seat, Stella was sleeping.

"Hurry up, Kenny." Anita was seriously starting to worry. Not to mention, the Traveling Titillator was goddamn uncomfortable to sit on. Hopefully it felt better once it was turned on, but right now it felt like sitting on a little pink bear trap.

That's when she heard the sirens in the distance.

"Fucking hell."

Grandma pounded on Rhonda's front door, "Bailey! It's me, open up!"

Bailey opened the door a crack and flew into Grandma Elise's arms. Grandma hugged Bailey tight. "What's Dan's Used Furniture and Supreme Meats cow truck doing here, and why does the cow have on a Mexican hat? Wait, I hear sirens." Grandma took Bailey's hand and walked toward the cow truck on the street. "Let's go find your mommy."

Kenny and Rhonda came around the corner to the front yard, and Kenny was instantly tackled by someone wearing an FBI jacket. They pulled his hands behind his back and cuffed him on the sidewalk.

"There's your mom, sweetie!" Grandma said to Bailey. She turned to one of the FBI guys as Bailey dashed off and hugged her mother around the waist. "How did you fellas know to be here?"

"We have ways of listening in," he said.

"The microwave…" said Grandma, tapping her forehead.

The FBI guy said nothing, only raised an eyebrow.

Anita saw the action going down, got out of the cow truck, and raced as fast as she could to the driver's side. At that moment, Kenny was rolled over by the police, his hip hitting the ON switch of the Traveling Titillator. Anita yelped and jumped; the Titillator fell and clattered to the pavement. Nacho the chihuahua barked after it, snarling ferociously.

"Holy Jesus!" screamed Grandma, watching the pink, crustacean-like creature spring to life and skitter in a circle. Grandma brandished her pickleball racquet and smacked it. It slowed, made a sad sound and buzzed in a circle. Grandma whacked it again, and it rolled into the storm drain.

"Damn bugs are bigger every year." Nacho yapped some more.

Two stretchers came around the corner, a sheet covering what had to be the little leftovers of a very stinky Not Todd. The other stretcher contained a furious and in pain Todd, his mangled hands cuffed to the gurney, with his fingers pointing every which way to Jupiter.

"You broke my fucking hands!" he screamed at Rhonda.

"Looks like she broke your fucking nose too," said Grandma. She kicked the wheel of the stretcher, making Todd scream in pain. "Lunkhead."

Rhonda fist bumped her.

The paramedics were looking at Rhonda's head wound; she insisted she was fine and refused treatment—there was no way she was leaving Bailey, whom she had picked up and was clinging to her neck. *Where the hell are Tate and Carlos?*

Kenny had a similar head wound from the same butt of the same gun. He still appeared dazed. "What's your name?" the paramedic asked him.

"Kenny…"

"What day is it?"

"Friday…"

"Who's the president?"

"That orange fella…" Kenny shook his head and grimaced. "No wait, it's that clumsy old guy that fell off his bike."

"He's fine," said Rhonda, Grandma, and the paramedic in unison.

The police yanked Kenny to a standing position and were dragging him toward the squad car; Nacho was tugging at his pant legs and snarling.

Anita slid into the driver's seat of the cow truck—no way was she going to jail! She jammed the key into the cow truck's ignition; to hell with this noise, she was heading to Vegas.

Being rich, happy, and maybe famous was in her cards! It was karma, it was fate, it was kismet, it was divine will!

It is my density.

The cow truck sputtered to life, and she took off at its top speed of about twenty-five miles per hour. The left front tire did a nose dive into the Sinkhole de Mayo and the truck's stereo system came alive:

> La cucaracha, la cucaracha!
> Ya no puede caminar.
> Porque no tiene, porque le falta,
> Marijuana que fumar!

Sheriff Jimmy Cruz put his hand on Kenny's head to dip him into the police car when Kenny saw Anita taking off down the road in the Used Taco wagon.

"Anita!!!" he called after her, "don't you fuck nobody!!!!"

Sheriff Jimmy Cruz—Andy to the townspeople—sighed like a man ready to retire, and let Kenny whack his head on the door frame. Nacho the chihuahua bit Kenny in the ass one last time for good measure, then turned his attention to the chihuahua-fearing sheriff. Andy lost no time sliding behind the wheel of the squad car and closing the door. "Fuck you, dog," Andy said out the window.

Nacho lifted his upper lip, showing off an impressive pair of canine chompers, "Fuck you twice, Officer Dipshit."

Tate, BJ, and Carlos ran from around the house. Red and blue lights set the neighborhood ablaze.

"What the hell's going on?" Tate asked his wife. "Oh god, you're bleeding!"

Rhonda, still having her wits about her, asked him, "What's that in your hand?" It was a shoebox-sized metal container covered in dirt.

Zane Holyworth settled back with a large drink into the plush cream leather of his private Learjet as it reached altitude, aimed toward Colombia. Dealing cocaine was sounding better all the time.

Chapter Twenty-seven

Bread & Butter, Butter & Bread

Three months later

RHONDA AND TATE sat in the living room of an eight hundred square-foot rental that used to belong to Grandma Elise's daughter Beth and her husband Jack. It was ten o'clock on a Friday night. The place had three postage stamp-sized bedrooms, a micro kitchen and a living room where you'd knock knees if more than two people sat in it at a time. Rhonda thought it was perfect—for the six months or so they'd be living in it.

Over at 291 Chestnut Street, the hazmat team had cleaned the small basement room and removed all of its questionable content. The construction crew had orders to demolish the entire space; maybe it would be a bathroom in the future. The carriage house was now a green expanse of lawn.

Tate took Rhonda's hand. "I hope we're doing the right thing."

"I know we are." She laid her head on his shoulder. "Have you ever seen our kids happier?"

Tate wrapped an arm around her. "That's what it's all about, right?"

Rhonda smiled. It was nice to know they finally were putting down roots. "I love having Carla and BJ close by." She laced her fingers with his. "We've made a lot of friends, and so have the kids. I have a job at Patton Elementary that starts soon, your work allows you to work remotely— we feel so…settled."

Rhonda looked up at the only pictures she'd hung so far, the blueprints of the original house at 291 Chestnut Street, one of Ethan's watercolor paintings of Antelope Reservoir, and a shadow box with Great-grandma's mantilla. It would take awhile for the construction work to be completed, but she knew it was the right move. Having the remaining three quads open for purchase had to be an omen. Hopefully not like the movie, but an omen nonetheless. Soon the house would be their home, restored to its original glory, wraparound porch and all. She and Egypt had saged the entire place again, just to be on the safe side, and even though the house was far from finished, she'd planted flowers (Grandma was right, all the ferns had died) in the old ore bucket.

Rhonda picked up a paperback novel she found in the hall closet. It was written by Blaze Bolivar, better known as Beth Harmon to the good people of Patton. *His Big Love* was printed across the front cover, along with a picture of a muscular, bare-chested man and his sultry black-haired, big-breasted lady love.

"I can't believe you're reading that."

"I think reading it is a right of passage for all permanent Patton residents," she said, and opened it to page one. "I'll give it to you when I'm finished."

Carlos and BJ were playing video games in Carlos's temporary bedroom. Nacho, now named Toby the chihuahua, was curled comfortably on Carlos's lap. He opened one eye, growled at BJ and then went back to sleep.

"Your dog's a stinkin' monster," BJ said.

Carlos scratched Toby behind the ears. "That's my good boy."

Bailey sat propped up on her bed in her temporary bedroom. In her new extra-large fish bowl, Goldie swam in happy circles with her new friend Buster. McJennifer was spending the night. The two of them were thick as thieves, and inseparable.

Bailey held up her little finger and McJennifer hooked it with hers.

"Bread and Butter."

"Butter and Bread."

One Year Later

Antelope Reservoir was filled with water from a fantastic Spring runoff and open to the public. Rhonda parked her car in the parking lot, got the wheelchair out of the back seat, and put on its brakes. She opened the passenger's side door and carefully helped Edna out. Her broken ankle from a year ago still had a hard time supporting her weight for longer than a few moments.

"How are you doing, Edna?" Rhonda asked her, placing a bag onto her lap along with her purse.

"I'm okay, sweetie, just take it slow."

Rhonda unlocked the chair's brakes and began to push her toward the water.

"I really am happy where I am," Edna said. "Leyta and Johnathan and Rosie…who would have thought I'd make such good new friends at my age." She smiled and took Rhonda's hand. "It was so good of you to donate Beatrice Wilson's savings to Harmony Hills, I've enjoyed every minute of living there."

Rhonda helped Edna stand, and took James's ashes from the bag they'd brought them in. She handed it to Edna.

"Are you sure you're okay with this? Do you want me to help?"

"I'm okay." Edna smiled as she lifted the lid to the urn and let her only child fly on the wind into the water.

Epilogue

Frank plodded over to an old cottonwood stump, set his lunchbox down between his feet, and took a seat. The lunchbox was mighty old and covered in dings and dents, but he'd never replace it. Phyllis had bought it for him the year they got married and he'd started his new job.

He opened the domed lid and pulled out a bag of cookies. His wife had made them last night. After all this time she still did the most thoughtful things.

Frank heard a rustle in the brush and looked up. "Hey there, Bob," he said through a mouthful of cookie, "where you been? We've missed you at work." Frank stood and held up a cookie. "You want a pecan shortbread? Phyllis made them last night, they're damn tasty."

Bob held his hand up and backed away. "I'll sit over here, toss it my way? I don't want you to catch what I have. Darla and the kids have it too, she's home now making up another batch of her secret medicine recipe."

"Lice again?"

"You got it," Bob said, scratching at a spot on his neck. "Again."

"Damn, that stinks," Frank said, "seems like your family never catches a break around cold and lice season."

"You know what else stinks?" Bob said. "Darla's medicine, that's what stinks." He laughed and scratched another spot. "Works, though."

"Well, I hope ya'll feel better soon, we miss you at work."

"Hey, Frank?" Bob said, "can I ask you a question? It's been on my mind for a few weeks, and it's driving me crazy."

"Of course, shoot."

"Remember that night back in June when we overheard those kids camping and they were talking about what a group of BigFoot are called?"

"Yeah, I sure do. Stupid kids."

"Well, what are we called?"

Frank thought for a moment. "You know Bob, I don't rightly know. A bunch?"

"Like bananas?"

"No, that can't be right." Frank looked at his friend. "To tell the truth Bob, I haven't a clue." He took another nibble of Phyllis's killer cookies. "What did those kids say? A sock? A boot?"

"They said a Shoe. A Shoe of BigFoot." Bob scratched lazily at his shoulder. "And the more I think about it, the more I like it."

"It's not bad," said Frank, "pretty clever actually." He laughed. "We scared the crap out of them that night when we shook the tent!"

"We sure did," Bob said, laughing. "Those kids high tailed it out of there like they were on fire."

"Except for the little one."

"No kidding. Brave kid. Think she saw us?"

"Naw," said Frank, "I doubt it. Well, maybe?"

"I better get going," said Bob. "There's a big pickleball tournament tonight." He lifted a hairy fist. "Go, Stompers!"

Bob chuckled and stood, then stretched and pushed his black horn-rimmed glasses up onto his nose. "I think we should bring up being called a Shoe at the next board of directors meeting. Maybe make it official." He turned to leave, giving his hairy orange rump a good scratch. "Hey, what's that thing next to your lunch box?" Bob pointed to an object partially buried by leaves that lay by the container that most likely held Frank's standard ham and cheese sandwich.

Frank bent and brushed off the partially buried thing and picked it up. "I think it's a gun." He examined it. "Actually, I think it's Elvis Presley's gun."

"You gotta be shittin' me. I thought Elvis was an urban legend?"

"I don't think so. I was watching a special about him on Netflix not long ago and damn it, Bob, this is his gun." Frank added, "It's loaded too." He put it in his lunchbox under his sandwich and bag of Fritos.

"Be careful with that thing, you might lose a toe."

"I promise," said Frank. "I don't know jack shit about guns."

"Tell Phyllis thanks for the cookie, it was great."

"I'll do that," said Frank as he watched Bob lumber off toward the forest. "Tell Darla and the kids hi for me." He waved. "And feel better."

"I will soon, I'm sure. Fucking lice… *again*. This here is some bullshit."

THE END

I'm a Pinecone Pioneer!
Filled with happiness and cheer!
Taking time each day for laughter,
We'll be friends for ever after,
Loyalty and trust abounds,
We lift our voice—a joyous sound!
We are Pinecone Pioneers!
Through all time and through the years,
Through the good times and the tears.
Always Pinecone Pioneers!

Bread and Butter
Butter and Bread